THE Scavenger's Daughters

Also by Kay Bratt

Silent Tears; A Journey of Hope in a Chinese Orphanage

Chasing China; A Daughter's Quest for Truth

The Bridge

A Thread Unbroken

Train to Nowhere

Mei Li and the Wise Laoshi

THE Scavenger's Daughters

A Novel

KAY BRATT

lake union publishing

The characters and events portrayed in this book are fictitious. Any similarity to real persons, living or dead, is coincidental and not intended by the author.

Printed in the United States of America.

Published by Lake Union Publishing, Seattle

www.apub.com

ISBN-13: 9781477805862
ISBN-10: 1477805869
Library of Congress Control Number: 2013912682

Dedicated to the many compassionate people in China who have opened their homes and their hearts to homeless children. Your efforts and kindness are an inspiration to the world.

Prologue

China, 1967

Benfu listened to the chorus of crickets and was relieved that evening was finally upon him. Carefully he paced the three feet of space with his hands tied behind his back, squinting in the dimness but knowing there was nothing new to see. Through his swollen eyes he saw the same murky shapes he'd seen since they'd dragged him there days before. He tried to take a deep breath but felt the crackling in his chest. The ragged breaths he was forced to take told him his ribs were bruised if not a few broken. He wished he could wipe the sheen of sweat from his brow, for it burned as it ran into the cuts on his face. It was a bit better since the sun had stopped beaming down on the tin shed but it still felt like he was being baked. He reminded himself to remain calm as he tried to focus on the thought that the cooler night temperatures were coming, a welcome reprieve that gave him the energy to move again and try to make sense of his sudden captivity.

By now he knew every step and each impression in the muck. He also knew from experience where the deep holes were that dropped to the pits of waste. He'd fallen into one that first night and had to be fished out of it like a flailing whale. He still reeked and his stomach rolled with nausea each time he thought of the squishy, putrid substance he had been covered in.

He was like a caged tiger, and though he was weak from lack of food or water, if someone else came through the door to beat him again, he'd fight just as hard as he had the last four days. He would not let them see him broken and he'd never give up and renounce his parents like they wanted him to do. Mao might be in control of most of China but Benfu would not let him take possession of his mind the way he had so many others. His parents were teachers, not revolutionaries! They'd done nothing but spend their lives molding intelligent minds and strong characters; he would not let someone tell him they were criminals.

At only seventeen, Benfu still knew right from wrong and had not joined in the obsessive following of Mao the rest of his generation seemed to have fallen into. Couldn't they see that they were only now starting to recover from Mao's failed Great Leap Forward? Benfu's own father had described to him how Mao's obsession for China to beat Europe's output of iron and steel had overcome his common sense, making him oblivious to leading them into the worst famine in their history. What did he think would happen when he pulled everyone from working the crops and instead had them running factory—and even backyard—furnaces to melt anything and everything in sight to make steel? Steel made from anything they could find from grain bins down to the smallest kitchen pots and utensils—done so haphazardly that most of it couldn't even be used!

Then without time to even recover completely, the government leaders had gone immediately from the failed Great Leap Forward to this new so-called Cultural Revolution. Even Benfu knew this latest plan of clearing out the superstitions and crushing Chinese traditions and artifacts to make way for modernization was not the answer. People needed to keep sight of their history to see how they were growing! When would enough be enough and the people figure out that Mao was not the leader they thought he was? Benfu could see it, but were he and his father the only ones in millions?

He shook his head and tried to shake the stench from his nostrils. Outside he could hear the work groups coming in from the fields, some trying valiantly to lead the others in a weak rendition of "The East Is Red," a song to exalt their glorious leader, the only semblance of music allowed.

When those in the work group had left that morning, their voices were stronger—ready to take on the challenge of meeting their ever-rising quota of gathering more vegetables, planting more rows, watering more crops. Now with the way all farmers were brought together to work toward one goal, many of them failed to see the irony that they were doing more work for less personal gain. Land that had been in families for generations was now owned and controlled by the government, and the people were poorer than ever! With the failure of the Great Leap Forward, the commune system was being reorganized, but not fast enough.

Benfu had kept quiet about it as long as he could but when he'd finally exploded with frustration, his sarcastic remarks had gotten him in trouble. He'd been called in to speak to the elders and he'd thought he'd settled them down enough. What he hadn't known at the time was his outburst had caused an investigation into his background, and they'd discovered he wasn't who he'd said he was. He'd immediately been accused of hiding the truth about his family line. It had only gotten worse from there because he'd refused to give up his parents' names.

After he had spent a few days locked in a small room off the commune kitchen, they'd moved him to the outhouse to try to break him. He had to admit they'd come close when the sun was at its highest and the temperature in the metal privy had soared. As his head pounded and he sweat out the remaining moisture in his body, the flies and mosquitos never let up from their relentless attack. With his hands tied, Benfu was helpless to fend against them or the stench of human excrement that filled his nostrils and mouth. To keep his sanity, he recited his favorite poem over and over, allowing his mind to focus on the words of long-gone poets rather than on the squalor around him.

"'The dragon sighs, the fine rains fall. . . .'" He paced as the whisper of his words punctured the silence of the small enclosure. The dragon was the heat, and he sincerely wished that fine rains would come and the roof would open so he could lift his face to the sky and take in mouthfuls of sweet water.

Twice already earlier in the day, before and after beatings, the commune leader had come to the shed to ask Benfu if he was ready to cooperate. Simple, he'd said, just tell him his parents' names and address and Benfu could go back to work with the others. Benfu knew if he did, his mother and father would be persecuted. They'd sent him to what they thought was a safe place to hide from the Red Guards who were so vehemently against those with undesirable family backgrounds—black families, as they called them. Teachers, landowners, business owners—in this tumultuous time, if a person didn't have ties to officials who could protect him, any sort of success or title gained in life could be their downfall, branding them as a counter-revolutionary. Benfu wouldn't put his parents in danger by revealing their identity.

But he wasn't the only one in the commune who came from a black background. There were landowners' family members as well as other people who'd come from some sort of undesirable line. The difference was that they had not tried to hide it and they gladly attended reeducation classes and renounced their family members, declaring to forever ban them from their lives—a last resort to find their way back in the good graces of Mao and his followers, and avoid persecution.

Benfu backed up gingerly and sat on the makeshift shelf over one of the deep holes. It was ironic that he was in misery from holding his bowels but was imprisoned in an outhouse. Only twice that day had someone come to unfasten his belt and allow him to relieve himself, ignoring his shame as they stood over him and watched as his dehydrated body expelled nothing but black waste. Only once had they sent a frightened young woman in with a cup of warm water to ease his swollen throat and cracked lips. He'd begged her to help him, to give him more water or bring him a ball of rice, but the girl had scampered away like a scared rabbit, too afraid to jeopardize her own freedom. He couldn't blame her; she was just a small peasant girl and would have never been able to withstand the punishment it would have earned her if caught.

The voices faded into the night and Benfu knew they were all now in the communal kitchen for dinner, competing in line with their coupons to get their rations before the food disappeared. Gone were the days of family meals and the joy of gathering around the table to connect. In its place Mao had convinced the people that communal kitchens were bonding the people together as a nation, but Benfu knew he wanted to eliminate the people's independence to function or fend for themselves. Total dependence would mean total commitment to his reign. Why couldn't the people see this instead of allowing themselves to be herded like blind sheep? Benfu couldn't understand it. Was the world going crazy around him? He once again wished for the calm assurance of his father and mother. But he'd never give up their names or tell the leaders where they were. He'd do all he could to keep them safe. Judging from the way the last few evenings had gone, Benfu knew he had about two hours before his next beating. It was usually after dinner and right before lights-out that they sent someone to do the deed.

He looked up in the dark as he heard the metal chain outside the door being rattled. It was too early! He wasn't ready! Yet he stood, proudly lifting his chin in defiance as the chain slid from the handles and the door cracked open. Quickly a young man darted in and shut the door behind him, the flash of light from the receding sun too fast for Benfu to make out who it was.

"Benfu?" the boy called out.

Benfu stayed silent. He wouldn't make it easy for whomever they'd sent. Even though usually they left the door open, Benfu suspected there were probably two or more others waiting outside to assist in dragging him out for his evening beating.

"I'm here to help you," the boy whispered in the dark.

Benfu straightened up. Help? He couldn't believe it. He hoped whoever it was had brought food and water. Anything—he'd eat anything at all. Even the tree bark he'd heard was the newest delicacy in the poorer circles that'd refused the life of communes. If he could only get to a tree, he'd strip it clean.

"What help? Who are you?" Benfu asked, trying to keep the pleading tone from entering his voice.

"It's me. Pei. I work on the other work team. You've seen me. I'm always at the end of the line."

Benfu struggled to remember who Pei was and suddenly his voice sounded familiar. If it was who he thought it was, the boy was several years younger than he and they rarely crossed paths due to the work teams' being segregated by age and ability. Here, everyone was assigned to a team, some inside the commune for the cooking, cleaning, or minding the children, and the stronger ones were sent to the fields to plant, collect, or water. It was a strict enforcement, and though in some communes around China, families were still allowed to live together, in this one, all males and females had separate sleeping quarters with each cabin assigned by age. Still, he'd seen Pei around a few times.

"Pei? What do you want? Are there more of your cadres out there?" Benfu didn't trust anyone at this point.

"No, just me. Come closer. I'm going to unbind you."

Benfu felt the young man's hands touch his shoulder. Then a sliver of light entered the shed again as the boy cracked the door enough to see him better.

He examined Benfu from head to toe and inhaled deeply. "*Aiya,* it's much worse than I thought. You're covered in welts and bruises. Is anything broken?"

"Why are you untying me?" Benfu asked, his swollen eyes frantically trying to see through the slit in the door to what lay waiting outside. He could handle a beating from one, but he didn't know if he could take on three or more tyrants. His body hurt so much and though he'd try, he didn't know how long he could remain strong.

But surprisingly, the boy was gentle and had brought a small kitchen knife. He moved around Benfu and cut cleanly through the rope around his wrists. With the sudden release, Benfu's shoulders throbbed and he rubbed his hands together, trying to restart the blood flow.

"I asked you why you are untying me?" Benfu stared in the dark, trying to see the boy's face.

"Let's just say I found my good sense again." The boy began rustling in his pockets. He brought out four balls of rice and a chunk of bread. With his overflowing hands, he reached out to Benfu. "This is my share of rations from the last two days. I've been saving it for you."

Benfu took the food and his mouth watered right along with his eyes. Food. He'd been dreaming of it all day. But why? He swallowed past the sudden lump of gratitude that rose in his throat and he fought the urge to stuff it all in his mouth at once.

He knew if he started, he'd look like a ravished animal and his pride couldn't take any more shame.

Then the boy unlatched the canteen hooked to his belt. He reached over and snapped it on Benfu's waistband. "And here's my water. I'll tell them I lost it in the fields."

Benfu looked at the canteen and shook his head in confusion. "You can't leave that here. They'll find it when they come back and your initials are carved on it."

"It won't be here when they return. Because *you* won't be here. I'm here to let you go but you have to hurry before they are done with dinner."

The boy spoke in such a low voice that Benfu had to strain to make out his words. But Benfu could have sworn he said he was going to let him go. Now he knew he was finally losing it—there was no way he would have said that.

"Did you say let me go?" he asked, his voice just as low but shaking now with hope.

The boy went to the door and peeked out, then gestured his hand toward Benfu. "Yes, the coast is clear. Just run through the cornfield until you reach the other side. You're about ten miles from Wuxi—follow the lights. From there, you'll have to find a place to hide for a few days. Then you need to keep moving far, far away from here."

Benfu knew where they were—he'd watched carefully when they'd been bused in from the city. But he couldn't believe what he was hearing. Was the boy really offering him his freedom? He tried to clear the tornado of thoughts in his head—he wouldn't let his confusion stand in his way of possible freedom. He stuffed one rice ball into his mouth and the others into his pocket. He'd eat them on the way. The bread he first held under his nose and inhaled the sweet aroma. Then he put it in the other pocket.

"They'll start looking for you soon. So you can't stop. Don't even turn around until you hit Wuxi. I'm going out there to trample down the field leading in the other direction. Then I'll double back. They'll think it was you and that might buy you some time, but be careful to not leave a trail."

Benfu's head was spinning. He still didn't understand why this boy whom he barely knew had come to help him. And suddenly he realized what would happen if the boy was caught. He sighed and his shoulders dropped. He spoke the hardest words he'd ever said.

"I can't go. I appreciate what you are trying to do for me but if they find out it was you, there will be nothing that can save you. Thank you, but I can't have that on my conscience. You're just a boy!"

Pei began stubbornly pushing him toward the door, ignoring his whispered protests.

"You *will* go and don't worry about me. I'm older than I look and I'm fast and smart—they'll never know who it was. I need to do this for you, Benfu. I've heard them beating you and stood in the shadows like a coward. You've already repaid me in ways I cannot say. Just go. Please, I beg you to just go!" With that he pushed Benfu harder than expected for such a small fellow and Benfu stumbled out of the shed. He looked around and, seeing no one, bent over and ran toward the first cornfield. At the edge he turned to see the boy one last time but he was already gone. Benfu wished he had thanked him for such a selfless act but now it was too late. He turned and ran.

Benfu watched from the safety of the cornstalks for a moment, then made a dash around the old shed and behind the kitchen building to the old well. The thing was dry and no one attempted to draw from it any longer, making it a great hiding place for the one thing in his possession that would have been confiscated if found. Yes, he'd taken a chance by carrying something that had been forbidden throughout China but he'd safeguarded it well. And he'd been lucky when he'd arrived; there weren't enough commune workers on hand to keep everyone together as they'd struggled to check them in, allowing Benfu to sneak away and find the well before returning to the line of new residents. It'd been almost a year since that first day and the well had remained the best place to keep his treasures.

Looking around to be sure he was alone, he leaned over the rounded bricks and began pulling on the frayed rope. He felt the weight on the end of it but didn't release his sigh of relief until his bag came into view. He quickly untied it and held it to his chest, then ran back to the field.

Pausing for a moment, he ate only a nibble from one more rice ball, scared he'd need to ration it for a while. He listened intently for voices, for he was sure there was probably a chase going on. But he didn't hear anything and once again he thanked the gods that perhaps Pei had successfully diverted them.

With one arm holding his ribs and the other clutching his bag, Benfu ran through the field until he thought his lungs would explode. As he ran, the stalks slapped his face and he could feel his cuts reopening, but he didn't let the sting deter him from his rush to freedom. Finally he stopped for only seconds to get his breath and take a sip from the most amazing water he'd ever tasted. He turned the canteen over and, sure enough, there were the initials of the boy, reminding Benfu he'd have to be very careful where he discarded it eventually. He sure didn't want the boy to face any repercussions.

He ran more until he reached the end of the row of cornstalks. There he stopped to rest and spread mud over the welts on his arms and neck. The mosquitos were still landing on him even in his sprint to safety, and the welts from the last few days burned like fire. Benfu quickly finished and took off again, by this time limping with each stride. He was halfway to town. He could do this, he told himself. *Don't stop, don't stop, don't stop.* The words became a mantra that kept him putting one foot in front of the other.

Finally he could run no more, so he staggered on toward the lights of town. He had plenty of time to think and marveled at how or why he had been given a reprieve. He took the time to barter with the gods that if he could just make it through the night, he'd spend his life finding ways to be just as selfless as Pei had been with him. As he walked he stayed close to the ditches, ready to jump at any moment. He knew he looked a sight—beaten and staggering like a drunken man. He hoped the late hour would keep anyone from seeing him. He unscrewed the lid from the canteen and drank the rest of the water, unable to stop himself.

At least three hours later, much longer than it should have taken him, Benfu found himself on the outskirts of town. He took a break and dropped to his knees, using his hands to skim just a tiny bit of water from the top of the mud in a pothole. It tasted oily and salty, but it was gloriously wet. With that small reward he felt he could keep moving a bit farther. As he stood, the rumbling and lights of a large truck came around the corner and Benfu stumbled to the high grass and hid as it went by. He figured it was the delivery truck coming from his commune, taking most of their day's crop intake on to Shanghai. No one cared there wasn't enough left behind to feed the people; their only directive was to bring it on to Mao's troops.

Still shaking from the close call, he stayed away from the main roads, choosing to skirt down the country roads until he came to one of the *hutongs,* the residential lanes that ran parallel to the major roads. He thought maybe he could find an old shed or barn to hide in while he rested. If he could get just a few hours of sleep, then he would set off again.

As he staggered down one quiet lane, he saw a small home with the gate open. The house beckoned to him and since his gut instinct had not failed him yet, Benfu quietly slipped through the gate. He looked at the front window and saw only a very faint light, and he hoped the homeowners were asleep as they should be at this time of night. First listening for noise from the inside and hearing nothing, he crept around the house toward the small utility shed. He wished it had windows as he could hardly make himself go back into such tight, airless quarters, but alas, he had no choice if he wanted to remain hidden. He hoped he could find space in it to stretch out for a few hours.

Spotting an old rusty water pump on the side of the house, he stood there, uncertain for a moment. He could take a chance and try to clean himself up a bit and get some fresh drinking water to refill his canteen, or he could wait. He shifted from foot to foot. He didn't want to get caught but he was so thirsty that his tongue felt swollen and rough like fabric in his mouth. If he didn't get water, he felt he would just die. He was dizzy and weak, and so thirsty that if he succumbed to his painful hunger and ate one of his last remaining rice balls, he might even choke on it. What a cruel fate to finally have food in his pocket but know his throat was too parched to get it down.

With precious moments wasting before daylight came upon him, Benfu made a choice. He had to drink. He only prayed the old pump would not moan and carry on, waking the family inside. With his ribs now in such intense pain he could barely walk, Benfu struggled over to the pump. He slowly and carefully lifted the handle and flinched when the old pipes began to rumble. Carefully he dropped to his knees. He'd be quick, just one drink. Turning his head to the side to catch the stream in his mouth, he heard someone behind him.

The quick movement to see who had caught him made his head spin and a wave of dizziness completely overtook him. As everything went black around him, he focused on the face of a girl about his own age. His last thoughts before he hit the ground were of how pretty and clean she looked as she stood there with her hands on her hips, a scolding frown making its way across her heart-shaped mouth.

Then all was dark and Benfu welcomed the curtain that fell across his vision and smothered the smell of his fear.

"If we could see the miracle of a single flower clearly,
our whole lives would change."

—Buddha

Chapter One

Beitang City, Wuxi, China, 2010

On a cloudy day in early January, Benfu stood outside his house and held the red pail under the spigot, waiting for it to fill. Today was a good day; when he pumped the handle, the old pipes didn't moan and rattle too much before deciding to cooperate. But he didn't mind it so much either way—like him, the piece of iron was ancient but stubbornly kept going. And anyway, they had a history together, and if a man could feel affection for a thing, then Benfu absolutely did. A silly fondness, but there all the same, for it was the very same temperamental water spigot that had been the matchmaker that brought him and his precious Calli together so many years before.

When the water reached the top, he pushed the pump handle down and carried the pail across the street to the old widow's house. Quickly he filled the tins for her chickens and used the last of the water on her pot of herbs hanging in her window box. He looked at the chicken droppings and considered cleaning them up, but that was a task Widow Zu usually took on and he didn't want to deprive her of that joy. And anyway, nothing was worse than the smell of chicken dung on a man's hands.

Chuckling, he returned to his yard across the street, got on his bike, and headed out for the day. Twenty minutes later, he pushed his rusted three-wheeled bicycle slowly up the steep hill and turned the corner. Around him the streets were coming alive. Morning vendors were opening their stalls and stacking displays of fruits and vegetables, sweepers cleaned the sidewalks, and early commuters bustled to work. As he strained to push the bike, the cars, electric scooters, and other bicycles rushed past him. Most paid him no attention, for he was just one of many laborers out at the crack of dawn trying to get an early start to the day. With his weathered brown face and deep wrinkles, he blended in, but unlike some of the men his age he passed who were doing their morning *Qigong* exercises or sitting at makeshift tables while playing cards, Benfu still had a job to do. Even though he had lived on earth for over six decades, he could not retire.

He struggled the last few feet, listening to his water canteen bumping against the metal bar it was tied to and thought about how much the city had changed over the years. At least his side of Beitang City—Old Town Wuxi as some called it—still kept some of the old charm, while new Wuxi had grown with businesses and even many foreigners coming in to make their mark. Benfu was a transplant—he'd been sent to Wuxi as a teenager by his parents to escape the danger of Shanghai during the Cultural Revolution. It was for his protection, they'd told him as they cried and bid him good-bye. What they had thought would be a better life for him was an unforgettable time of trauma and hardship. And though he'd never intended to stay for so long, fate had intervened and Wuxi had become his home. But that was long ago and he'd survived many more hard times since then—times that were better left unspoken of, times that made a day like today feel like child's play.

At the top of the hill, Benfu mounted the bike again and with shoulders bent over the handlebars to add more weight, he pedaled slowly. He was already tired and that irritated him. He'd always been known to be bigger and stronger than most, but for the last year he just couldn't shake the cough and heavy feeling that had enveloped him. Passing the line of street breakfast stands, he winced at the sudden squeaking from the rusty back wheel of his bicycle. As it began to bump and turn haphazardly, he hoped it would last the day, at least until he could ask his daughter to take a look to see if she could repair it. If she could, that would save him some valuable coins that he could avoid paying the local repairman. He was lucky to have the transportation, and the three-wheeled bike was fitted with a makeshift cart on the back, allowing him a way to haul things home without carrying them in a basket on his back as he'd done for years before.

Benfu passed the cigarette store and for a moment he fought the sudden craving that overtook his thoughts. His wife had finally got her way when he'd stopped smoking a few years before, but there were days he could almost taste the sweet tobacco, he wanted it so badly. It was a welcome distraction to hear his friend call his name from where she perched on the next front stoop, peeling peanuts. His mouth watered at the sight of the treats in her bowl. He would have liked to be able to bring some peanuts home to add to their own simple dinner. Occasionally the woman saved a small bag behind her to hand over to him, but not today. He had many friends in the neighborhood and one had even complimented him long ago by telling him he was a big man with an even bigger presence. He didn't quite know how he had a big presence but it had sounded nice. Always known as soft-spoken and wise with his words, he found that when he had something to say, others usually listened.

"*Zao,* Benfu. Cold day, eh?"

Benfu raised his hand to the woman and smiled. "Good morning to you, too, Lao Gu. Yes, very cold. But don't worry, spring is coming soon!"

These days he was so used to being cold that he no longer thought much about it. At least there hadn't been any snow this season—saving him the trouble of carrying his load when he couldn't get the cart through. Sure his cough was worse in the cold, his old joints ached, and his gnarled hands cramped from the hours spent wrapped around the handles, but instead of dwelling on it, he chose to focus on other matters—matters like finding enough discarded items to earn enough for a day of meals for his family and if he was lucky, enough to put some savings toward their monthly rent bill. But first, his self-imposed obligation needed to be fulfilled for the day.

"*Zhu ni haoyun,* Benfu." She wished him luck and went back to peeling. No small talk was needed because there wasn't anything new to discuss. They'd been passing each other for the last fifteen years and only stopped to catch up every month or so, unless either of them had news worth interrupting their chores. The woman was widowed and Benfu had known her husband back in the hard days. But those were times they didn't talk about.

Benfu continued with his cart and hoped his morning would be uneventful. He didn't wish to find anything out of the ordinary as he turned past the block of buildings. He really didn't. He always wished to find nothing except trash. But sometimes something other than trash found him.

Now in the alley between two buildings, he guided his bike around soiled refuse bags and a line of jumbled bicycles, then heard the first mewl coming from a pile of boxes. He hoped it was nothing but a new kitten, strayed from its mother. That would be the best scenario, for Benfu could help it find the rest of the litter and then go on with his day as usual. But the closer he got to the huge pile of trash, the more that hope faded. He'd heard this same sound before and he scolded himself; he should have known the difference from the start.

Sighing, he stopped the bicycle and climbed down. He walked over to the pile of cardboard boxes. Lifting them carefully and tossing them aside one by one, he dug down until he finally found the right one. As he paused to look at the labeling on the side of the cardboard, a couple at the end of the alley stopped and pointed at him, then moved along.

Gently he picked up the box and carried it to his cart. He carefully set it on top of the pile of trash he had collected on the way over. Opening the two flaps, he peered into the box and immediately connected with tiny dark eyes.

"Aiya," he muttered softly, so as not to scare her. The baby was very young—maybe only a few hours or possibly a few days old. She lay in the box fully unclothed save for a scrap of a red shirt with frog ties and a few balled-up newspapers scattered around her. Benfu wrinkled his nose as the smell of urine wafted up from the soaked box. He noticed her umbilical cord still hung from her tiny button, already turning dark from the lack of sustenance running through it. From the weak sound of her mewling and the mottled color of her skin, she didn't have much time left.

Faster than most would think an old man could move, Benfu struggled out of his worn red overcoat and laid it on the ground in front of him. He then lifted the infant and set her on top of it. As he knelt down to wrap the material around her, he ignored the throbbing in his knees and rubbed her tiny feet and hands. He counted under his breath as he quickly massaged each petite toe and finger. While he worked to get the blood running in her body again, his eyes met hers and held.

With the surprise of being suddenly discovered, she had quieted and serenely stared up at Benfu, her dark eyes twinkling at him. She was beautiful, this one was, and he wondered what sort of ailment she might have that would have prompted her parents to relinquish her to a new fate.

"Hello, *nuer*. I've come to take you home. Just hold on and we'll get you all fixed up. And we'll add one more scavenger's daughter to the world, yes we will." He wrapped the coat all around her, making sure to double the sleeves around her icy feet. He gently laid her back in the box and after checking to make sure he had made a sufficient tunnel through the material for her to breathe through, he closed the flaps again. Looking around, he hoped the remaining cardboard would be there when he returned, but for now he needed to hurry.

Turning the bicycle around, he shivered from the sudden gust of wind that blew through his clothing. He climbed aboard and slowly began to pedal, willing the stiffness in his knees away. As he picked up the pace and began his journey home, he sighed and looked over his shoulder again at the box his newest treasure was nested in. He ignored the nervous fluttering in his stomach that reminded him how hard it would be to feed one more hungry mouth, and instead gave thanks to the gods that he had found the baby girl before it was too late.

Chapter Two

Fifty minutes later Benfu pulled his cart onto the sidewalk and around the low concrete wall to the lane of small buildings. Their house, like others along the row, opened up onto a small backstreet. The narrow *hutong* was only wide enough for pedestrians and bicycles to get through, creating a quieter sense of community that with the ever-increasing number of trucks and vehicles on the roads was getting harder to find in China these days. The downside was that the small homes were all very close together and most times that meant a lack of privacy.

He pedaled the bike much faster than the neighbors were used to and the sound of the squeaking wheel soon brought the people out. Like statues, they stood silently, watching him go by. They knew by the pace he kept that he carried something more than his usual trash. As he passed, they eyed the box lying on top of the pile in his cart.

"Calli!" he called, struggling to get his breath. *"Guo lai!"*

Within seconds his wife popped out of a doorway ahead. Around her a few more heads of different heights began appearing. Peony was the first to burst out the door to meet Benfu, skipping as fast as she could—so fast her braids took turns dancing in the air.

"Ye Ye! Do we have a new sister?" She rushed to him and ran alongside the cart as he pedaled, trying to peek into the box.

"*Dui le,* Peony. You have another sister. But if we don't warm her quickly, she won't survive."

Calli met him at the low gate to their tiny courtyard. He had caught her in the middle of wrapping up her long, wet hair and she struggled to pin the strands into a bun on the top of her head as she hurried to him. Benfu reached into the box and picked up the baby girl, then breathed a sigh of relief as he handed her over to his wife. He saw a flash of pain cross her face, pain from too many years of bending her body to pick up trash, but Benfu knew that if the baby could be saved, his Calli could do it.

"She's very cold." Benfu shook his head and shoved his hands into his pockets to warm them and stop the trembling.

"I've told you to take a blanket with you, crazy old man. Now look at you standing there shivering without a coat." She tsked as she carried the baby into the house. "Peony, stoke the fire and get your Ye Ye his sweater. Ivy, get the can of flour and the milk powder, and plug in the kettle."

Everyone hurried around the small house as Calli sat down in her chair and opened the bundle. Beside her, their youngest, Jasmine, stood and watched everything happening. At five years old, the little girl had never uttered a word since they had found her over a year before; she only stared at everyone with her big, knowing eyes. The infant stared up at Jasmine and when the cold air hit her skin, she gave a pitifully weak wail. Maggi, another daughter, strained to see the baby from her pallet on the bench lining the wall.

Benfu nodded his head. "That's a stronger cry than the one that helped me find her. So we've got more of a chance than I thought to save her."

He met his wife's eyes over the bundle of the baby. Her expression told him what she was thinking. It was the same thing he was—about the first little baby girl he had brought home many years earlier. Benfu had found her wrapped in a thin sheet in front of the train station. He'd walked up to find a crowd standing around the white bundle, yet no one was doing anything other than staring. He had broken through them and picked up the baby and brought her home. She was so cold that her tiny body was frozen stiff. They had wrapped her in a burlap sack and warmed her as best as they could, and she had responded for a while, even beginning to wiggle in Benfu's oversized hands. A quick check by the doctor and he had released her to their care. She was a gift that had healed a hole in their hearts and they had named her Rose, but tragically she had died a few weeks later. The short time they had her made Benfu realize that they had been depriving themselves of the joy a young one could bring to one's heart.

Since then, Benfu and Calli had made it their life's mission to care for the castaways that fate brought into their lives. For Benfu, it was a self-imposed penance of a sin only one other knew. For his wife, the girls helped to fill an empty, sad void deep within her soul. In her younger years, she'd been called Mama by the girls she'd taken under her wing, just as he'd been Baba. But a decade or so ago their newer daughters instinctively called him Ye Ye and her Nai Nai—the affectionate nicknames used for grandparents in Chinese families.

Many of the children they had rescued were out in the world thriving now, but Benfu felt a small bit of relief that those who hadn't made it had at least felt a bit of love as they passed through to the next world.

Calli unwrapped the baby and handed the coat to her nearest daughter. She pulled the quilt from the back of her chair and wrapped the infant inside the folds, exclaiming over the creamy hue of the child's brown skin.

"Put your inside jacket on, Benfu. You'll have pneumonia," she scolded her husband. Their home, like others in their neighborhood, was still quite chilly inside, despite their best efforts to keep it warm.

The kettle began to bubble and shake. Benfu rushed over to supervise his daughter as she made the baby's first meal.

"Only one spoon of powder, Ivy." With his thumbs hooked through his suspenders to keep from interfering, he coached the girl as she measured the powder into the bottle. The milk powder was very expensive and he had taught her to ration it carefully. Ivy opened the bag of flour and added a heaping spoonful to the mixture. She poured the steaming water over it and put the nipple on and shook it.

"I already know that, Ye Ye. I made all of Mallow's bottles before she died. And you don't have to tell me how lucky we are to have milk powder, or the story of how when I came home, all you could give me was flour and water." The girl grinned at Benfu and he winked back. Next to his little Jasmine, Ivy was one of his favorites, though he'd never let the others know. It amazed him how all of his daughters remembered those who had left this world and were able to fondly speak of them. He was getting so old he struggled to remember how many had died over the years, but he knew it was at least a half dozen.

"Hand it to me, Ivy." Benfu took the bottle from her and opened it again. He didn't mention that their first found baby wasn't even lucky enough to have flour and water. That came with the second child but Rose was fed broth right from their supper pot. That was all that they had at the time and it was given with a spoon, a few drops at a time. Since then there had been many more children and they had learned to keep a small amount of milk powder locked away in the cupboard, ready for emergencies.

Benfu reached over and lifted the pitcher of cold water from the counter and added an inch or so to the bottle. He shook it, then hurried over to his wife.

Calli held the baby close to her body, rocking and humming to her. She had pulled her chair as near to the old coal stove as she could. She took the bottle from Benfu and as soon as it touched the baby's cheek, the tiny girl frantically bobbed her head back and forth, instinctively rooting for the nipple. Calli slid it into the open mouth and everyone around breathed a sigh of relief when the baby successfully began to suckle. Calli and Benfu would take the baby to see the neighborhood doctor later in the day but she had learned over the years that the children had the best chance of survival if she worked to stabilize them at home first.

Peony, Ivy, and Jasmine crowded around their Nai Nai, watching the baby suck the lumpy mixture. Lily—Ivy's twin sister—sat at the table, listening intently to what was going on around her. Even Maggi stretched herself as far as she could from her perch on the bench, trying to get a glimpse of the baby's face.

"Nai Nai, do you think she misses her mother?" Peony asked pensively. She was the next to youngest in the group and usually the most vocal and probably the sassiest, too, Benfu would say. There was no doubt that Peony was of mixed blood and by the streaks of auburn in her hair and the slight rounding of her golden-colored eyes, Benfu suspected her father was Caucasian. At nine years old, Peony still remembered her own mother and even recalled the day only a few years ago that she was told good-bye and set on a bench outside the train station. Her mother told her to wait and someone would be along to take her to have the peach-sized lump removed from her head. She said they'd be together again when she recovered.

Lucky for her that someone was Benfu and he had begged and borrowed to get the money for her surgeries. To make things harder for the child, postcards had started to arrive for Peony soon after her first treatment. Obviously the woman had been watching to make sure her daughter was found and had followed them home to see where they lived, always staying elusive enough to avoid being discovered.

Before the end of the three freezing treatments and final procedure for Peony, two more postcards arrived. They were brief, only a line or two, and while there was never a return address, the sender claimed to be Peony's mother and said she was watching the girl from afar and wanted her to know that when her circumstances changed, she'd be back for her daughter. He and Calli had agonized over whether to give the girl the postcards or not but in the end, Calli reminded him that they'd always been totally honest with their daughters. They hadn't wanted to start keeping secrets. Since the first postcard, Peony had started acting quite ornery. However, Benfu was gentle on the girl because he knew she was hurting inside.

Benfu didn't know if the woman would ever really come forward and claim her child, but he did know that the postcards were a thread of hope that Peony clung to with all her might. She even slept with them under her pillow, taking them out one by one and gazing at the scenery on the fronts as she probably tried to imagine where her mother was. He only wished he had a way to find the woman and reunite the two, even if it would be painful to lose the girl. It never failed to sadden Benfu when Peony talked about the gentle kiss her mother had given her before walking away.

"*Bushi!* She doesn't miss them. They are cruel for leaving her in the cold with barely any clothes on. If her parents had their way, she'd already be dead," Ivy blurted out, and received a chastising look from her Nai Nai.

Benfu saw Peony visibly wince, then lower her head. "My mother didn't mean for me to die. She wanted me to get help. She told me so," she said, picking at the threads in the colorful rug she sat on.

Benfu shook his head. The girls knew he had a strict rule about criticizing parents for leaving their children. He always told them no one knew the entire story or what was truly in the parents' hearts. He even believed that sometimes it wasn't the mothers who did or even agreed to the abandoning of their children. He knew that from experience—a hard lesson he'd learned years before.

"Zheng Ivy, we mustn't make rash judgments. Perhaps her mother was sick herself and someone else took her baby from her. We just do not know the truths of the story. All we know is that it is fate that she is a part of our family now," Benfu gently chastised her while pushing away a forbidden memory that threatened to invade his thoughts.

Ivy hung her head, her cheeks flaming. Benfu patted her on the back. Ivy and Lily were their only set of twins—identical at that!—and had been with them for nine years. At first he'd got their names constantly confused but he'd finally stopped calling them the wrong names. Now they were fourteen and Ivy's emotions seemed to be all over the place as she struggled with feelings about her birth parents. She was a loyal one—he'd give her that. She'd always been the eyes for her blind sister and totally devoted to caring for her. Lily had so far been a gentle-mannered girl but lately Benfu could sense some discontent behind her unwavering stare.

He knew she needed to be enrolled in a school for the blind but so far his requests had gone unheeded by the council of affairs. The whole family continued to let her be as independent as possible but the truth was that she needed more assistance to learn the ways of the blind than they could give.

Ivy didn't lift her face to meet his gaze; she didn't like to be scolded. And in return he didn't like to see his girls unhappy and rarely worked up the energy to discipline them. He didn't see life through rose-colored glasses, though. He'd admitted before that some of the girls who'd passed through their doors had taken months and even years to soften. Many of them had been physically or emotionally abused—sometimes even both—but he and Calli always remembered that all children had some good in them. With the most difficult cases, they'd focused on giving them a stable home, and Lao Tzu was right when he once said, "Kindness in giving creates love."

Benfu sighed as he thought about how dearly he loved all twenty-four flowers that had bloomed in the fields of his life.

Chapter Three

As the sun set and the nighttime chill invaded their house, the rest of the family arrived and they all gathered around the room, ready to sit down for supper. The concrete floors had been swept clean and mopped, the colorful braided rugs beaten and returned to their places. The fire had been allowed to die down, the usual routine to keep the girls from breathing in too much coal smoke as they slept. Benfu also kept their supply of coal rationed, in case the weather turned bad and he couldn't buy more. Coal used to be inexpensive but nothing was cheap these days. It was inevitable that the cost of living in Beitang would soon catch up to the bigger cities. Every yuan needed to be carefully accounted for.

The modest home could only accommodate a small table that sat three, so all but Jasmine scattered to other perches. Some balanced on overturned crates and some on short stools. Benfu always told the others that he liked to have Jasmine at the table beside him so he could watch and make sure their tiny sister ate her dinner. The other girls didn't mind—they knew his affection for Jasmine and, bundled up in coats and scarves, they sat quietly, their cheeks flushing a healthy pink hue.

Benfu looked around and smiled at his daughters, proud of their attempt to look proper for dinner. Although they couldn't change their clothes for another day or so, until their allotted bath day, they had all washed their faces and combed their hair. He and his wife had raised many children, and most of them were now out living their own lives, but he had always made it a point to teach them to be proud of who they were no matter what their status. The children in the room were meant to be the last ones but the new arrival today had changed that plan—once again.

Linnea, currently the oldest daughter in the house, held the baby. She had arrived home and stopped to repair the loose wheel on the bicycle before taking her turn to get to know the newest member of her family. At seventeen, the girl had an unusual ability to understand mechanics and could fix most anything. Still, like some of her adopted sisters, she had not been allowed to attend school past the fifth grade, as her birth was unregistered. Instead she held a job as an assistant to a street-side bicycle repairman. It earned her only a few yuan a week, but her contribution to the family income was needed and appreciated. Benfu also liked that her job kept her busy; he dreaded the day that she would become interested in boys, as she was already turning into quite the beauty. Luckily, he thought, she hadn't realized it yet.

It was Ivy's turn for kitchen duty, and she scooped the rice from the cooker and distributed it evenly among the bowls as another sister handed out clean chopsticks. When finished, Ivy took the first bowl to her twin. Lily felt Ivy approach and Benfu watched her serene smile slowly appear, her hands out, ready to receive her supper. Then Ivy picked up another bowl and took it to the bench where Maggi stretched out. As she approached, Maggi pushed herself up on her elbows, eager to eat.

"Xie xie." She thanked her as Ivy handed her the bowl and then took the time to pull the coverlet over the girl's feet. Even though Maggi couldn't feel anything from the hips down, Ivy didn't want her toes to be cold. They all took great pains to make

sure the girl was always treated with the utmost care. The doctors had said she would never be able to walk because her spina bifida hadn't been treated soon enough. But other than her sometime grumpiness from pain caused by the lump on her spine, and her embarrassment at her incontinence, Benfu rarely remembered her ever complaining in the three years she'd been with them. She was one of the sweetest eight-year-olds he'd ever known.

"You're welcome." Ivy returned to the bowls and took the next ones to Nai Nai and Ye Ye at the small table. She took Linnea's bowl to her and set it down beside the stool the girl sat on. She quickly finished handing out the rest and sat down with her own bowl in one hand, chopsticks in the other. They all sat still, waiting for Benfu to give the word to begin their dinner.

"Linnea, put the baby down into the cradle," he reminded her.

She gently laid the baby in the wooden bed and tucked the blanket around her. The child still slept, as she had done almost nonstop since her first bottle hours before. Benfu was worried about her, but he knew that they had done all they could and her destiny was now out of their hands.

"Let's eat," he said, and the room erupted into a clatter of chopsticks against porcelain. Tonight's dinner was only steamed rice and eggs with tomatoes, but around the room the girls ate as if tasting one of the greatest recipes on earth.

"Ye Ye, when will we have pork again?" Lily asked, then shoved a bite of rice in her mouth. Lily couldn't see the expressions everyone held as they looked up to see what Ye Ye's response would be. However, she was startled at the sudden silence brought on by her question.

As the eldest, Linnea looked up to answer for their Ye Ye. "Lily, we all look forward to the nights that a bit of meat or vegetables will accompany our rice, but you must learn to keep that thought inside your head and not let it pass through your lips," she said quietly. When she finished, the eating began again and noise filled the room.

Benfu looked up from his bowl just in time to see a sad shadow cross Lily's face. He held his tongue, knowing that each child must learn the lesson of a humble life and pass it down to the younger ones. He had no doubt that in time Lily would learn it, too.

For Benfu, Lily's question brought back a lot of memories. During the revolution and the years after, meat was allowed only once a week for most families. And that was only if they had the proper food coupons, which were mostly given to the red families—those without questionable backgrounds of ties to counter-revolutionaries. Of course questionable backgrounds included anyone related to an official, teacher, landowner, or intellectual, so many families were automatically out of the equation. Since all the persecution had ended in the early seventies, he'd had meat more often, but since he was getting older and money was getting scarcer, they had to depend more on rice and noodles for their daily meals.

After dinner his daughters gathered around in a circle. Benfu brought in a large box of scrap from his morning collection and set it in the middle. The girls reached to grab remnants but Benfu held up his hand. Their nightly sorting of empty plastic bottles, newspapers, tin cans, and other treasures could wait a few minutes.

Benfu went and picked up the infant from her bed. He brought her with him to the rocking chair and sat down, cradling her in his big hands.

"Wait. First, we name the baby. Who has a name they'd like to offer up?"

The girls all made various expressions of concentration. Benfu looked over their heads at his wife and smiled. Calli had taken the baby to the doctor and he had given her a once-over and declared her fit to stay in their home. They still weren't sure she would live or even if they would be given custody of her after the police reports were made, but instead of waiting the traditional one month, they always gave each child a name right away so that if she died, she could enter the spirit world knowing who she was. Some in China might call their initial dubbing only *milk* names, to be changed after they started school or married, but with Benfu's girls the names would be permanent. After so many daughters, it was getting harder to come up with new names and these last few years he had made the important decision a family affair. His daughters took the naming ceremonies very seriously.

"What about Fang?" Ivy offered. "It means fragrant. Zheng Fang makes a nice name."

Behind her the infant stirred and let out a small cry. The girls giggled. The baby then began to coo and do her best to give all of them a piece of her mind.

Calli laughed. "I don't think I've ever heard such a young infant be so vocal. I think she wants a say in if she should be called Fang."

"I don't think she likes that name and anyway, it isn't a flower, Ivy," Linnea said, rolling her eyes.

"Close enough, because a flower smells good!" Ivy retorted, crossing her arms sullenly.

Benfu chuckled, remembering how *fragrant* the infant had been when he found her. He was glad that his wife had washed the strong smell of urine off her once she had settled. Now she smelled only of the flower water Calli made and distributed each week to the girls.

The girls began chattering among themselves, too quickly for Benfu to keep up with. He looked at his wife and pointed toward the kitchen cove.

Calli stopped her rigorous massaging of Maggi's legs and went to the cupboard. She took the key from around her neck and unlocked the door, opened it, and removed a pencil and a thick leather-bound book. Sitting down at her stool at the table, she untied the twine and opened the weathered cover. Benfu smiled at the sight of the red book embossed with a golden 家, the character representing *Family*.

Calli picked up the pencil and waited with it poised in the air, ready to record the new name once decided, as well as the baby's finding spot. Every small detail mattered; where they were found, what they wore, contents of any note left with them. Calli often stated that if any of her children wanted to find her birth family one day, they would have every clue she could give them to start their search. In addition, Calli recorded dates of the child's milestones and for those who were grown, their most recent addresses. No one but Calli had ever looked in the book, but she made it clear that when they were grown, the daughters would be welcome to their pages. So far none of them had ever asked for the information.

The girls quieted when they saw Calli sit down with the book. Bringing it out always settled them down. They all knew the importance it held. As far as the girls were concerned, the book was the most sacred possession in the house, for it contained all of their histories.

"Other ideas?" Benfu asked. He had given all the girls his own surname, so Zheng was already decided. They only needed to find a fitting second character. Years ago and in still many households today, names were picked by the grandparents or given by the local fortune-teller. The choices were usually dictated by the day and time of their birth, their parents' zodiac signs, and other factors. But Benfu was always one for breaking traditions and superstitions. "Lily, do you have a name you'd like to suggest?"

"What about Poppy? She was found on such a cloudy day and poppies are strong, even in storms." Lily smiled serenely. Benfu knew that some would wonder how she knew it was cloudy, since she could not see, but the girl had an uncanny ability to know what the weather was at any time. She could feel changes in the atmosphere before anyone could see them. Most of the time she could even forecast the weather for the next day, and Benfu was very proud of her gift.

Around the room everyone nodded in agreement. Even Ivy looked satisfied at the alternate choice. Benfu met eyes with each daughter, as he wanted the choice to be unanimous.

"What do you think, Calla Lily?" Benfu asked after each girl gave her approval.

Calli nodded her agreement, a small smile twitching at her lips. She reached up and tucked a stray hair back into the loose bun on her head.

"That's perfect, Lily. She is now officially our little Poppy." Benfu didn't mention that the older generations felt the poppy was a symbol of China's humiliation at the hands of European powers. But he pushed the thought back, not wishing to educate his daughters on such rubbish. And anyway, any mention of the opium that had at one time brought his country to such a low level could make him instantly angry.

Behind them Calli bent over the notebook and scrawled the new name inside on a fresh page. She recorded the few other details her husband had shared, including the date printed on the crumpled newspaper that had been in the box with the child. The pages were part of a newspaper from a neighboring town and were dated only the week before. It was a small clue but a clue all the same. The paper and the shirt Poppy had been wearing would go in her own small box to be stacked under the high bed with the rest of them.

Calli closed the book and retied the rope, then put it back into the cupboard and turned the key. She turned around to her children and smiled, clasping her hands together in front of her.

"Another Zheng flower is suitably named," she said, initiating a loud burst of applauding and giggling from the girls.

Linnea went to the baby girl, pulled her from the cradle, and held her high in the air. The layered split pants and jacket Calli had dressed her in after her quick sponge bath had swallowed her up, making her look even smaller than she was despite the thick layers.

They all laughed as their *jie jie* swung the infant around and sung her new name to her. "Zheng Poppy, you have come, Zheng Poppy, you are the one. . . ."

Benfu chuckled, then cleared his throat to get their attention. "Okay. Enough fun. Now we get to work." Around him the girls obediently scattered to their tasks, some to clean the supper dishes and others to sort through the day's collection.

Chapter Four

Linnea rose earlier than usual in her attempt to be out the door before any of her sisters woke up. Walking softly around the room, she tried to be quiet as she dressed and then as she weaved her hair into a simple braid down her back, but Nai Nai heard her stirring and rose to make her a quick breakfast of congee. Linnea turned around and placed her hands on her hips, sighing her frustration.

"Nai Nai, please go back to bed for a while. I don't need any breakfast," Linnea whispered. She knew her Nai Nai had a long day ahead of her and she wished she would rest longer.

Nai Nai ignored her and bent to pull her pot from the cupboard. After filling it halfway with water, she set it on the burner and lit the flame. From the canister on the counter she dipped out a few cups of rice and added them to the pot.

Linnea shook her head and took a seat at the table. She looked down at her watch and gave another dramatic sigh that her Nai Nai ignored.

Within minutes Nai Nai had served up a steaming bowl of congee and set it in front of Linnea. She ate quickly, eager to get on her way. She took care not to tap her spoon against the porcelain bowl, but even though she made no noise, her sisters began to stir.

Now with the comfortable lump of hot rice in her stomach, she briskly walked the half mile or so to the corner where her *laoban* had chosen to set up that week.

This morning her mind was on other matters—stuff that she didn't want to discuss with anyone else. These days she was feeling more and more pressure to do something to change the fate of her family. She was tired of being poor but more than that, she wanted to do something that would give her Ye Ye and Nai Nai some peace for the short time they had left on earth. They were old. It was a hard truth to accept, but Linnea knew they wouldn't be around too many more years. Already her precious Ye Ye coughed constantly, and Nai Nai got slower and stiffer every day because of her raging arthritis. Most days she didn't even pick up her beloved knitting. Linnea had seen her eyeing it with longing when her hands hurt too badly to work the needles. It just wasn't fair. They had given so much to give girls like her a chance at life, and despite their years of hard work, they still lived at almost the lowest level of poverty in town. Scavengers—Linnea hated the ugly label put on her and her family. Ye Ye had taught her to be satisfied with her station in life and as far as he knew, she was—but lately Linnea was fighting a discontent that refused to leave her. All around her, people were moving into the future with their fancy cars, computers, and other possessions they took for granted. Yet her family was lucky to be able to eat meat once a week and only had one bed in the house, not to mention the hand-me-down clothes that had made their way through dozens of girls. It was just unfair.

As she crossed the busy street, she passed a line of schoolgirls about her age coming from the other direction. Looking at their squeaky-clean white and blue uniforms and shiny running shoes, Linnea felt self-conscience and reached up to smooth the loose hairs around her face toward her braid. She looked down at her stained jeans and ragged shoes and her cheeks flushed with embarrassment. Her coat was also nothing to be proud of, as she had worn it since she was thirteen and the sleeves were at least an inch or so too short. She reached down to yank at one, trying to cover her pale wrist. She shouldn't have worried; the girls didn't even notice her. It was like she was invisible as they continued to skip ahead, giggling and chatting to one another, oblivious to her discomfort.

Just an added bright spot in another monotonous day, she thought sarcastically as she hurried down the street. She refused to allow herself to even think about the day ahead for the schoolgirls. The books, neat classrooms, and free time with friends—she remembered those days. Because she was considered a *child of the state,* she'd been allowed only eight years of schooling before they'd pushed her out.

She thought of her battered spiral notebook tucked deep into her backpack. She hoped to have time after work to go to the park and spend some time drawing. She knew she was good and wished she could attend art classes to show others that a poor girl from the old side of town could still have talent. And she'd put her reading and writing skills up against any of them. If only she were allowed to take them, she knew she could pass the historically ruthless university entrance exams. Her Ye Ye had taught all of them calligraphy and insisted they learn at least a hundred new characters a month, along with memorizing many famous lines of poetry. He was a fine teacher and Linnea felt a spark of guilt for wishing she were still in public school.

She strained her eyes and could see the bicycle repair stand a block ahead and already a few people waiting to have repairs done. She picked up the pace, hoping to get there in time to share in the profits of the early jobs.

"Zao." She called out a morning greeting to Lao Joh.

In reply he tossed a bicycle tube at her. "Find the hole and fix this."

Despite the short warning, Linnea caught the tube in midair. The customers gave her a curious look and then went back to minding their own business. She was used to Lao Joh's curt attitude and most of the time she just ignored it. She took the newly inflated tube and began rolling it through a bucket of water, looking for the air bubbles to form that would show her the hole.

Finding a gathering of small bubbles, she covered them with her finger and pulled a rag from the supply box. She dried the tube, then used a piece of chalk to mark the hole. Using her hand tool, she scraped and brushed at the bad spot to prepare it for adhesive.

"See how slow this girl works beside the master," Lao Joh stated to the crowd, breaking Linnea's concentration. He was already working on another tube for another customer. Linnea quickened her pace until she heard a flurry of whispers.

She looked up to find everyone around them grinning at the silent competition. She considered slowing down as she knew her boss would lose face if he was beaten by a girl, but something in her refused to bow and she picked up her pace again.

She grabbed the tube of glue and very precisely squeezed out just enough to cover the hole. She didn't want to get chastised for wasting too much, especially in front of the growing audience of gawkers around her. Beside her, Lao Joh picked up his glue and slopped a big patch of it on the tire tube he held.

Linnea glanced over at Lao Joh as they both waited the agonizingly long few seconds for the patching to dry. She saw him take his lighter from his pocket and light it next to the glue, cheating to dry it faster.

"Here." A young guy watching them from the crowd caught her attention and threw her his lighter. She caught it with one hand and hesitated, looking over at Lao Joh. He could've saved his glaring look of warning; she knew how he felt about her ability to use a flame properly. She wasn't allowed—short and simple. Using the flame could result in owing the customer a new tube, a mistake that would cost her *laoban* dearly. But if he was going to do it, she was, too. He shook his head at her but she ignored him and flicked the lighter, holding the flame to the glue just as he had, causing a murmur of amusement around her.

Instead of the short flick of flame that she expected, the flame jumped and ran the length of the tube. Linnea jumped up and using her hand, slapped out the fire. Ignoring the sting on her palm and the one to her pride, she tossed the lighter back to the stranger.

"I told you that you weren't smart enough to use the old ways," Lao Joh snorted.

Linnea didn't reply. Anything she said would mean trouble for her. But she still wanted to beat him. She couldn't help herself.

Simultaneously she and Lao Joh both turned to their customer's bicycles. Linnea quickly made sure the glue was dry, then rolled the tube once more through her bucket of water, searching to make sure there weren't any more holes. Then she pressed the almost-deflated tube into place inside the tire. Now biting down on her lip in concentration, she used her thumbs to push the tire into the frame, flinching when she pinched her skin next to the metal.

"*Aiya,* the girl is quick," remarked one of the customers over her shoulder.

Linnea didn't look to see what stage Lao Joh was at; instead she picked up her tire iron and used it to pry the rest of the tire into place. Beside her she heard the thump of Lao Joh's tire iron hit the pavement and knew he was right behind her.

The spectators—at least a dozen now—began to chant around them. "Go, go, go. . . ."

Linnea wasn't sure if they were rooting for her or Lao Joh and she didn't care—she just wanted to prove to him she was faster. Finally the tire was in place and she reached behind her for her air pump. Around her the crowd broke into laughter. She looked beside her and saw Lao Joh lunge for his, trying desperately to keep up with her. Linnea smirked, knowing the crowd's chanting and amusement were making him nervous.

A few pumps and the tire inflated perfectly. Linnea threw down the pump and lifted the tire into place on the bike frame. From her peripheral view, she could see Lao Joh doing the same.

Her hands now shaking, she picked up the wrench and quickly tightened one screw, then moved to the next. Lao Joh began tightening his first screw and Linnea started on the second one, trying to hide the smile that lurked in anticipation of beating him. At almost the last crank of her wrench, Lao Joh suddenly jumped to his feet and threw his tool down, narrowly avoiding hitting her with it.

"Go!" he yelled, pointing his finger at her. "Go away now! You are fired. From now on no girls will work for me!"

Linnea stopped working and stared up at Lao Joh. Neither tire was completely ready, so neither of them had won, but she knew she was only half a second from the crowd's declaring her the winner. She also knew she should've let her boss win, but she was so tired of always being the subservient one—taunted for being a girl. Now she was going to be jobless, all because of her stubborn streak that her Ye Ye had always warned her to control.

Lao Joh had gotten angry at her before for silly reasons and she knew if she just held her tongue, he'd finally calm down. But as she waited, he stepped forward and shoved her. Linnea stumbled backward and would have fallen if someone behind her hadn't reached out and supported her, then given her a gentle nudge to set her back on her feet. Embarrassed, she didn't even turn around to see who it was, but instead straightened up, refusing to let Lao Joh scare her.

At his manhandling, the spectators around them stopped chanting. Gasps could be heard from a few and others showed their disapproval of his poor sportsmanship by walking away. Lao Joh stood glaring at her with his hands on his hips.

"I told you to get lost." He glared at her, even angrier now that the crowd appeared to be turning against him. Though only a corner-bike-shop repairman, he took great pride in his small success and thought himself an important businessman. Linnea had learned long ago that any conceived slight against him would set him off.

"Lao Joh, *dui bu qi*." Linnea lowered her head in an attempt at a sincere apology, her cheeks flaming with the indignation she tried to hide. "Please, don't do this. I need this job."

When she raised her eyes to see his response, he still pointed at the street, adamant in his decision. Linnea picked up her bag and that was that. She was officially unemployed.

Linnea stayed on the sidewalk, walking along the busy town street and kicking at the few pieces of trash that found their way in front of her path. She felt humiliated, angry, and scared. All sorts of ill feelings wrapped up in one heavy lump sat in the pit of her stomach. Her pride had lost her a good job—one she was good at. Lao Joh had refused her apology and told her to leave. She didn't want to go home and tell Nai Nai what had happened. Even though she knew that her Nai Nai would probably comfort her and assure her it wasn't her fault, she dreaded seeing the flicker of concern her loss of income would surely bring to the old woman's eyes.

She stopped when she came to a low wall in front of the Bank of China. She sat down and pulled her notebook out of her bag, along with a pencil from the bottom. She flipped through until she found a blank page, then staring up at the majestic gold-flecked lion statues on either side of the glass doors, she began doing the only thing she knew would calm her nerves. She sketched.

A half hour had sped by as she stayed bent over her paper, making lions come alive under her pencil. The rapid movement of her pencil and the concentration on the lines calmed her and let her forget for many precious moments that she was in a tough predicament.

Suddenly she felt someone tug at her sleeve and jerked around. It was a tall guy and at first she didn't recognize him. But then suddenly she remembered.

"You!" she spat at the stranger accusingly as he grinned at her. Her abrupt movement made his hand slide down her arm and rest on top of her hand. Linnea jumped at the slight tingle that climbed up her arms at his touch on her skin, then jerked her hand away. She wasn't used to being touched by strange guys, even if they were cute.

"Me what?"

"If you hadn't tossed me your lighter, I wouldn't have made my boss so mad. Now I don't have a job. And we have a month-old-baby in the house for whom I had hoped to buy some milk powder today. There goes her milk powder and the bushel of corn I was going to get for a treat for my sisters. So thanks. Thanks a lot."

"Wow, you're going to blame me for all that? It looked to me like you were determined to show your *laoban* up in front of his customers. It's not my fault he got angry. I was just there to see what was drawing such a crowd. And if not for me, you'd have landed on the concrete on that little round butt of yours."

Though he kept his voice neutral and didn't seem to be offended, Linnea's cheeks burned at the truth he spoke. He had disappeared from her view for a moment and had obviously walked around to stand behind her. It really could have been his arms that caught her when Lao Joh shoved her so roughly. If that was the case, she was glad he had broken her fall, as she didn't know if her pride would have withstood that much humiliation.

"You're right. *Dui bu qi.*" She apologized and turned away from him.

She stuffed her pencil and pad into her bag and began walking. She'd gone only a few paces when the guy caught up with her again. He wasn't giving up easily.

"Hold on a minute. No need to apologize. Tell me your name. Where are you going so fast?"

Linnea was irritated that even her rudeness hadn't removed the smile still plastered on his face, along with an expression of determination.

She didn't have anywhere to go, honestly. She no longer had a job and couldn't go home yet. She was still trying to think how she was going to confess her mistake.

"I'm Linnea. And I don't know where I'm going. Just going."

The guy laughed and linked his arm through hers. Linnea almost pulled away but had to admit the sound of his voice was like a salve, soothing the ragged edges of her bruised dignity. She resisted her instincts, at least for a minute, to see what he wanted.

"Well, how about we *just go* together? I'll buy you some breakfast to make up for throwing you into the fire, so to speak. You can show me more of your work. I saw that picture you were drawing and you've got some real talent. Oh—my name's Sur Li Jet. Call me Jet, okay?"

Linnea hesitated. The guy was not much older than she, but he looked like he was from another world with his smartly cut black jacket and polished shoes. Usually she was invisible to people like him. So why was he interested in her? She knew it was obvious that she was from the poor side of town, so his attention didn't make sense. But before she could say no, he had guided her to the doorway of a local noodle shop.

He grimaced. "I know what you're thinking—and yes, my parents are fans of Jet Li."

Linnea shook her head. He was definitely sure of himself. *Maybe too much so.* "No, that's not what I was thinking, actually. I was thinking I need to get moving and find a new job."

"Please, Xiao Linnea. I swear I'm harmless. I just want to treat a pretty girl to a nice breakfast. And I might have an idea for how you can get a new job immediately. Spare just a half hour for me. *Hao de?*"

Linnea took a deep breath. No one except for her Ye Ye and Nai Nai had ever called her pretty before. And what could a simple breakfast hurt, after all? Or maybe just a cup of tea and then she'd leave. But would this be called a date? She'd never been on a *real* date before. Suddenly she realized she was overthinking everything and he was looking at her as if she were acting strange.

She exhaled slowly. "Okay. *Jet.* I've already eaten, but tea would be nice."

Jet held his hand up high in the air. "Great. High five! Starbucks or Mr. Li's Corner?"

Linnea tentatively reached up and tapped his hand weakly. Starbucks wasn't on her usual list of shops, as it was reserved for the rich Chinese who could afford to pay ten times the usual price for tea or coffee—definitely not an option for her small pocketbook.

"Mr. Li's Corner, if you don't mind. They know me there." She thought it couldn't hurt to have just a measure of safety and to let the guy know it in case he tried to pull anything creepy. That was all she needed after the day she'd had—and if he did feel brave enough to try something, he'd better be ready for a fat lip. She was tired of the meek act to let the men in her life get away with their macho ways. Her Ye Ye had raised her to be stronger than that.

"The Corner Shop it is then, pretty girl."

Chapter Five

Benfu walked slowly back to the house from his long trek to the post office. He didn't want to get home too quickly before deciding how to present what he held in his pocket. They'd received another postcard from the woman claiming to be Peony's mother. His first instinct was to throw it away or hide it, but he couldn't do that. It was a part of his daughter's life—her history. It simply wasn't his to throw away.

Yes, he and Calli had decided long ago to give Peony the postcards and let her make her own mind up about her so-called mother, but still he knew each word brought the child a certain level of grief that her mother had not come forward to claim her. This time, even without his glasses, Benfu could see the scratchy, barely legible characters that the woman had used to say she was going to be away for a while and unable to communicate.

With it still in his hand, he turned the corner and before he could even make up his mind what to do, there was Peony at the gate. She leaned over the metal rungs, her pigtails almost touching the dirt below as she swung herself back and forth. Benfu could still see the scar left behind from her hemangioma, as the doctor had called it. But she looked content. Unlike other children her age, Peony didn't need fancy toys or games to entertain herself. She was easily placated with only her imagination and the warmth of the sunshine on her face. Once again he was struck with what a wonderful daughter the woman was missing out on. And for what? If someone waited until they were financially able to have children—or in this case *keep* their children—there wouldn't be much procreating going on. And if he'd managed to raise dozens of daughters, he didn't see how the woman couldn't take care of just one.

Peony raised her head as she heard Benfu's footsteps. "Ye Ye! Why didn't you let me go to the post office with you?" She gave him her most petulant look, her lip hanging so low Benfu wondered how she didn't trip on it.

He shook his head. "Well, Peony, I didn't see you out here when I left. You must have been hiding somewhere or did you take your invisible potion? Wait a minute—I can't even see you now! Where did you go?" He frantically looked around, pretending not to see her right in front of him.

Peony laughed and Benfu sighed. He hated to break her cheerful mood with the postcard that he knew would cause her to be unhappy. But he also never wanted his girls to think he kept anything from them. Truth had always been the only answer in his book and he was too old to start changing now.

"I'll tell you what." He patted her head. "How about you and I go for a stroll? Hurry up now before any of your sisters see us." He opened the gate and Peony shrieked as she rode through the wide arc it made. Then she jumped off and stuck her hand through one of his suspenders, holding on until she steadied herself.

He looked toward the window and saw Calli peering out. He nodded at her, then put his arm around Peony, leading her out of their courtyard. Calli would know they needed a moment alone.

Benfu and Peony headed to the busy street and they stopped at a sidewalk vendor. After the old woman running the tiny kiosk finished telling him what a healthy-looking granddaughter he had, she then looked taken aback when she saw the color of her eyes. Benfu let Peony pick her yogurt drink and reached in his pocket for the three coins. He paid the speechless old woman, then led Peony to a bench alongside the sidewalk. They weren't far from home, but just far enough that they wouldn't be interrupted. Other pedestrians and commuters passed back and forth, paying no attention to what looked like an outing between a grandfather and his granddaughter. Even in the sea of people Benfu felt a sense of privacy and security.

"Sit down, Peony."

Peony sat quickly and peeled the tinfoil from the top of the cup rim. She took a deep gulp and when she brought the cup down, Benfu couldn't help but chuckle at the white mustache she sported.

"*Xie xie,* Ye Ye." She took another swallow. His girls loved the yogurt drinks and he tried to treat each of them at least once a month.

"You're welcome. Hey—listen. I brought you out here so we could be alone. I want to tell you something. You got another postcard." He pulled it from his pocket and handed it to Peony.

She eagerly grabbed it and first turned it to see the photo. She stared at the picture of a white cat embroidered across a beautiful red tapestry.

"Look, Ye Ye. I used to have a cat just like that!" Her eyes widened as she stared at the postcard.

"You did? You've never mentioned it before. Are you sure?"

Benfu was caught off guard, not expecting any revelations from that side of the card. It had been two years since he'd found Peony and not once had she ever mentioned having a pet. And he was sure that even if she did have a cat, *this* one wasn't hers. This was just another piece of artwork and white cats were a common decoration for the Chinese, as they represented fortune.

"I know but I just remembered when I saw the photo. Her name was Xiao Mao—little cat. She used to play with my pigtails when I'd get on the floor with her. She batted them around." Peony stared so hard at the photo, Benfu wondered that she didn't bore a hole through it. Then she flipped it over and strained to read the haphazard calligraphy. Parts of it were smeared and must have gotten wet somehow, and Peony struggled to make out the words. Benfu watched her face turn solemn. Then she handed it back to him.

"Ye Ye, can you read it? I don't think I understand."

Benfu took the card from her. He also couldn't read parts of it but he thought he could make out most of the message. He cleared his throat.

"To my dearest Mei Jin Zhen, for that is your name. I have heard you being called Peony but in case you wanted to know, you were named after a beautiful golden pearl," Benfu read, then looked at Peony to see her reaction.

"Mei Jin Zhen . . ." She spoke in a low whisper, letting the name roll off her tongue softly.

He could tell she was happy to know her real name and he felt a stab of disappointment. Even though she was seven years old when she last saw her mother, Peony had only remembered that her mother called her Mei Mei, the common nickname meaning little sister. Giving her the name Peony had made her very happy at the time.

Benfu patted her leg. "It's a beautiful name, Mei Zhen."

Peony looked up at him quickly. "No, Ye Ye. I want you to still call me Peony. I don't want anyone to call me Mei Jin Zhen until my mother comes back and I hear it from her first. Don't tell the others, okay?"

He nodded his head. "Okay, let me finish here, Peony."

Peony leaned back and through the corner of his eye, Benfu could see her mouthing her name silently to herself.

"She says, *'I need to tell you that I will not be near you for some time. I have to go to a place far away to work. But when I am able, I'll return and then hopefully we can be together again.'*" Benfu stopped reading. Just as he thought, Peony looked crushed. Even though they wondered if the woman really was near, it was an idea the child had held on to. And truthfully, the woman knew too much about them not to have been watching once in a while—even knowing she was called Peony told him she had indeed been near. The thought made him wonder just how many mothers out there had hung around his home to check on offspring who landed there.

"But where do you think she's going?" Peony asked.

Benfu put his arm around her and gave her a little squeeze.

"I don't know, Peony. Maybe she's a migrant worker. That would explain why she moves around to find work." That really was the most logical answer, as the investigation into where Peony had come from had turned up nothing from the locals. It was as if the girl had been brought to Wuxi from far away, but even she didn't know what town she was from.

Peony didn't answer. Benfu wished he could see what was rolling around in her little head. He felt so helpless.

"Peony, I know this makes you sad, but maybe she really will come back. And in the meantime, you'll always be a part of this family. We all love you dearly—you must know that. Right?"

A lone tear slid down her cheek before she quickly rubbed it away and jumped to her feet. She plucked the postcard from his hands and held it to her heart.

"I know, Ye Ye. And she's coming back. She said so."

Benfu watched her face transform from one of complete desolation to one filled with hope.

The constant resilience of the girl amazed him. It took so much to faze her and nothing could keep her down for long.

"Yes, Peony, that's what it says. And you didn't let me finish. But if you look along the bottom, she also says when she returns she'll bring you a present. Now you have even more to look forward to."

Peony smiled and then began skipping ahead. Benfu was glad the talk was over, and he was even glad that he had made it through another difficult moment and was able to remain straightforward. Life was hard but deception and lies would only make it harder. Perhaps the woman would never come back. He didn't know but he hoped she would stand by her promise. But if she never did, at least Peony would grow up knowing that he and Calli had done their best by her and never hid the truth.

He stood and followed her down the path, back toward home. Hopefully he'd have a calm afternoon, but in a house full of women that was highly unlikely. He smiled as they walked, secure in the knowledge that though very poor, his was a home full of truths, cheer, and a measure of love some never got to experience.

Chapter Six

Benfu paused when he came to the intersection. Most days he would take a right but today he'd gone through another part of town to make a visit to a certain bicycle shop owner. Linnea had been fairly secretive about how she had lost her job but after a week, the details of the event had finally made it through the *hutong* grapevine and to Benfu's ears.

He hadn't reacted to his neighbor's gossip; he had simply listened and nodded. But inside, he had immediately decided that Lao Joh needed an attitude adjustment. By the time he'd simmered over it all night, he'd left that morning with such a thunderous look on his face that none of his neighbors had even raised their hands in greeting as he went by. They didn't know it but his concentration was from his intent on having a *conversation* with Lao Joh. Benfu wouldn't stand for anyone putting his hands on any of his daughters. Ever.

Lao Joh had been surprised to see him, but even more shocked at the strength an old man like him still possessed as he brought him off his feet with just one large hand around his scrawny neck. It was more than just the week's pay the man owed his daughter; Benfu felt it important that Lao Joh learn he wasn't allowed to treat women just any way he wanted. He didn't think the surly street vendor would be so quick to do it again to other young women, and the expression of humility on his face was a satisfaction Benfu didn't expect. After his feet finally found solid ground again, Lao Joh had asked Benfu to convey his deepest apologies and gladly handed over Linnea's back pay plus a tidy bonus. Benfu couldn't wait to give it to her but for now he needed to return to his usual path and get back to work. Feeling much better, he had moved on.

As he pedaled through town, he appreciated the change in his routine, seeing people he'd never seen and vendors selling items much different than those on his usual path. At one corner an old man hawked his wares to the young women briskly walking by.

"Louis Vuitton! Gucci! Coach! Three hundred reminbi for top quality!" Behind him hung a makeshift wire display of purses, bags, and scarves that Benfu knew had to be counterfeit from the prices the vendor was quoting. A few girls were already there inspecting a bag, looks of envy splashed across their faces.

He didn't approve of selling fake items as it sullied the reputation of China, but he respected the tenacity of the man and nodded his head to him as he passed. He knew life was harder for some than others and he tried not to judge anyone his choice of livelihood. Though he'd never purchased such things, he expected that soon the man would have a few foreign women to haggle with and the local girls would disappear. The foreigners overpaid for everything, so they were where the real money was, and all the vendors competed for their attention.

As he came closer to a block of restaurants, he heard music pouring from one of them. People were coming and going and Benfu thought they must be having some sort of wedding banquet. Always the curious one, he stopped his bike and stood before the poster to see if it involved any families he knew.

But it wasn't a wedding. The flyer advertised a Cultural Revolution reunion for those in and around the city of Wuxi.

How ironic that he should choose a new path that morning and pass the restaurant at just this time. Could it be karma? Benfu had no desire to reunite with most of the people who surrounded him back then, but he did wonder what had happened to his old friend, Pei. He owed his life to the young boy and had thought about him for years; he even hoped Pei's path had smoothed out and he'd prospered after the revolution ended.

Using his hand to shadow the sunlight over his eyes, he peered through the glass door. Suddenly it moved out from under him and a young woman dressed in an old Red Guard uniform beckoned him in. Just like back in the day when the young people were proudly sporting their Red Guard clothes, this girl's green army uniform was too big and quite baggy, held up strictly by the security of her scarred leather belt. Only the recognizable red armband emblazoned with gold letters looked bright and shiny. Benfu thought she must not have been able to find any remaining vintage armbands to use and instead made a new one. Even knowing those days were long gone, Benfu felt a shiver of revulsion at the memory the girl's costume prompted.

"Please, come in and join our Cultural Revolution celebration," she cheerfully invited him. Behind her the tables were filled with people, many his age, drinking and chatting loudly. Decorations hung from every chandelier and long tables of food lined the outer walls. With a quick sweep of the room, Benfu didn't see anyone he recognized. And why should he? It had been at least forty years or so, way too much time for him to remember a face.

But a celebration? Benfu shook his head and opened the door to leave. There was nothing about the revolution that he wanted to celebrate. Or even remember. The entire historical event had boiled down to a tyrant conducting a war between classes—the peasants against the upper classes—enforcing Mao's vision of a new China. The Cultural Revolution—as Mao had named it—had resulted in more devastation and hardship than anyone could have ever predicted.

The ripples from all of those years were still felt around the country and some who had lived through it would never recover from their emotional, financial, and physical wounds. And on second thought, he knew he didn't ever want to lay eyes on those who'd given him his own beatings as they tried to beat the so-called bourgeois tendencies out of him. Benfu also knew the reunion probably had people from both sides and he couldn't possibly stay and listen to any still-naïve Mao supporters. If he did, more than likely he wouldn't be able to hold his tongue. Over the years, he'd rarely talked about his experiences and he knew they were just simmering, waiting for a reason to explode. He couldn't take that chance. He quickly moved out of the door and was back on the sidewalk where he had started.

He climbed back on his bicycle and adjusted the mirror he'd bumped in his hurry to read the poster. With one foot up and ready to start rolling, he heard a voice behind him.

"*Ni hao*. Are you here for the reunion?"

He turned and found a small woman about his age peeking out the door. Peeking around from behind her was the young waitress dressed as a Red Guard, pointing his way. Benfu turned to see if they were looking at someone behind his cart but no, they were after him.

"Um, no. I'm just leaving. I'm not really dressed for the event." He looked at her fancy dress, then down at his work clothes, and hoped the excuse was enough to get her to leave him alone so he wouldn't need to be rude.

She flicked the corner of her dress. "Does it really matter what we dress ourselves in? You are still the same person on the inside, right? I saw you look around in the dining hall and was compelled to speak to you, but you left too quickly. Do you have comrades here?" She stepped outside and came closer.

Benfu sighed. He'd never get rid of her now.

"Well"—he touched his hat respectfully—"I really don't know. I was only looking for a friend I knew many years ago. But I didn't see him. Now I really need to get back to work."

The woman put her hand on Benfu's arm.

"Please, just come in for a moment. Perhaps we can find your friend, and from the look on your face, I think you would be sorry if you didn't give just a moment of your time. If he isn't here, you can leave. But at least take a look at the sign-in log to see if who you look for is here. Okay?" she asked sweetly.

Benfu debated. How could he not just give a few minutes of his time to see if he could thank Pei in person? Only a boy at the time, his comrade had risked his life that dark night to save Benfu. He could've been branded a traitor; yet he took that chance to do something no one else would—to stand up for what was right. When Pei had removed the lock, gave him food, and handed him his freedom, Benfu had run as fast as he could and never looked back.

The woman smiled at his hesitance.

"It's decided. You can come in and get a bite to eat as my guest. You don't even have to sign in if you'd rather not."

Pulling on his sleeve, she practically dragged him off the bike and Benfu reluctantly followed her into the restaurant. No one looked up as they entered, as everyone was busy with their own conversations and reminiscing.

"Over here's the log, if you'd like to see if your friend signed in. Then we'll go fix you up a heaping plate of dumplings and other juicy tidbits."

Benfu trailed behind her, still unsure why she had taken such an interest in him. Finally she stopped at a podium and flipped open the book that lay on top.

"What did you say his surname was?" she asked.

Benfu shoved his hands into his pockets. He was the only one in the room so under dressed and felt like he stuck out like a beacon. "It was Pei."

"First name?" She tapped the top of the wooden podium with her red manicured nail.

He shook his head. He realized he didn't know Pei's first name. He went only by his surname.

"I just don't know," Benfu answered, scratching his head. "He never told me."

"Did you say Pei?"

Benfu turned at the sound of the deep voice behind him. There, only a foot or so away, a man stood, his eyebrows raised with curiosity. Benfu stared. He wasn't sure, but it could have been the boy he knew so long ago.

"Are you Pei?" he asked.

"Yes. And who are you?" The man stood before him in his baggy dress pants and a pin-striped vest buttoned over a dingy white shirt.

"Zheng Benfu." He looked for the scar that should be running up one side of the man's cheek. Benfu remembered instantly the day the bungling city boy had mishandled the scythe and given himself quite the injury. Benfu had been standing outside the canteen when they'd brought him back for medical care from the commune's doctor. The young, inexperienced physician hadn't really known how to stitch up such a serious wound. Benfu examined both sides of this man's face, but could not find any scars. Could it have really healed so clean? He thought it next to impossible.

Benfu looked him over from his snazzy shoes to his bald head. What he'd thought for a moment might be an amazing reunion was not to be.

"Were you in a commune a few miles outside of Wuxi in 1967?" Benfu asked.

The man shook his head. "No, sorry—I was in that commune, but I didn't arrive until 1968. It must have been a different Pei. There are a lot of us in here in the Jiangsu province and back then, we were spread all over the place."

With that the lady turned and began to walk away. She gave a little wave and moved quickly toward the center of the room. "Not the reunion you'd hoped for, but it looks like you have something in common. I'll leave you boys to it now. Please help yourselves at the buffet and when you finish, if you'd like to give a donation to our Wuxi Ladies Charity Group, please see me at the door."

"I'm sorry to have bothered you," Benfu said, turning to go.

The man put his hand on his sleeve. "No bother. Actually, I haven't met anyone here who I remember; would you like to join me for a quick bite to eat? Like she said, we have something in common, after all."

Benfu sighed. He really had a lot of work to get done. He regretted he'd even stopped, but the man looked so earnest and though he was dressed to impress, Benfu could feel an air of awkwardness about the fellow. He felt sorry for him.

"Okay, a quick talk and then I need to be on my way."

Benfu and the new Pei settled themselves at a corner table, deciding to forgo a plate of food for the moment. Instead they sipped at their glasses of water and talked. Benfu couldn't believe how easily he got on with the stranger, and their conversation flowed seamlessly.

As others around them reminisced about Mao and his so-called accomplishments in bringing about a newer, more modern China, Benfu and Pei spoke quietly of the collective they had in common. They compared the abuses they were forced to bear in Mao's directives of *thought reform through hard labor,* when all over China the urban classes were exiled to the country and forced to learn by the example of the peasants. However, Benfu carefully guarded the truth that he was there quite by accident. It still nagged at him that what his parents thought would be the safest place for their teen son turned out to be a much harsher place than they'd imagined.

Pei rattled on about being pulled out of school, as so many were because of Mao's directives. Benfu was surprised he'd found someone who wasn't afraid to give a true opinion as to what damage they thought the Cultural Revolution had wreaked. Many were still afraid of repercussions, even decades later.

"So, did you ever get to attend the university and finish your degree?" Benfu asked. Back then it was a common dream that once the revolution was over, some could go back to the education they had been robbed of.

Pei nodded. "I tried, but it wasn't what I thought it would be. Once I finally made it back in, we were only allowed to study approved newspaper articles and rewritten textbooks to exalt Mao and his followers. Tales that bent the truth about his supposed victories."

Benfu shook his head in disgust.

"And each afternoon was still set aside for discussions and self-criticisms. Nothing had changed and I was miserable with the lack of intelligent studies and conversations. It was torture. After a few years of that, I gave up and started a business exporting tea." Pei frowned.

Benfu nodded politely, his face blank of expression. What he wouldn't share was that while some were supposedly getting new revolutionary educations, Benfu was being hidden by Calli's family. If Benfu had confessed to his bad background in the beginning, life would have been easier, but since he and his parents hid it, if he had been found, he would have served time in prison or worse. What Pei described as torture was a fantasyland compared to what Benfu would have endured if he'd been caught.

"And all Mao's carefully thought-out plans did what?" Benfu asked. "Resulted in the loss of all China's history and left nothing but a dehumanized nation. What satisfaction did he find in the wrecked old towns, smashed temples, and ruined pieces of art, all in his quest to make a new China, emptied of all past history? How could anyone desire that for a country he supposedly loved?"

"I know! And even today there are millions who think he was some sort of god and that he brought our country to a new level of success! Where? I ask—I see nothing he did except break apart families and cause destruction. He used his people to fulfill his sick goals of complete dictatorship." Pei looked genuinely upset and a vein in his neck began to pulsate.

"Well, those days are gone. Let's talk of better times while we have the chance," Benfu suggested, worried by the sudden quickening of breath his new friend took on in his stress. He looked around to see if the man's outburst had been noticed. He decided they needed a break before Pei caused a scene.

"How about that lunch? I think I can manage another half hour or so." Benfu stood and gestured toward the buffet bar.

Soon they both filled plates with goodies and over their lunch conversation turned to their families and the blessings in their lives. Before Benfu knew it, he'd been at the restaurant for over two hours. He was shocked how good it felt to find someone who could truly understand what it had been like in the same commune he had endured. The constant fight for clean drinking water, the weeks without bathing, the hard labor, and frequent self-criticisms to prove to their commune neighbors that they'd improved their integrity and loyalty to the new China had taken a toll on all of them. Many had not survived.

"This has been amazing, Pei, and it has been a pleasure to meet you, but I probably need to go. I still have a lot of work to do today," Benfu said, deliberately leaving out the details of his profession. He'd let the younger man believe he was a collector—which was close enough to a scavenger, just not as undignified.

"Okay, but one more question. Were you able to save anything from the rampage of those who led the destruction of Chinese relics?" Pei asked, his expression reminding Benfu of an inquisitive boy, despite the deep lines and age spots peppering his face.

"Save anything?" Benfu was confused.

"Yes, you know—from their intent to rid China of anything that represented our history?"

Benfu hesitated. It was indeed a miracle that he was able to save his violin when so many musical instruments across the nation were confiscated and lost forever. Maybe his new friend would appreciate his story. "Well, did you ever see that dried-up old well behind the kitchen?"

Pei shook his head. "I don't think so."

"While I was at the commune, I hid my violin in an old well, but I rarely got to play it—I was too afraid I'd get caught with it."

"Now that is luck! Who would've thought to see what was down there? Back then it was said that those old wells were used to dispose of unwanted infants. My team stayed far away from it, scared of unsettled spirits haunting it, I suppose."

Benfu had also heard that rumor and on the few times he'd raised up his instrument, he refused to look deep into the well for fear of what he'd see. It was a disturbing thought, and one that he had no trouble believing to be true in an era during which so many horrible acts were committed.

"Do you still play?" Pei asked.

Benfu shook his head. For years everything except songs praising Mao was forbidden. By the time real music was allowed again, Benfu had lost his desire to play.

Pei looked disappointed. "Well, that's very sad to hear. Mao tried to take away everything that brought us joy—art, books, and even music. Zheng, I learned a lot about antiques during my time after the revolution. Even though many things were lost, some treasures were safeguarded. Good for you. Do you still have the violin?"

Benfu hesitated as he watched the man nervously tap his fingers on the table. He'd never forget how his parents had told him to keep the family heirloom safe from all others. He thought he could probably trust Pei, but in China it only took one slipped word to lose something of value. He looked around at the packed restaurant. Who knew who was listening to their conversation?

Benfu shook his head. "Unfortunately I haven't laid my fingers across it for many decades. Everything was lost to me in those days, even my desire to make music."

Pei rubbed at the middle of his forehead, his eyes closed for a moment.

"You weren't the only one with a secret, you know."

Benfu raised his eyebrows, waiting for him to continue. He thought perhaps Pei had hidden a romance of some sort. At the time, relationships between non-married individuals were absolutely forbidden. Yet nothing could stop the magnetic pull of young love and despite the repercussions, it still happened; even in his commune he'd seen a few stolen moments here and there.

"When my parents' library was ransacked and everything destroyed, the Red Guards thought they'd gotten everything. But I hid a collection of classics from them. I kept one concealed with me at the commune and the rest in a safe place. No one found the books and after everything was over, I was able to retrieve them from the inside of the walls in our house."

Benfu was taken aback. Pei must have been a very brave lad back then. If he had been caught with any books other than the party-approved listed ones, he would have been severely punished. "*Aiya,* that was quite a chance you took, Pei."

"I know." Pei looked around nervously and Benfu could see he was afraid to talk of it. Though Mao was dead, there were still many devoted followers who would love a chance to prove their loyalty by settling old scores.

"It took me a few years, but I was finally able to reconcile my thoughts to the truth that what Mao was doing was quickly erasing all the pieces of China that would help us remember where we came from. When I started to show dissension, they tried to starve my body but they could no longer control my thoughts. I'll never forget those days," he whispered across the table.

Benfu nodded. He also would never forget the ache in his stomach from days without food or the hundreds of welts that covered his body from the hordes of insects in the shed. He wished he *could* forget, and he had tried to for years, but the memories were still as vivid as if it were yesterday. But at least the night he was freed was a part of it all, softening the horror. He still remembered the clink of the metal against the lock and the first fresh breaths of air when the door was opened. He'd expected another beating to be waiting but instead had met a boy's worried face and his first bit of food he'd had in such a long time. It was an amazing moment he'd treasure always. He still wished he could have found the real Pei.

With that Benfu stood. "It's time I must get back to work."

Benfu led the way out of the restaurant and through the door to the sidewalk. He glanced over his shoulder to find Pei following closely. Though a bit embarrassed about the shape of his only transportation, Benfu pushed those thoughts aside and went to the front of the bike.

"See this?" he asked, pointing to the battered water canteen hanging from the handlebars.

Pei nodded.

"This was given to me from the Pei I was looking for today. It's a long story I can't really speak of, but this canteen is a symbol of an extraordinary night that sealed a friendship between us. Many times I almost dropped it in the river but I couldn't make myself do it. It's my only solid reminder of him—the one person in that commune to show me mercy. I always hoped I'd be able to return it to him." He was surprised at the sudden mist of tears that threatened to come.

"That's amazing that you kept it so long," Pei said, taking the canteen and flipping it over to see initials carved on the bottom. "This is definitely an antique now, but more importantly it helps keep your memories intact. In any other case, I'd try to buy it from you for my collection, but I know you would not part with such a special piece. So thank you for showing it to me."

With that Benfu chose to ignore the old tradition of avoiding emotion and displays of affection in public and he approached the smaller man. Pei saw it coming and opened his arms. Benfu embraced him, clapping him on the back heartily.

"Comrades for life," Benfu said gruffly. He knew their paths would probably never cross again but still, he was glad to have had the chance to meet someone with some small connection to this past. Even if they hadn't actually crossed paths, they had walked the same one for a time. And if he could admit it, perhaps meeting someone who held opinions close to his own had helped to heal one tiny part of his broken history.

"Comrades for life," Pei agreed.

Chapter Seven

What a difference one month could make. It was only February and already spring was making a subtle entrance. The unusually warm day was consolation for the fact that Benfu was so tired—even more so than usual. As he pedaled home, he was pleased at the balmy weather and best of all, relieved that their newest addition was still with them and doing well. The mandatory police report and newspaper listing had not brought anyone forward to claim her and despite Benfu's worries of caring for another infant, he was glad to have her. Curiously, his little Jasmine had silently become Poppy's unofficial guardian and had to be reminded constantly that she was only five and not big enough to carry the baby around. Each time she was reprimanded, she solemnly nodded her head and stepped back. The truth was that Benfu was glad she had finally perked up and was showing interest in something for the first time since he had found her the year before.

Unlike most of the children who were found near the train station or down secluded alleys, Jasmine he had discovered on a late-afternoon trip through one of the famous parks of Wuxi. While most patrons had left for the day, Benfu and Calli were spending a rare afternoon alone and were taking advantage of the last light of the day. As they walked hand in hand through the park, he had spotted a tiny girl of around four years old playing in one of the small ponds, the only thing there with her a ragged cloth doll. He still remembered how magically the goldfish swam around her hands as she gracefully weaved them in and around the water in tiny swirls.

Benfu was suddenly jolted from his memories when his bicycle tire hit something. He stopped to get off the bike and bent down to pick up a few empty plastic bottles. He tossed them into the back of the cart and climbed back on, resuming his ride in deep contemplation.

In the park that day they'd stopped to ask the little girl where her parents were but she wouldn't—and still hadn't—spoken. Benfu had reported finding her to the police, but nothing came from the so-called investigation and after her photo was run in the local papers for a month with no one coming forward, she was officially placed with him and Calli. By then she'd felt like theirs anyway, as the department had allowed them to keep her in their home during its search. He still wondered if she was actually abandoned or just lost, but at least the girl seemed content to be with them. And he had to admit, the child was one of the most special he had known. His affection for her was huge.

Benfu was surprised Jasmine had taken to the newest daughter so well. With Poppy's arrival, Jasmine had lost her ranking as the baby of the family but it didn't seem to register for her yet. He hoped that her unusual attachment to the infant would bring a breakthrough to cause her to finally speak. But so far it hadn't happened. Even though they wanted her to have the best chance at life, which he thought would entail communicating, they never pushed her. Benfu felt that of all their children so far, Jasmine was the most introverted. She was really shy—even preferring her hair to fall around her face like a curtain, almost as if hiding from the world. He hoped to hear her speak just once before his own days were over, just to hear the sound of her voice, which he imagined would be soft and pure.

Benfu looked up and saw the blue sea of caps—the first signs of home. At the end of the narrow *hutong,* men wearing blue Mao caps bent over makeshift tables playing mahjong or cards. A few of them lifted their hands in greeting as he passed. Some days—especially like today when his bronchitis was acting up and he felt as if he couldn't catch his breath—he wished he could be like them and pass his days with games and naps, but most days he wouldn't trade his life for anyone's. He was close now and felt he couldn't get home fast enough. His old legs were tired of pedaling and he looked forward to a cup of tea.

Picking up the pace, he turned the corner and pedaled down the lane to his courtyard. Just on the other side of the gate he paused when he saw a large basket of corn sitting on the ground. The unexpected bounty brightened his day and he gave silent thanks for the generous neighbor who had left it.

"Ye Ye *hui jia le*!"

Benfu heard Ivy's loud announcement of his arrival before he even saw her. He parked his bicycle beside the house and turned just in time to brace himself for the onslaught of hugs from a few of his daughters. After peeling Peony's and Ivy's arms from around his waist, he reached out and settled Lily, who had been jostled and looked like she was going to fall over. The girl had used her gnarled old stick to find her way out of the door and to his side, her small hand already holding on to the back of his coat to let him guide her back to the house.

"What are you girls doing? Why aren't you finishing up your afternoon chores? I let you stay home today because you promised to help your Nai Nai," he gently scolded. Some Saturdays he allowed them to stay home instead of taking them out around town to help him collect. He felt at their age, they needed some time to just enjoy being children without the constant pressures of earning income. Now that some of the girls were getting older, he knew it was embarrassing for them to be seen picking up trash.

"We *are* doing chores, Ye Ye. I was just emptying the mop water and I heard your bicycle. Guess what, Ye Ye? Someone left us corn and milk powder again and we still don't know who!" Ivy answered, hopping up and down with the dripping bucket still in her hands.

Benfu smiled. Ivy was a smart one, listening for the sound of his bike. Linnea had fixed the loose wheel yet again, but it still squeaked and the girls loved that they could hear him coming down the lane and rival one another to be the first to greet him each day. For him and his tired old legs, knowing what was waiting for him made those last few yards easier.

"Indeed we've had a secret visitor again, haven't we? How lucky are we? And they didn't leave their name, so they're an example of a true giving heart. Ivy, pick six of the best ears from the bunch and take them over to Widow Zu. Let's spread the gift." He picked up the basket of corn with the can of milk powder on top and carried it to the door. He set it down and took off his outer jacket, hanging it on the first nail beside the row of ten. He never wore his work jacket inside, as it reeked of trash.

With his daughters around him, he entered his home. He stopped to remove his shoes and set them on the low shelf. He reached into the basket for his slippers and dropped them on the floor, sliding his feet into them. He nodded when he saw his wife sitting in her rocking chair and cradling the baby. On the other side of the room, Maggi waved at him from her perch on her bench.

"Maggie Mei, *ni hao ma*?" he teased as he reached for his indoor jacket from the nail inside the door and slid it on, buttoning it to the top.

"Fine, Ye Ye," she answered, beaming back at him.

As usual for this time of day, Maggi leaned over a rickety ironing board, happily ironing a large newspaper. He knew it made her proud that despite her disability, she was able to contribute to the family's well-being by straightening and smoothing all the paper they gathered each week. After Maggi ironed them neatly, the other girls worked together to stack and bundle them for Benfu to take to the recycling center for selling. Each time he returned, Maggi was like a little jack-in-the-box on her bench as she excitedly urged him to tell her how many yuan the papers she'd ironed brought in. Paper was probably the least valuable of all his finds, but it was much easier to collect than the more-coveted abandoned bicycle and auto parts he sometimes came across. And goodness, when he was lucky enough to find discarded televisions and computers, the internal guts if still intact brought in his biggest income for the month. But everything helped and he was lucky he had a family that wanted to do its part in any way possible.

"Poppy *hao-bu-hao*?" he asked, moving to the small sink to wash his hands. The baby had brought a new level of energy to their home and despite his concerns that they were getting too old to raise any more children, he thought the presence of so much youth did a small part to keep him and his wife young.

Calli looked up, her eyes tired. "She's fine. A bit colicky today but I think she'll be okay."

Benfu crossed the room and looked down at his wife. He put the back of his hand to her forehead. She didn't feel hot and he was relieved. They couldn't afford for Calli to get sick, as she was the glue that held his family together. She always had been and always would be. Without her, Benfu wouldn't have the strength or desire to move forward in such a hard world.

"She might be okay, but what about you, Calli? You look tired." He was concerned. Usually Calli never showed her fatigue.

"*Dui,* I was just getting ready to take a nap, if I can get this little beetle bug to sleep." She sat rocking in the chair, while she held the baby over her shoulder and thumped her repeatedly on the back.

Benfu reached out for the baby. "Let me take her. You go lie down."

His wife handed the baby up to Benfu and she stood, straightening the wrinkles from her apron. "Oh, I forgot to tell you, the new officer from the district came by today to ask if we have any more room. He brought our stipend."

Benfu's face darkened into a scowl, even as he settled Poppy gently in the crook of his arm. The local officials were very aware of the home they ran and had even brought at least a dozen of their daughters to them over the years. There just weren't many places for homeless children to be sheltered and Benfu had gained the reputation of taking them in. Just in the last few years they began paying a small allowance for each child that came from them, though nothing for the ones Benfu brought home himself and not near enough to take care of all the girls. For the state, the monthly pittance was a small price to pay to avoid opening the orphanage. Ironically a beautiful building stood empty on the richer side of town because it was too expensive to staff and keep running. Instead needy children were bumped from place to place, some ending up back on the streets where they were found.

"I hope you told him that we cannot take any more children." Benfu was glad he had missed the meeting with the official. He was already dreading the day that he was too frail to work and he didn't know who was going to support the daughters he had remaining in his care. Though he would never turn away a child, he preferred that now the officials start to find new families—younger parents—to open their homes. There were some scattered throughout the area but not near enough.

"I did." Calli moved slowly across the room and sat on the edge of the one bed in the house. She bent down and removed her slippers, then lay back on her pillow. At her cue, the girls one by one stopped what they were doing and went to the corner and pulled their bamboo mats out, unrolling them to get ready for their afternoon naps. Maggi folded her last paper and pulled the plug out of the wall to disconnect the iron. She was visibly tired and though she would never voice a complaint, Benfu thought she looked relieved it was nap time.

He looked down at the baby girl in his arms and smiled. "It's time for you to close your eyes, Mei Mei." Half the time he called all the girls by the same nickname. These days it was harder and harder for him to pull the right names out of his old brain, and for the most part the girls seemed to like to be called little sister, anyway.

In his strong, warm arms the baby began to relax. Her droopy eyelids were soon closed. Benfu stood and took her to the cradle, laid her in it, and then tucked the cover tightly around her. He rose from the chair and stretched, yawning.

From the bed, Calli shook her head. "Five minutes with you and she's sleeping like a baby panda. How do you always do that? You just have the magical touch, I suppose."

"I guess I do. At least the gods have blessed me with something other than my good looks."

Calli laughed and Benfu beamed at her. Nothing cheered him more than her giggles that still made her sound like a young girl to his old heart.

"Peony, I think it's time you told Ye Ye what you did today."

Benfu looked over to see Peony hang her head, two bright spots of red appearing on her cheeks. "What happened?"

Peony didn't answer fast enough for her sister. Ivy piped in. "I couldn't find my lucky coin until I looked in her bag. She took it!"

"Did you take your sister's coin?" Benfu asked Peony. He wanted to take her outside and have a one-on-one talk with her but that would wait for the next day; right now her actions and his reprimand would be a lesson to all.

She nodded, her cheeks turning even redder.

"Then you'll take her chores for the next week. We don't steal from one another or anyone else." With that it was over and Benfu reached in his pocket and pulled out a letter. "I stopped by and picked up our mail. Looks like a letter from one of our girls. Which one?"

He walked over and handed it to Calli. He knew how to read but his eyes had gotten so bad he could barely make out the characters in the dim evening light. He needed glasses but that was an expense he couldn't afford. Leaving the letter with Calli, he ignored the hopeful look he saw in Peony's eyes and instead went to Maggi. He didn't want to make a big deal that Peony waited each day to see if another postcard arrived for her, to see if the woman had begun corresponding again. It was when that wistful look came over her that he regretted ever giving her the cards.

"Hello, Maggi Mei, how are you doing today?" He bent, letting her slide her arms around his neck in a tight hug as he slipped his arms under her. He lifted her and took her to her waiting pallet. As soon as he dropped to one knee and set her down gently, her sisters moved to arrange her legs and settle her under the coverlet. Benfu slowly stood and rubbed his aching back. He wasn't sure how many more years or even months he could continue lifting the girl as she was getting bigger each day that he grew older and frailer.

Calli watched him and shook her head and sighed. She pulled her glasses from her apron pocket and perched them on the end of her nose. She smiled as she looked at the neat characters on the envelope. The paper was tattered and by the looks of all the chops imprinted on the front and back to show various signatures of approval, it had passed through many hands. It was a miracle it had made it to them.

"It's from Mari." She ripped open the envelope and unfolded the letter.

The girls all quietly sat up on their mats, anxious to hear news from their older sister. Marigold—Mari, they called her—was one of the few who, after a rocky start, now led a more exciting life than the others. Her letters were a welcome dash of drama to her family. They often got mail from the girls they had raised, but not all of them—as some worked too hard to have time to write—but enough of them that they received mail at least once a month. Each letter was treasured by all, but especially by Benfu and Calli, who worried constantly about each of them.

Benfu sat down beside his wife and pulled at the slippers on his feet. He scooted closer to the wall and leaned back on his own pillow. He sighed, glad to be horizontal and not moving for the first time all day. He took a deep breath and rested his arms across his belly. He didn't want to tell Calli that he felt feverish. Instead he hoped if he didn't bring it up, it would prove to just be exhaustion.

"Let's see what Mari has been up to. Girls, *anjing*. Nai Nai will only read it once, so you'd better listen closely. Tomorrow you can all take turns reading it aloud to see if you can recognize each character."

Jasmine popped up from her mat and, dragging her quilt behind her, ran to the bed. She crawled up and settled herself beside Benfu. He readjusted his arms so that she could use one for a pillow. He was glad she was still little enough to want to snuggle with them and couldn't bear to make her return to her pallet. The smell of her hair wafted up to his nose like a gentle perfume and he inhaled deeply as he reached to pull her quilt up and over her.

Calli cleared her throat. The large room was quiet as she began reading the letter. Benfu watched the smiles form across the girls' faces as his wife described Mari's latest adventure when one of her husband's camels tried to run away with a foreigner perched on top. Mari had married a farmer's son from a neighboring province but instead of farming, her husband had taken his early inheritance and spent it on a camel and camera equipment. Together they made their living from taking tourist photos at one of the places on the Great Wall. Benfu dreamed of seeing the historic structure one day but at this late time in life he doubted he ever would. It made him happy that some of his daughters had seen it—at least he could live vicariously through their descriptions of the magnificent project his people had accomplished.

"She says the foreign devil was from Germany and he made the camel mad because he was too fat."

At that the girls erupted into giggles, earning a scolding look from Calli as she folded the letter and tucked it into her pocket. They loved it when Mari wrote about the camel adventures and the spitting and bucking that went on when their temperamental camel didn't like some of the foreigners it was forced to carry. The amusing tales sent them into hysterics every time.

"Shhh, you'll wake Poppy. When Linnea gets home I'll read the rest of it. She'll want to hear what her favorite sister has been doing, too. Now, let's take a nap so we can get up and shuck that corn for dinner."

The girls groaned in disappointment, then turned over and quieted. Calli lay back down again, her back to Jasmine and Benfu. Within seconds Calli emitted a small but constant snore.

Benfu drifted off to sleep thinking of his older daughters and the lives they were leading now. Each of them had started with sad stories but he hoped that they still remembered they had a home with him and Calli. He wished he could see all of them and his new grandchildren, but traveling around China was much too expensive and, like him, most of them were not well off.

With his eyes closed, Benfu could still recall all of their faces, though he sometimes struggled to put names to them. He chuckled one last time before he went to sleep, picturing a fat German foreigner on a spitting, farting camel with his petite Mari running after it.

Chapter Eight

Linnea looked around her to be sure she wasn't being followed. She was meeting Jet again, this time at the park on the edge of town. She'd told Nai Nai she was leaving for work and she had earlier, but later she'd decided to enjoy the afternoon with Jet instead of working until dark. She wasn't proud that she was hiding him from her family but she knew Ye Ye wouldn't approve. He still didn't know that the gift of corn and milk powder had come from her new friend, and if he did, it probably wouldn't change his mind about the young man. Even though without Jet she'd have never been able to start her new T-shirt business, it probably still wouldn't sway her Ye Ye. He'd told her to be responsible in repaying her debt but warned her not to get too involved with someone she knew nothing about.

Sadly, he was right about that much. They had been seeing each other for over a month and so far all she knew was that Jet was in training to take on his own position in a year or two, something involving working with the community, he'd told her. She tried to talk herself out of falling so hard, and on the way to the park had searched her memories for reasons he wasn't a good catch. First, he smoked. *But so did most of the boys and men in China.* Second, he was maybe just a little bit arrogant.

Finally the only other thing she could find as a mark against him was her usual disdain for boys her age from the upper classes.

But unless he was a great actor, he wasn't anything like the ones she'd met before! She bit her lip, shaking her head at herself. To have fallen for someone like Jet was embarrassing and so unlike her—but she couldn't help herself.

She looked up and spotted him on a blanket under a tree at the top of the hill. He stood and brushed his hands off on his jeans. She waved and he waved back. Even from a distance she could see the handsome lines of his face—his strong jaw and white teeth.

"Ni hao!" he called out, then reached up and smoothed his hair back. Linnea liked that he hadn't followed the latest trend of the long, shaggy style for guys but instead kept his hair neatly trimmed.

Linnea blushed at the huge smile that spread across his face. She picked up the pace and ran up the rest of the way, almost barreling into Jet at the top. She wasn't worried that he wouldn't catch her; unlike some his age, Jet carried himself on broad shoulders and a tall frame.

He caught her in his arms. "Whoa, there."

Linnea pulled away, though reluctantly. Other than a few crushes and some careless flirting, this was her first taste of something real—and she couldn't ignore the sparks his touch sent rushing through her.

"*Ni hao,* Jet." Linnea was still shy around him, though with each date she got a bit more comfortable. She didn't understand why such a handsome and successful guy was interested in her—basically a poor orphan working on the street.

"How's my little designer doing?" he teased.

Linnea laughed. "It's going slow, but I think I might make a profit at the end of the month!"

She was still surprised at that discovery. From a bicycle repairwoman to a small shop owner—it was all such a fluke. The day she'd met Jet, she had told him about her dream of designing vintage T-shirts. Over their tea that turned into a long two hours stretching into the lunch hour, she'd described taking old subway tickets and street signs and using them for inspiration. She loved combining the old with the new and had so many more ideas to bring to life. When she'd showed him her sketches, Jet had been impressed enough to use his contacts to find her someone who'd sell her shirts at a great wholesale price. Then he'd also loaned her the start-up funds to open a small kiosk. From the local Internet shop, she'd found someone in Beijing to do the screen printing and she was suddenly a businesswoman! It was hard work but for the last few weeks she had felt more alive than she had in years. She was doing something with her own brain—not just getting her hands greasy on bicycle tires. Right now it was only a small rolling cart with cables to drape shirts on, but it was profitable and someday she hoped to have a real store.

Jet grabbed her hands and pulled her down on the blanket. He began to unload a basket, pulling out small cardboard boxes of every size.

"Earth to Linnea . . . Okay, dreamer, you can tell me more later. I can see you've got some more ideas floating around in that pretty head of yours. Can you slow down long enough to eat lunch? My *ayi* packed it and just wait to see what all we've got here."

Linnea didn't answer. She was glad to see the bounty of food but was still embarrassed when he mentioned having house help. What he didn't understand was that she would be fortunate to find work as an *ayi* herself. A job as a housekeeper for a rich family would be a dream come true, because then she could make enough that her Ye Ye would no longer have to work.

Jet stopped pulling out boxes and looked at Linnea, his brow puckered together.

"Are you okay?" he asked. "You have a strange look on your face."

Linnea laughed uncomfortably. She couldn't help but see the huge difference in their lifestyles just with the array of food he'd brought. "I'm fine. But that's a lot of food for just two people!"

"Oh, we'll eat it. Don't worry about that." Jet began opening the top flaps of the food boxes, showing small pieces of watermelon, lumps of rice, loquats and even chunks of spicy pork. Linnea's mouth watered at the feast before her. She picked up the box of spicy pork and inhaled. She had been eating only noodles for weeks now and she would never complain, but to see something different made her smile. Jet handed her a wooden set of chopsticks and they dug in.

"Okay, now let's talk. How's business?" he asked.

"It's good." She blushed. "Thank you so much for the loan, Jet. I've got everything I need and many of my old customers are coming to me now to see what I'm selling."

"Well, see, it's all about how you treat people. You made an impression on them and now they want you to succeed!"

Linnea smiled. "Yeah, and some of them still want me to fix their tires! But anyway, I should be able to pay you back really soon." This was the first time she'd ever borrowed money and the burden of owing someone weighed heavily on her. She couldn't wait to hand him the last of it and have it paid back in full.

Jet shook his head. "No, I told you that I don't want you to make any payments until you've made a profit for at least six consecutive months. That was our deal. And it's a good one."

She lowered her eyes. "Good deal for me—not so much for you."

"Good for me, too! I get to hang out with the prettiest designer in town. And you've given me something worthy to spend my money on for the first time in my life. Just think, you are helping me grow up and make adult decisions." He winked at her.

They were in their own happy little world, and it was as if they were the only ones in the park as they laughed and ate until she felt she would pop. Each time she stopped putting food in her mouth, Jet would hand her another box to try. Finally she took the last sip of her yogurt drink and set it down.

"No more. Please." She sighed and held her stomach.

"Me, too." Jet flopped down on his back and pulled Linnea down to lie beside him.

"*Xie xie*, Jet. That was the best lunch I've had in a very long time." She eyed the leftovers from the corner of her eye and felt a pang of guilt knowing her sisters would love to have just a morsel of what she had devoured. She wondered if he would offer her the leftovers.

"No thanks needed. You don't eat enough. You're too skinny," he teased, grabbing her hand and tracing her slender fingers with his own.

She let him fill her up with the nonsense. What girl didn't like to hear how skinny she was, after all? He finally stopped and they were quiet for a moment, enjoying the balmy day.

"Linnea, I want to ask you something." Jet sat up and his face took on a serious expression.

She cringed. She still had not told him much about herself. She felt she had a better chance of keeping him if she remained mysterious. After all, who would want to date a girl whose own mother didn't want to keep her? Now he was going to ask and she dreaded telling him the truth.

"What?" she asked hesitantly, avoiding meeting his eyes. Under his intense gaze she felt so exposed, as if he could see right through her.

"I don't know much about you."

Linnea sighed. She knew what was coming. Now he would want to know everything and would never want to see her again.

"So what's your favorite color?" he asked, twirling a blade of grass between his lips.

Linnea let out a loud laugh. Color? That's all he wanted to know? That was easy. She could handle questions like that all day.

"Blue. Like the color of the water in an exotic ocean."

He laughed. "How do you know about exotic oceans?"

"It's in a book my Nai Nai reads to us." Linnea smiled, thinking of their almost-nightly ritual of bedtime stories that she liked to pretend she was too old for but really loved. Most of their stories were old Chinese folktales or legends taken from history, but sometimes their Nai Nai bent to the whims of the latest fads. Just last month Peony and the other girls had been spellbound on the nights they'd read from the famous British series of Harry Potter. Their Ye Ye had scooped the series up from the Chinese knockoff market and, in the last book, they'd all laughed at the Chinese rendition of Harry and his Chinese circus acrobat sidekick named Naughty Bubble, and their adventures traveling to China to track down Chinese Porcelain Doll to stop Yandomort. Her Nai Nai had barely gotten through it without rolling her eyes at the silliness of what she'd called unbelievable sorcery.

"Hmm . . . you always talk about your Nai Nai. What about your mother?"

Linnea felt a wave of uneasiness. There it was—the question. She had thought she was off the hook, so it hit her like a ton of bricks. But suddenly Linnea was tired of always trying to find excuses or make up lies about her story. For once she wondered what it would feel like if she just said it. What was the worst that could happen? Jet would leave and never come back, and if he did that—then maybe he wasn't as perfect as she thought anyway.

She sat up and took a deep breath. She looked him straight in the eye.

"My mother left me when I was little."

Jet looked taken aback and sat up quickly.

"What? Left? What do you mean?"

"Left. Abandoned—whatever word you want to use. It all means the same. She didn't want me."

"I'm so sorry. But you don't live in an orphanage, right?"

Linnea couldn't hide the sharp intake of breath. To most in China, being abandoned automatically made people think the person lived in an institution. And if they thought someone lived in an institution, many jumped to the conclusion that the person had mental issues. Even the thought of being branded as institutionalized made her feel sick.

Jet cringed. "Never mind, I didn't mean—"

Linnea held her hand up. "No. It's not your fault. Let me finish. I've never told anyone this and I'm ready to finally say it. My mother didn't want me. She kept me until I was three years old and then she left me sick and alone in the meat market. A scavenger found me and took me home. He and his wife nursed me back to health and have taken care of me since. He is my Ye Ye and she is my Nai Nai. I'm not proud of my birth story, but it is what it is."

She lifted her chin proudly. She'd done it. She had told the truth. She silently dared him to say anything about her beloved Ye Ye or try to say he wasn't a man of honor because of his trade. She knew no other man in the world could be as kind and loving as her Ye Ye and she was ashamed that she had at first been hesitant to talk of him.

Jet took her hands in his and brought them to his lips. The soft touch of his mouth on her skin sent a shiver all through her.

"Linnea, I don't care whose daughter you are. I only care about you, don't you know that? I'm glad you told me so I can share your pain with you. I can see in your eyes when you talk about your mother that she hurt you very badly. You don't have to carry your sorrow alone. If you let me, I'll help you carry it."

Linnea hung her head and one tiny tear made its way down her face. Jet reached up and rubbed it away with his thumb.

"Nai Nai tells me my mother probably loved me so much she was willing to leave me for someone to find me who could pay for me to see a doctor. Turned out I didn't need a doctor but that doesn't change what happened."

"Now, no more sad stories. I brought a kite! Let's get it up in the air and see who can keep it up longer. You in?" He nudged her chin up so he could look her in the eyes.

Linnea felt a heavy weight lift from her heart as Jet pulled her to her feet. Maybe this new thing she had found was real. And maybe—*a tiny chance of a maybe*—it could be something meaningful. She had always thought herself unworthy but could she be wrong? She didn't want to jinx herself, so instead of pondering that thought too much, she grabbed the kite and took off running, letting Jet chase her down the rolling hill.

Linnea walked home from the park in a daze. She didn't know what being in love was supposed to be like, but if the goofy, weightless feeling she was experiencing was it, she didn't want it to end. Because of him she had done something she'd never done before—danced. She still couldn't believe that he had talked her into waltzing along with the senior citizens at the square. They had only walked up to watch and Linnea was mesmerized and amazed that despite their bland, Mao-style clothes of dark blue pants and jackets, the old men guided their partners around the square as gracefully as anything she had ever seen. Some of them were at least as old as her Ye Ye and Nai Nai, making it even more romantic that they appeared lost in another world, oblivious to the sounds of traffic and people around them. When Jet had grabbed her hand and led her to the middle of the couples, Linnea had tried to refuse, but the smiles and laughs of approval all around her, along with Jet's insistence, had kept her there, and surprisingly she had been able to follow his lead. She sighed as she thought it had to be the most magical moment of her life so far.

Afterward Jet had bought them ice cream, and they sat on a bench and talked for another hour or so. Because he asked and seemed to genuinely want to know, she had told him all about her family. She described each of her sisters and was surprised at the interest in his eyes with each story of abandonment. He seemed hungry for every detail she tentatively gave until she'd described their personalities and told all she could about each of them. She finally worked up the courage to ask him why he was so interested in her. She'd never forget his answer and it kept reverberating in her head as she unseeingly passed all the familiar sights on her path home. She could repeat it over and over, and she wished that she had the nerve to tell it to her Nai Nai and ask her to record it in the book on her page. But since she didn't, she'd just have to hold it in her heart. She silently mouthed the words one more time.

"Lin, I knew you were special from the first moment I saw that look of determination cross your face. You didn't care that you were a girl and were racing against your own boss. Even with the weight of the world on your shoulders, you're obviously driven to find a way to succeed. I've never met anyone like you. The more you tell me about yourself, the more smitten I am."

Smitten? She was confused and more than a little embarrassed to have to ask what it meant.

"Smitten means I'm going to spend as much time as I can getting to know you, and if you'll let me—I'll try to make your life just a little easier. Let me earn favor from the gods by showing you that I'm something more than just an official's spoiled son. Give me the gift of letting me share in your world."

Chapter Nine

Benfu rose with the sun. He picked his way through the rainbow of colored quilts that covered the girls as they lay sleeping around the room on their pallets. Today he'd decided that he would attempt to collect in a different location than his usual path. He really didn't want to resort to the plan, but money was tighter than ever and collecting within town was getting harder. For the last few days he had been forced to pick through cabbage leaves, egg shells, and uneaten noodles to find even a small bounty of paper or cardboard that could be sold. And this week he had found no plastic bottles before other scavengers had beat him to them. The spring festival to greet the New Year was coming soon and in addition to squaring up all his accounts as was tradition at the end of each year, Benfu wished to give his daughters a worthy celebration.

After going outside to the small outhouse he returned to the house and found Calli already pouring him a cup of tea. Behind her the large pot of congee was steaming, the aroma making Benfu's stomach growl. He was thankful for any breakfast the gods saw fit to provide his family but the sweet corn soup from the night before still lingered on his mind. They had made the bounty go far with several tasty recipes, including *yumi lao,* his favorite sweet deep-fried corn fritters, but it was finally all gone.

"Zao," Calli called out softly.

"Good morning," Benfu answered as he went to the sink and washed his face and hands. He quickly brushed his teeth and turned the water off. Peering into the mirror tacked above the sink, he used his comb to slick his hair back. He scowled at the color. There was a time he kept his hair jet-black with Calli's help and a bottle of dye. But once the gray had declared war, he'd finally let it take over. Yet still there were times he didn't recognize the old man in the glass and he wished for the younger version of himself that was still rooting around in his mind.

He went to the stove, opened the hatch door, and stoked the coals to warm the room. Already Calli had sewed sand up in long lines of cloth to put around the cracks of the windows and the door, small barriers but at least something to catch the chilly drafts that would soon turn frigid. Some of his neighbors had upgraded their houses to propane heating or small electric portables, but Benfu couldn't afford such luxuries and was glad the old stove still performed.

Satisfied finally that his morning rituals were complete, he sat down at the table and sipped his tea, trying to hold back his urge to cough. Behind him the girls began to move around and awaken. Poppy stirred and let out a cry and Linnea rose to see to her.

"Ivy, please care for Maggi," Calli quietly spoke as she stirred the congee, her voice hoarse from the long night in the cold room.

Benfu let his cough out but continued to face the wall to allow Ivy the privacy to change the pad underneath Maggi. The girl's paralysis was such that she didn't even know when she was soiled, but every morning one of her sisters tended her and made sure she was fresh to start the day. At eight years old, Maggi had spent her entire life unable to care for herself and knew nothing different. In their household, Maggi was the most optimistic of all the girls and when things were tough, she was the first to find good in every challenge. Benfu was thankful for the day he found her on the street corner, lying on a mat with a cup in front of her, begging for coins. She had fallen into the clutches of a gang and at an innocent five years old, probably brought in a worthy take each day. But the thieves should not have been so confident to leave her alone during the noon hour while they left for the mid-day lunch and nap.

Benfu had worked in the area and watched them for an entire week, until he was sure he knew their routine. Then one day he had swooped in and rescued her. No one around them had said a word when he pedaled to her and quickly climbed off, picked her up, and put her in his cart. To stop any questions, he had muttered to those around her that the girl was his granddaughter. Maggi didn't resist; she was accustomed to having no say in her fate and Benfu thought she had acted like the interruption to her day was somewhat welcome.

Benfu drained his cup of tea just as Calli brought him a heaping bowl of congee.

"*Xie xie,* my love," he said as she set the bowl and spoon in front of him. Calli went back to scoop up more bowls and left Benfu to eat and finish his thoughts about his Maggi, who lay waiting patiently for him to eat his breakfast and take her to her bench—just as patiently as she had been that day in the cart of his bicycle when he had rescued her.

As he had pedaled furiously away that day three years ago, he had felt a moment of fear that the gang leader would come after him. He was naught but an old man and couldn't possibly fight for the girl. But fear for the fate of the child won out and he continued his getaway. Once they had traveled far enough away from the scene, he'd turned his head and told the child that he was taking her home to meet her Nai Nai. The moment Calli had met them at the gate and enveloped the girl in her arms, she was theirs. The girl had given them her name but said she never knew her parents. After asking for her permission, they had renamed her Magnolia—shortened to Maggi—because they wanted her to know that although she had been introduced to an ugly part of life, it was now time for a fresh start and all the anguish and suffering that had come before could be forgotten. In his home she would be loved and cherished—not taken advantage of.

Finished with his breakfast, Benfu rose from the table and went to Maggi. Ignoring the sudden pain in his chest, he bent down and lifted her in his arms. It was worth the discomfort he felt each day just to feel the affection that she gave as she squeezed his neck tightly and smiled up at him. He set her gently on her bench and straightened her legs. Pulling the coverlet around her, he gruffly reminded her not to work too hard. He thought once again that if he had the money one day, he'd take her to Shanghai for a second opinion; perhaps someone could give them hope for her future.

He turned and gathered his things. Linnea brought him his coat and he put it on, buttoning it to the top. Calli came and stuffed a clean handkerchief in his pocket and handed him his bottle, filled with tap water. He tightened the cap and put it in his other pocket. He headed for the door but stopped in front of Jasmine, who had crawled up to snuggle in his warm spot on the bed. He touched the tip of her nose and was rewarded with a shy smile.

"Daughters, be good and mind your Nai Nai today," he said as he looked around and made eye contact with each of them. He knew he need not even have reminded them, as he was lucky that all the girls were well behaved, save for some occasional bickering.

"But Ye Ye, why are you going to work today? It's Sunday," Ivy asked, her brow already creased with worry. She sat on the floor as her twin sister, Lily, stood behind her and braided her long hair.

Benfu patted her on the top of the head as he walked to the door and picked up his shoes. He took them outside and sat on the bench to put them on. Ivy waited another second for Lily to finish rolling the elastic around the end of her hair, then, always the little questioning one, jumped up and followed Benfu.

"Ye Ye? Why?"

"Because, Daughter, I need to pick up some more things. The spring festival is coming and you want fresh fruit and dumplings, *dui*?" He put first one shoe on and then the other before he erupted in a fit of coughing. Ivy quickly knelt down and tied the shoes for him, then looked up. Beside her, tiny Jasmine appeared like a silent dark-haired ghost, her big eyes staring.

"But why won't you let me go and help you, Ye Ye? I can walk as fast as you can ride, and I can pick up the trash you point out so you don't have to get off your seat," Ivy said.

Linnea walked up behind the girls, her hands on her hips.

"If you're working today, then I should work today. Ivy can stay home and then Lily won't be sad. I'll help you," she said. Her stubborn streak was showing and Benfu struggled to keep from chuckling, which would have made her lose face. Linnea was a very proud young woman. And if their estimate of her birth date was correct, her personality was a perfect match for her zodiac, the dragon.

"What's with all this bossing around?" Benfu softly scolded. "Today is a day of rest and after you have helped your Nai Nai with making the tea, you girls should spend the afternoon doing something fun. Play outside, read a book. Don't worry about me. I might even stop and have a game or two of mahjong with Lao Gong."

Benfu planned to do no such thing, but the girls were protective of him and he had to tell them something to get them to stop worrying. As far as he knew, his old comrade Lao Gong was still in Guilin visiting his son. He sure hadn't seen him around in weeks.

"Ye Ye! *Zai jian!*" Maggi called from her bench, doing her best to peer around the doorframe to see Benfu. As usual, her voice was cheerful and optimistic for the day. *At least she isn't mad at me for leaving,* he thought to himself.

"Maggi, on second thought, I'm coming back in to pick you up. You need some outside time today while it's such mild weather."

Benfu went back into the house and after guiding her arms into her outside coat and buttoning it, picked the girl up in his arms. He was once again glad he was much stronger than the average sixty-something-year-old man.

"Maggi Mei, I do declare, you are getting heavier than a bag of potatoes," he teased, making the girl giggle. "Maybe we ought to throw you in a pot and boil you with some garlic. I think you'd make a tasty treat!"

With Calli fluttering about behind him to make sure he didn't drop her, Benfu carried Maggi out and set her on the bench, then tucked the coverlet around her skinny legs. Maggi smiled from ear to ear from the special attention.

He looked around to find Jasmine still directly behind him. He bent down and touched the tip of her nose, then pointed at the sky.

"I love you to the moon and back, Jasmine," he said, then felt his heart lighten at the smile that spread across her face. Oh, how he wished she could return the sentiment.

He straightened up and looked around one last time.

"Linnea, please make sure you watch out for your sister and take her back inside in about an hour," Benfu said.

"*Hao de,* Ye Ye," Linnea answered, settling herself next to Maggi on the bench. Calli gave one last check to make sure her daughter was secure, then returned to her tasks in the kitchen cove.

"And bring her that bag of plastic bottles from last week. She can peel the labels as she sits and they'll be ready for me to take to town tomorrow." Benfu knew Maggi didn't like to feel useless and peeling labels would be a welcome diversion from her usual job of ironing the papers. He once again thought about the vendor on the corner who sold puzzle boards and he hoped to be able to get Maggi one for Chinese New Year. She needed something other than meaningless tasks to combat her boredom.

After checking the spot where Poppy had been found, as well as a few other places abandoned girls had been discovered over the years, Benfu pedaled his bicycle toward the edge of town. As was usual for a Sunday, he passed many people out shopping or strolling about, enjoying the day off from their usual responsibilities. In front of one merchant stand he smiled when he saw a man holding his daughter on his shoulders as they waited in line to buy one of the bright red candy sticks. The small girl saw him looking and gave him a friendly wave. After the initial jolt of regret it brought, the sight warmed Benfu's heart to see a father appreciating the joy of his daughter, instead of bemoaning that she was not born a male. China was changing and would do so faster if only more of the older generation would get on board with fairness for girls instead of trying to manipulate their grown children to strive for the male heir. It still infuriated him that most girl baby abandonment was the result of pressure from old-fashioned grandparents. He shook his head, also shaking off the negative memories that threatened to invade his day.

Farther along, he marveled at the number of young people he saw walking along with mobile phones in their hands—pecking away at the buttons, oblivious to everything around them. It amazed him how they could walk and reach their destination almost without looking up at the path ahead of them.

Mobile phones. Laptops, fancy televisions, bahh! He didn't see what all the fuss was about and why everyone felt the need to waste their money on fancy gadgets. Why couldn't everyone go back to using face-to-face contact and letters? Even if he could afford his own mobile phone, he wouldn't want one. He felt technology was one of the biggest reasons for the chasm between family members. In his younger days, he went to visit his grandparents every week no matter what was happening in his life. When he had married, he and Calli even lived with her parents until their early deaths. And they did it with pride and joy at the long evenings spent as a family. These days the younger generation thought a weekly phone call or note through a computer was sufficient to show their loyalty and respect. It was a travesty, Benfu thought as he pedaled on.

Just outside of the busiest part of town he passed a park and gazed at the rolling green hills that held colorful patches of blankets. Families all around sat eating or napping or were up and about chasing kites. Benfu could see more than one affectionate couple and smiled at the heart-warming scene, feeling content that some things never changed. He wished he could stop and ramble up the path and across the bridges, maybe even find a spot to rest under a weeping willow tree and reminisce about when he and Calli used to spend their weekends there so many years ago when they were newly married. But alas, he had to get moving. He started to take off, when he thought he saw a familiar face in the crowd. He paused and stood up on the pedals, making himself taller to see over the many couples.

Yes, he was right. It was Linnea. And if his old eyes weren't playing tricks on him, his daughter was strolling along the sidewalk with a boy, not holding hands but definitely closer than they should be.

Benfu sighed. So it was her turn to grow up. It made him sad but he knew it was inevitable, just like with his other girls who had left the nest. He just wished Linnea would not try to hide it. If she wanted to start seeing someone, she needed to come forward and talk about it. For a second he thought about calling her name. Then he dismissed the idea. She would be mortified and he didn't want to embarrass her. He decided he'd keep it under his hat for a while and give her a chance to tell him herself.

Benfu pedaled on and finally made it to the outskirts of town. Ahead of him he could see the line of blue trucks, waiting their turns to dump their loads. He thought being a Sunday it might be a quiet day at the landfill, but already he could see other collectors with arms looped through the handles of baskets on their backs, searching through the piles. Others poked at the trash with pitchforks and tossed empty cans, jars, and paper into bags set around their feet.

Benfu shook his head at the scene before him. *"Aiya . . . ,"* he mumbled. He had gone from heaven to hell in an instant.

He had not been there in years and had no idea the site had grown to such proportions. He shook his head. There was a time that the piece of land held acres of bountiful crops tended by him and others—though most of what they reaped was trucked to Shanghai to feed Mao's officials and troops. While they worked the land, the cadres had watched over them to ensure nothing would be stolen, looking past their haggard faces and skeletal frames to pretend they didn't realize how hungry the people were for fresh vegetables. And when the rice coupons were no longer valuable because all the rice had run out, there were many days

Benfu had survived off only one stolen potato cooked and split among at least a half dozen others. And that was on a good day—a day they weren't subsisting on grass and plants cooked like a stew. But that was before the people in his collective had turned on him. The memories came pouring back and Benfu felt the old rage surge up inside. He looked over the heaps of trash to the place where the tiny outhouse once stood and he remembered the beatings and the isolation. All because of who he had been born to. People who had claimed to be his friends, even his new family! They'd turned on him like a lynch mob because of his *bad family background.*

Toward the end of the revolution, the crops had eventually shriveled to nothing and were abandoned, and the land was used for the people in the outskirts of town as a landfill. Obviously they were now getting all of their village trash, as well as the Wuxi city trash transported there. The dump was huge, appearing to go on for miles with tall mounds of rubbish every few feet. Not only were the piles an unseemly sight, but the smell that hit him was worse than putrid. All around, mountains of waste sat decomposing, much of it consisting of unrecognizable items from a distance.

Benfu could see children, like shadows against the hazy landscape, following along behind their parents, mostly migrant families joining in the task of searching for salvageable items among the tons of trash. He felt a wave of pity for the kids forced to live such a life but also felt relief that thus far he had never had to resort to recruiting his own daughters to such a place. In his opinion, other than the mines, there couldn't be a worse situation to make a child work than in the horrid landfills.

He paused to pull his handkerchief from his pocket and tied it around his face, then pedaled his bike to a place away from the line of trucks—he didn't want to lose his only transportation to a careless truck driver.

Pulling his own basket from the cart on the back of his bike, Benfu struggled to work his arms through the handles and balance the basket on his back. He took his trash stick from the cart and made his way closer to the site. He looked around and, choosing a huge pile of junk, began to look for anything he could use to make a yuan. He shook his head at the evidence of the new generation of disposable items. Microwave food boxes, instant noodle bowls, wooden chopsticks, paper slippers—so much trash made from the desire to move ever faster in the modern world. He wished again for the older, slower pace of life where less was more. At least in his home they hadn't felt the pull to succumb to—or keep up with—the new ways.

As he searched the littered ground below, he swatted at the hundreds of mosquitos that swarmed around him. He had only stabbed a few soiled newspapers and dropped them into his basket when he had to stop and straighten himself, the gases from the piles of waste making him more than a little dizzy.

An hour later, besides a few soiled papers, Benfu had only been lucky enough to find a dozen or so plastic bottles and a few cardboard boxes. Each time he spotted something more valuable and began toward it, another collector would beat him and snatch it right out from under him. He was really disappointed when he saw the remains of a computer and a petite woman beat him to it. Though years younger than he, the others had no mercy for his age and didn't give him a second glance as they competed for each scrap. With the combination of being away from his usual route through his beloved town and missing the interaction with familiar neighbors, he conceded that the depressing atmosphere of the landfill slowed him down more than usual. He felt as if he were wading through water in slow motion.

Even so, he pushed on but eventually stopped his hunting when he was interrupted to bandage the cut foot of one of the migrant children. The child, just a toddler, had stepped on a shard of glass and sat crying and holding his bloody foot as his preoccupied mother ignored him. Benfu made his way over the hill of trash between them and comforted the boy. He took the handkerchief from his face and after using his only bottle of water to clean the wound, he wrapped the child's foot and made him promise to stay in a safer area until he healed. His mother didn't even stop her collecting to thank him, but he didn't blame her. It was people like her family who, if they didn't find anything that very day, just wouldn't have the money to eat. Theirs was a desperate situation and his wasn't. Not yet, anyway.

Benfu walked toward his bicycle, his shoulders hunched as he coughed violently from the assault on his senses. His chest hurt terribly and he grasped it with one hand, willing it to behave. Unable to continue without his handkerchief to filter the stench, he decided to call it a day and come back later in the week.

Through watering eyes, he looked around at the rest of the people still fighting to gain a closer spot to the latest load dumped by a truck and his heart felt heavy. It was a shame that some of China's people were so desperately poor, especially when it was well-known that anyone working for the government lived a posh life full of benefits. All of his adult life he'd hoped he would see major changes and reform that would unite the people. He hoped the government would step in and set up a welfare system. They had barely done anything about the problem in all his years; what was done was all fluff and propaganda. In China, the poor were like dung on the bottom of the rich man's shoe.

He shook his head in disgust. Benfu had survived the atrocities of the so-called Cultural Revolution only to see even more of a gap between the rich and poor, instead of the classless society

Mao had aimed for during his reign. Benfu was thankful that Mao had backed down and called a cease to the revolution when his prospective rival, Liu Shao-chi, was expelled from the party back in the late sixties. Even though the *Chaos*—as most of the locals tended to call the revolution—lasted at least ten years, things finally settled down and they'd begun the long road to recovery. With that, Calli and her family had struggled to regain the hope and sense of security that had been so callously snatched from them. And Benfu still didn't regret his choice to stay by their side. They'd been loyal to him and nursed him back to health—even given him refuge during his darkest moments. How could he possibly abandon them? His parents hadn't been happy, to say the least, but he'd chosen to remain with his new family rather than return to the life he'd known before the nightmare had begun.

With another look at the people on the hills rummaging through piles of stench, Benfu marveled that only a few miles away people were living in new high-rise apartments with luxuries such as those he'd never seen and probably never would. It proved that despite it all, there was still a huge gap between the classes. He wondered if Mao was pleased looking down from his place in the afterworld. His legacy of hardship may have been interrupted, but it still refused to be broken.

Chapter Ten

At the parking lot of the government building Benfu hopped off his bike and wheeled it into a gap in the row of others. He really didn't want to be there and debated turning around and leaving. Then he thought of his girls and, taking a deep breath, pushed back his reservations and climbed the steep concrete stairs.

Unlike the unkempt parking lot, the inside of the building was pristine. Benfu passed an elderly woman using an old rag mop to swipe wide arcs of soapy water back and forth across the hall. He did his best to walk close to the wall and keep out of her path, but she still muttered her irritation as he went by. He was relieved to turn down the next hall and be rid of the slippery feeling under his feet.

There his shoes echoed eerily and he shook his head at the extravagance around him. He thought it ironic that he was coming to ask for assistance to give his girls a decent holiday while the offices looked like a palace with their marble floors and artistic pieces of calligraphy art hung on the wall. He passed several closed doors until he came to one marked CITY WELFARE OFFICE.

He hoped they were still open. It was right before the New Year celebrations and most offices were being manned by only a skeleton crew while the rest of the employees left for their extended vacations. He hoped he hadn't waited too late to come.

At the door he hesitated, then turned the handle and walked in. Benfu looked around to find the clerk sitting behind a large metal desk, instructing a couple in front of her on which sections of a form to complete. Benfu took a seat to wait until they finished.

"State your intent on this line," she told them, pointing to a bold black line on the piece of paper.

"Intent?" the middle-aged man asked. He squinted at the woman, his eyebrows coming together in one straight line.

"Yes, intent. Why do you want to do this?"

"I already told you we want to earn some extra money to help pay our son's university tuition. Our neighbor said we could be foster parents."

"Then write that," the woman sharply answered. "Finish all the other boxes and bring it back to me with both of your city resident permits."

She waved her hand toward the seats around Benfu and the couple got up and joined him. The man handed the clipboard to the woman with him and told her to finish it. Benfu thought he looked more than irritated and that didn't bode well for him. He wasn't surprised, as he hadn't been to the welfare office in over a year but remembered nothing ever went easy there.

"Next," the clerk announced, not looking up from her paperwork. She picked up the red-handled chop from the pad at the corner of her desk and gave several hearty stamps to a sheaf of papers in her hand.

Benfu looked around to be sure no one was ahead of him, but it was still just the three of them, so he got up and approached her desk. He sat down in one of the chairs and waited for her to look up.

"Can I help you?" she asked, eyes still on her papers and her lips a tight, white line across her face.

Speaking quietly, Benfu leaned closer to the desk. He could feel his face heating up and hoped the couple couldn't hear him. "Uh, yes. I'm already a foster father, but I'm here to ask for some help with our family festivities this year."

The woman finally looked up. "There are boxes of oranges in the closet. You're entitled to one box. Do you have your resident permit with you?" She tapped her red lacquered nails on her desktop. Benfu thought she must have had a few of the oranges herself and they must be on the sour side, judging from the lines around her puckered lips.

Benfu pulled his *hukou* out of his pocket and put it on the desk. The clerk flipped it open and looked at it, then quickly shut it again and jotted his name down on a yellow piece of paper in front of her.

"*Xie xie,* I appreciate the oranges but I need more than that. I have seven girls at home right now and they need clothes, shoes and we need supplies for our festival dinner. I've been fostering for years and have never asked for help before. Can you make an exception this once?" Benfu asked.

With that long speech he fell into another fit of coughing, one of many that day. He was so ashamed that he'd had to come and he wished there were another way. He'd just felt so terrible lately that he hadn't been able to make as many treks around the town to search for goods and his income had dropped dramatically.

The woman took a pencil from her canister and used it to scratch rapidly at her scalp, sticking it in the middle of her tight bun of hair. Benfu could see she was losing patience, but so was he, darn it. Behind him the door opened and another couple stepped through, this time with a small toddler trailing behind them. The clerk heaved a sigh of exasperation.

"The office closes in thirty minutes," she said over Benfu's head. The couple nodded and took a seat anyway. The toddler wailed and the quiet room turned into a tense prison.

"Now, back to you. Let's get you finished up. Did you already receive your monthly stipend for the foster children approved by the state?"

Benfu nodded. "I did receive it, but we only get stipends for a few of the children and like I said, I have seven at home. The allowance is barely enough to keep a roof over their heads. I need a loan, an extension, or something. Don't you have some sort of assistance program?"

The clerk shook her head. "Lao Zheng. I don't know who told you that we are in the business of loaning money but they told you wrong. You chose to foster the children and you know the rules. We don't give special treatment to anyone. Now, I've got other customers waiting, if you don't mind."

"But I think I should get stipends for all the children in my care. If not for me, they'd be put back in the welfare system and you'd have to find a home for them anyway. The system is flawed." Benfu hated that he sounded like he was begging, but she was his last resort, even if she wasn't any older than the pair of rugged boots he wore.

"What you are talking about has nothing to do with me and my position. You will need to come back after the festival when the other personnel are here."

With that she shut him down and Benfu got up. He grabbed his *hukou* and put it back in his pocket. With his face flaming, he made his way past the two couples and to the door. He didn't look at them and hoped no one would speak to him. He'd never be back here again—they could count on that. The government officials hadn't changed in all the decades since the Cultural Revolution; they still held all the power. It was a sham and Benfu despised himself for even asking for their help.

He was almost out when he remembered the oranges. He really didn't want to take anything from them if he couldn't get financial assistance, but he knew the girls would love to have the fruit. Backtracking, he looked around and saw the closet she had nodded toward and went to it. He opened the door and removed the top crate of oranges. Without making eye contact with anyone, he made his way out of the building and down the stairs.

Outside a beggar followed him, swinging his cup at him asking for money. Benfu was so upset he felt like slapping the cup out of the man's hands, but then he stopped in his tracks. He was ashamed of himself. He wouldn't let *them* change who he was! Carefully balancing the crate on one arm, he dug a yuan out of his pocket and dropped it in the man's cup, then patted him on the shoulder. He held the crate out and invited the man to take a few. At least he had a warm home and a family to return to for comfort. The beggar probably had neither.

At the sight of the silver coin the beggar chuckled and nodded his thanks. He grabbed four oranges and practically danced on down the sidewalk. Benfu smiled briefly. He knew one yuan would buy several meals of steamed rice and that thought made him feel a bit better about his initial reaction to the man.

At his bicycle he sat down and waited until his heartbeat slowed. He could feel his blood pressure pounding in his ears and the nausea roll in his stomach. Now what were they going to do for the festival? He'd let his family down and he felt like a failure.

He stood. It was time to be a man and go home to tell the girls.

He backed the bike up, then set out for home. He thought perhaps if he rode slow enough and thought hard enough, some sort of idea would come to him on the long way back. Or more accurately, he *hoped* an idea would fall out of the sky. But at this point, he was all out of ideas.

Chapter Eleven

Benfu sat in Calli's chair and watched the flurry of activity around the kitchen. It was a bittersweet day for him—on one hand he was pleased that his daughter had proved to be so responsible and was growing up. However, if he was to be honest, his pride was bruised that this was the first year someone else would provide for the spring festival treats and sweets. Linnea's new business venture was proving to be much more lucrative than working for someone else. He couldn't be prouder that she had taken a dream and was making it a reality.

After he'd told them the news about the tough year on their family finances, Linnea had stood up and said she'd take care of everything. With her profits from the last few weeks she had purchased all the supplies needed for their spring festival meal, even the cooking wine! But he wasn't completely lacking in morals. He would swallow his pride and be thankful to the young man who had secured the proper loan for her, at least glad that she hadn't been forced to borrow from shadow lenders—the groups of underbelly loan sharks that charged exorbitant fees.

Though he could easily see it in the sparkle of her eyes when she talked of him, Linnea still hadn't mentioned if she was serious about the boy, and Benfu knew it was because she didn't want to have to answer questions about him. Benfu didn't tell her that he'd seen them in the park that day. So finally today he would meet him, and Benfu was curious to see what sort of fellow could have transformed his stubborn Linnea so effectively into such a lovesick girl. It had happened with many of his daughters but he had not seen this coming with Linnea so soon. He also meant to dig a bit and see if the boy was truly up to his standards and good enough for his girl.

He'd never forget the day he'd found her wandering alone in the meat market. Most children didn't even like to be around the hanging carcasses of dried ducks, snakes, and pig parts. Mornings there were crowded as all the *ayis* and grandmothers came early to get the best meats. Benfu hated how the sidewalks would be peppered with blood that leaked from the cheap plastic bags as they carried their prizes home. If it wasn't scary enough to see so much blood around, the stench alone was enough to make them cry. He couldn't imagine what Linnea's mother had been thinking to pick that place to leave her little girl when there were many other more pleasant sites.

He'd found Linnea crying as she held the hem of her ragged shirt over her face. He'd bent down in front of her and asked her where her parents were. She had mumbled through her tears that she didn't know and began sobbing loudly. Benfu had spent the rest of the afternoon carrying her from one end of the open market to the other, weaving in and out of the crowds as he called out, asking if anyone knew the girl or her parents. Everyone either turned away or gave him a curt shake of their heads. It was obvious that she was newly orphaned, but Benfu held out hope that he was wrong as he searched.

Linnea had warmed up to him after he'd spent a few of his valuable coins to buy her a corncob on a stick. She'd stopped crying long enough to gulp it down and hand over a cob that was clean as a whistle. With that hungry look still in her eyes, he'd bought her another. Then he'd bought her a cup of yogurt milk as they'd walked the half mile to the police station to register her as a foundling. He was ashamed to remember that he had debated taking in another child. Money was as tight as the living space he shared with the other foster daughters he already had. They'd told him he could leave her there and they'd process her, but at those words she had clutched his leg and Benfu had been unable to leave her behind.

Thank goodness for that. Now all these years later he couldn't stop looking at her—a beautiful and headstrong young woman bent on paving her own road to success.

Benfu was jolted back to the present by the smell of searing ginger that wafted up his nose and made his stomach growl. It had been months since they'd had anything as expensive as pork to eat. With the delicious smells floating through the house, he knew they'd have a memorable day.

He smiled at Jasmine, Peony, Ivy, and Lily as they stood around the small table, pinching the tiny squares of dough together over bits of minced pork to make dumplings. He'd wait until they finished before sneaking over to slip a lucky coin in one. He was moving slower than usual today after a sleepless night of waking up with the sweats and coughing. Though they hadn't complained, he knew he'd been a hindrance to all of them, keeping them up with his tossing and turning. But instead of being upset, they'd spent the day refusing to let him do anything but rest.

Benfu inhaled deeply to enjoy the spicy aroma of the pork and it set off a coughing fit. Jasmine ran over and stood in front of him, patting his leg as he struggled to get his breath. His coughing disturbed little Poppy and she fidgeted. Jasmine stared at him with big eyes as he reached over and gently rocked the cradle to lull the infant back to sleep.

"I'm okay, little one. Go back to work." At that she ran back to the table and picked up another piece of dough.

Calli stood at the counter, cutting the pork into small cubes as she gave directions to Linnea for her dish she was making with the wok.

"Now just get a good coating of oil on the ginger and then add the sugar. Don't do it too early or you'll ruin it," she calmly told the girl.

Benfu could see the impatience in the bend of Linnea's shoulders. She didn't like to wait for anything. He always compared her to a pot of dumplings constantly on simmer; one had to watch it carefully or it would boil over.

"When do we add the pork?" his daughter asked.

"After the sugar dissolves," Calli softly answered. "Then we'll add the soy sauce, cinnamon, and wine last, then our braised pork dish will be complete."

Benfu cleared his throat. "I can't wait to get a taste of that. The smell reminds me of years ago. Did you girls know that same dish was a favorite of Mao's during the Cultural Revolution?"

That got their attention; he chuckled and began rocking back and forth. His girls loved to hear about the revolution and the ways the poor people had to step up and teach the exiled rich families how to survive on almost nothing. Those days were definitely a time of extreme role reversal in the country. Benfu had lots of stories—though some were too sad or terrifying to share with his daughters.

Linnea turned to him. "Why was this dish his favorite?"

Benfu smiled. He knew one of them would ask. "Because the pork shoulder usually has a lot of fat, which Mao considered an element crucial to boosting brainpower. His chef recounted later that Mao made him cook the dish before every battle or political meeting so that he could ready his wits for quick thinking and making smart decisions."

"People in the Hunan province still consider the pork shoulder the best brain food," Calli added.

Maggi piped in from her spot on the bench. "Thank you, Linnea, for bringing home food to make all of us smarter!"

Calli had given Maggi her scarf and needles to keep her busy and told her she expected at least a few inches completed before dinner. Benfu knew that more than likely, his wife would have to pull the stitches out and start anew, but he loved her for always finding something to keep the little one engaged. Maggi was just learning how to knit and had already shown a love for it and with her inability to move around, knitting was proving to be a great diversion to boredom. She still needed more practice, as it was difficult for her tiny hands to maneuver the needles quickly. Maggi always wanted to be doing something, and Benfu refused to allow her to peel bottle labels or iron papers on such a big day.

Benfu heard a bell outside and turned to look out the window. He saw the pedicab stop in front of the gate and out stepped the young man Linnea had told them about.

"It's Jet!" Linnea cried out, leaving the wok and smoothing the loose pieces of her hair back. She looked in the mirror over the kitchen sink and grimaced. "Go meet him, Ye Ye. I don't want to look like I was waiting."

Linnea's cheeks reddened and she appeared so flustered that Benfu had to chuckle. With her quick blush she reminded him of Calli in the early days. The girls around the table began teasing Linnea and Benfu almost felt sorry for her. They were as excited to meet the young man as Benfu was, but they knew not to come out and that their Ye Ye would be first to meet the visitor. Over their heads he met Calli's eyes. She gave him a knowing smile and nodded. He wondered if like him, she was remembering that feeling of anticipation they had shared the day he'd met her parents so long ago—the day she'd finally stopped hiding him in their shed and decided to bring him in and plead for him to stay. Lucky for him her parents were just as compassionate as their daughter. It was their kindness that had given him a new beginning.

Benfu stood and went to the door and opened it. Outside he met the eyes of a tall young man following behind a pedicab loaded with a couple pails of fruit and vegetables, and a box. The boy held his hand up and waved. Benfu walked out, shutting the door behind him. They approached the courtyard gate at the same time. The pedicab driver stopped and waited to be told where to unload the goods.

"Nice to meet you, Lao Zheng. *Gong xi fa ca!*" The boy came and reached over the low gate, extending his hand as he kept his eyes to the ground out of respect. Benfu was glad to see him use traditional manners.

"Nice to meet you, and wishing prosperity back to you. So you're the famous Jet we've been hearing about? Please, welcome to my home." Benfu opened the gate, and the driver of the pedicab hopped off and quickly set the boxes and pails inside the courtyard.

"What is all this?" Benfu looked down at the supplies.

Jet wrung his hands, eyes still downcast. "Lao Zheng, I'm not worthy to join your family on this special day. Please accept my gifts of gratitude."

Benfu hesitated at the stylish picture the boy presented of himself, then clapped the young man on the shoulder. "According to the praises my daughter has been singing, you are worthy. Come meet the girls. I believe at least one of them is very excited you are here."

Jet looked up and finally made eye contact. Benfu could see there that despite the trappings of wealth the boy's clothes and shoes showed, he also offered evidence of honesty and kindness.

"Can I take your daughters the gifts I brought as I meet them?" Jet asked, looking around Benfu at the box.

"*Dui,* your gifts will be deeply appreciated." Benfu swallowed hard. Besides the food situation, this was also the first spring festival he had been unable to scrape up enough money for gifts for his girls. Linnea had come through for the meal and the gods had been good to him, instead sending someone to deliver the gifts in his place. He would take this as a moment to be thankful and not allow the damper of disappointment in. He would get to know this young man and decide if he was worthy to court Linnea, and try to get to the reason why a person so obviously from such a different class would be interested in only a poor scavenger's daughter.

Linnea watched her Ye Ye carry in the biggest pail of fruit while Jet followed him, carrying the box. Her sisters sat quietly for once, waiting to meet their big sister's new beau. Linnea had warned them not to say anything to embarrass her, but she was still so nervous her hands were clammy with sweat. She'd promised Ivy an extra share of dumplings from her plate just to get her to swear to keep her mouth shut. That girl was always doing something to make everyone laugh and Linnea didn't want it to be at her expense today of all days.

"Jet! *Ni hao,*" Linnea called out, coming to meet them. She wished the courtyard had more decorations—flowers, grass, or anything to brighten up the barren dirt square. Other than a few piles of trash left to sort through, it was embarrassingly empty.

She'd never voice her complaints as she knew it was a sore spot for her Nai Nai. Decades ago Mao had issued instructions that all grass and flowers be pulled up, that such extravagances were bourgeois habits and should be replaced with cabbage and cotton, even if it wasn't the correct type of soil to grow such things. To have grass or flowers was a sure sign of being counter–revolutionary and could bring an onslaught of violence against the family. Nai Nai's parents had made her pull the grass out by the roots, an endeavor that was extremely hard because of the deep, intertwining roots that crisscrossed the courtyard. Since her family eventually lost everything they owned except the house, they were never able to afford to return the courtyard to its original glory. It remained stark as did most of the others in the *hutong* and even the neighborhoods outside of it. There had never been any extra funds for frivolous things like flowers or grass seed.

Linnea tried to ignore her embarrassment as she gestured toward the pail her Ye Ye carried. It overflowed with mandarin oranges, pomelos, and plums. "And so much fruit. Thank you." She hoped Jet wouldn't try to hug or kiss her in front of her family; she knew that wouldn't go over well at all with her Ye Ye's modest ideas about *courting* as he called it. Even though in many parts of China, the younger generation was finally catching up to the rest of the world in its willingness to be less sheltered and more worldly in the matters of dating, her Ye Ye still believed in a slow friendship building into something more only after time and family acceptance. So far, like her sisters, Linnea had always respected his traditional attitude toward dating.

Her Nai Nai took the fruit from Ye Ye and gestured to the rocking chair. "Sit down, Benfu. You are tired and shouldn't be carrying such heavy things."

He let her take the pail but then waved his hand impatiently. "I'm fine, woman. Don't treat me like an invalid."

Yet Linnea was amused to see he went back to the rocking chair like an obedient child.

Around them the girls chuckled, and Linnea was glad for the diversion during the awkward moment. Jet set the box at his feet and nodded to her Nai Nai first, and then at each sister. Linnea cringed as he looked around the one-room house, then spoke to divert his attention from the sparse décor.

"Jet, this is my Nai Nai; you can call her *Lao* Calli."

Jet approached Nai Nai as she fumbled to dry her hands on her apron.

"Thank you for inviting me to join your family meal, Lao Calli. I am honored." He bent low at the waist, kowtowing in the old way that most his age wouldn't.

Linnea smiled at his effort to show traditional respect. She was amused that he was so nervous, too. At least she wasn't the only one feeling the discomfort.

"You are very welcome here," Calli answered. "We've heard a lot about you for the last few weeks. Please, make yourself comfortable and thank you so much for the fruit—the girls will really enjoy it." She gestured to a stool that the girls had left empty for him.

Jet picked up his box and went to the stool and sat down. Linnea caught his eye for a brief moment; then he bent his head again, digging in the box.

"I have something for you girls," he said, a sly grin spreading across his face. His voice teased her sisters and all around they rewarded him with shy smiles and giggles.

Linnea felt her heart flutter as she watched him interacting with her sisters. She'd thought she would be embarrassed when he saw her humble home but was relieved that he didn't seem shocked or disheartened. He acted comfortable in the meager setting, and that put her at ease. As she watched, he pulled out several rolls of red paper and a small bag filled with child-sized scissors.

Ivy clapped her hands together. "Oh! For paper cutting!"

Jet laughed. "Sure is—you beat me to it. I was going to tell you. Here, Ms. Smarty-Pants, you're in charge of handing out scissors."

Linnea smiled at the sudden excitement in the air. This year her Ye Ye hadn't bought paper lanterns or other decorations but now her sisters would get to have them after all. And instead of cheap store-bought ones, they'd get to make them the old way. In her opinion that was much better, anyway.

"I know what to do," Maggi said. "We can draw flowers and cut them out to represent all of us."

Linnea could tell her little sister was anxious to get her hands on the paper and she took the first roll to her, along with a pencil from the bag of scissors. Jasmine plopped down beside her sister and patiently waited to be handed some paper.

"You make the first drawing, Maggi. Show us your flower." The girl knew exactly how to draw a magnolia; Linnea had seen her do it many times before.

"I want to do some paper folding next," Maggi answered.

"No, we aren't doing origami today. We're doing paper cutting!" Peony called out.

"Girls, did you know origami is a Japanese word?" Nai Nai asked, and Linnea smiled. Since Linnea was a little girl, their Nai Nai had always found a way to fit lessons into their daily lives. Linnea was used to it now.

"I know—I know! *Ori* means folding in Japanese, and *gami*—really supposed to be *kami*—is paper," Peony said.

"That's right, Peony, but the Japanese got credit for inventing paper folding in the sixth or seventh century. In the old days paper was very expensive, so only the rich had access to it, no matter which country they were in. In Japan the samurai folded paper around dried meats or bits of fish and gave it as gifts. Later they started folding paper butterflies around tiny bottles of sake or rice wine used when presenting the new bride and groom at weddings. But there are those who argue that the Chinese were already doing paper folding in the first or second century, long before the Japanese discovered it."

"Because the Chinese are smarter," Peony said under her breath. "And better-looking."

Linnea choked back a laugh. She loved some of the discussions her family got into. She hoped Jet found it just as entertaining; she didn't want to bore him to death.

"Peony, that's not nice," Ye Ye called out from across the room. "Actually, our paper folding began not as celebrations for life events, but as a way to give honor at funerals. Just as we do today, in the Sung dynasty they were folding paper money, clothes, and even dishes to burn at funerals for their deceased to use in the afterlife."

"So we did beat the Japanese, then," Ivy said, looking up at Nai Nai.

"Okay, that's enough talk about who did what. I think that's a debate that will continue until long after I'm gone, but I didn't know my history lesson would turn into a competition," Nai Nai said.

"Now, which one of you is Lily?" Jet teased as he diverted their attention by rummaging around in his box again. Linnea saw Lily smile as she stared blankly ahead of her. Jet knew which one was the blind sister, but it was sweet for him to pretend not to.

Jet pulled a book from the box and took it over to Lily. He gently put it in her lap and opened the cover, then guided her hand to the first page.

"This is a book about animals, printed especially for the blind. I know you can't read Braille yet, but you might one day. And each page has an illustration made of different textures. Feel this. It's a lamb."

Lily's smile spread wider as Jet guided her fingers across the soft cottony substance that made up the picture in the book. Jet left her with the book and returned to his stool.

Linnea met her Ye Ye's eyes as they both heard Lily whisper to herself, "I wish I could see this."

Neither she nor he addressed the comment, as it wasn't one made to get attention. Her heart ached for her sister and she was glad Jet had been so kind as to think of her disability.

Linnea watched Peony as she stood and walked over to stand in front of Jet. In her usual sassy stance she put her hands on her hips, waiting.

"Peony! Leave him alone!" Linnea could feel her cheeks start to burn again.

Jet chuckled and pulled a stack of postcards from the box, then handed them to Peony. "Share these with your sisters, *hao le*?"

"Okay," she answered, already engrossed in flipping through the detailed photographs of the Great Wall and the terra-cotta warriors on the fronts of the cards. Linnea could only imagine how fast Peony would be using them to pen notes back to her mother—notes that would never be sent because the woman was still missing in action. It infuriated her to think of the nerve the woman had in giving Peony false hope, and she truly wished she'd disappear once and for all. But she wasn't going to let thoughts of another runaway parent ruin her day.

Jet reached in his shirt pocket and took out a deck of cards and set them on the table. "Do you all already have playing cards?" he asked, looking around.

"No, we don't have cards," Linnea answered softly. Cards were a luxury they'd never splurged on and it embarrassed her that Jet immediately saw them lacking such a small thing that for most Chinese families was a staple for entertainment.

"Well, later I'll teach you all how to play *Dou Di Zhu*. It's the most famous card game of all now and I am thus far undefeated," he answered, winking at her. He looked at Calli standing in the kitchen cove. "I've also brought a pail of corn, peppers, and zucchini."

Nai Nai nodded her approval at the boy, and Linnea was amused that she looked a little bit shy. But then she wasn't surprised; Jet had the good looks to match his movie star name and her Nai Nai obviously wasn't immune to it, either.

Next Jet bent down and pulled out a small silk satchel. He stood and took it to Maggi. She put down the paper and scissors and held out her hands for the gift.

"I hear you're becoming quite the accomplished knitter. I hope this helps."

The little girl grinned from ear to ear—a shy smile that caught every heart in the room. She pulled open the drawstring of the bag and gasped when she looked inside.

"What is it?" Ivy demanded to know, ever the curious one.

Maggi pulled out a beautiful bundle of copper-colored yarn and a small set of bamboo knitting needles.

"For my very own?" she asked as she held them to her chest.

"Your very own. The needles are imported from Japan and said to be the best. Now your hands will never need to be lazy," Jet replied, and Linnea could have sworn he had a tear in his eye but he turned away too quickly for her to tell. She felt a burst of pride for her sisters' good manners and hoped Jet noticed how well-behaved they were.

Linnea's Ye Ye cleared his throat to get everyone's attention. He waited for the girls to quiet down so he'd have their full attention.

"So, Jet. Where's your family on this special day?"

Linnea met Jet's eyes from across the room. She already knew that his father wasn't too pleased at all the time he was spending with her. Jet had wanted to be honest with her and they'd discussed the situation after she invited him over. Jet told her to be patient, and that he was working on them. She was sad that his family didn't want to meet her but she could understand their reluctance to let their son be involved with a girl from the poor side of town. Even if he hadn't told them she was a scavenger's daughter, he did mention where she lived and that was enough.

"My father is meeting with his contemplation group today. They follow the old ways and will be spending time under the trees until dark, drinking rice wine and smoking. My mother was napping when I left. We just returned from our family visits yesterday. I couldn't wait to get back to see Linnea and meet all of you. And I want to thank you for allowing me to join your celebration and giving me the joy of seeing your girls smile at my humble gifts."

Her grandfather nodded but Linnea could tell he knew there was something Jet wasn't saying. Ye Ye was a smart man and it was rare to get anything past him. She hoped he wouldn't question Jet too much in front of the rest of the family, and she held her breath as he started to speak again.

"So what do you do, Jet? For a living, I mean."

Linnea could see Jet swallow hard and could almost hear the blood pounding in his ears from where she sat. She knew he was dreading this question. They'd discussed her Ye Ye's aversion to positions of power, and how it was a touchy subject.

"I—uh—I graduated from the University of Shanghai a few years ago and now I'm doing an internship at my father's office. My goal is to one day do something to help the people, possibly in welfare reform—but I, uh, might have to be elected to an official position to do it."

Benfu nodded slowly, and Linnea's heart felt like it would pound out of her chest. Finally he spoke.

"Well, I don't know about you, Jet, but I want some red paper lanterns to hang outside beside all the girly flowers they're making. How about it? You up to helping an old man trace and cut?"

Linnea breathed a sigh of relief. He wasn't going to give Jet an inquisition and maybe he wouldn't find out that Jet's father was an official. At least not until after the festival.

"Absolutely!" Jet answered, pulling a beautiful leather sketchbook from his box and jumping to his feet. "But only if you promise to tell me some stories about the Red Guards later."

As he crossed the room to come to her, Linnea saw a bundle of red envelopes poking out of his front pocket. She shook her head in amazement. He'd thought of everything and saved their spring festival.

He handed her the sketchbook and took a step back. "Linnea, a true designer needs a real portfolio. This is for you."

Linnea held the book in her hands and couldn't speak. It was the nicest thing she had ever owned, and all she could think about was opening it and filling it with all the ideas floating around in her head.

Benfu broke the moment. "I'll tell you about those Red Guards—if you're sure you can handle a few horror stories."

Nai Nai called out from the kitchen cove. "Good. You men keep yourselves busy while Linnea and I get this meal ready. We don't need you underfoot anyway."

With that Linnea joined Nai Nai back at the small stovetop. Her pork was simmering and it was time to drop the dumplings. She looked over at her Ye Ye and he gave her a wink of approval. She smiled and thought how happy she was in this moment—happier than she'd ever thought possible.

Benfu leaned back in the rocking chair and crossed his arms over his too-full belly. They'd finally finished eating and all of them except the designated dish-washing crew, Calli and Peony, sat around the living room. The other girls lay scattered around the floor, tracing and cutting out paper lanterns and dragons. Even Jasmine had dragged her paper across the room and knelt at his feet as she cut out the flower Linnea had sketched for her. Maggi perched on her bench, knitting with her new needles. Poppy lay in her cradle, entertaining herself with her own fingers.

It hadn't gotten past Benfu that Jet and Linnea sat side by side on the floor, leaning against the edge of the bed. They were close but not brave enough to touch in front of everyone. He still watched them closely. He wasn't happy about the boy's aspirations to work in the government sector but he wasn't going to ruin a good day by dissecting it. He'd let it go for another time, when he could talk to Linnea about it alone.

"Calli, you and the girls made a mighty fine meal. I thought I'd died and gone to the afterworld when I tasted those dumplings."

Calli waved her dish towel in his direction. "Oh shush with you, Benfu. They weren't that special." She went back to drying and stacking bowls on the counter, a satisfied grin on her face.

"Ye Ye, you promised to tell us a Red Guard story," Linnea said.

Benfu began rocking back and forth. He thought it was important his daughters hear the real truth about the Cultural Revolution, and not the fairy tales they would be taught in school. "I just might. But who can tell me what a Red Guard is?"

Peony moved quickly from her station in front of the dishpan of soapy water. She jumped up and down excitedly.

"I can, Ye Ye! I can. The Red Guards were students that followed Mao Zedong and did anything he wanted."

Benfu nodded. "Yes, you are right Peony, except it started out only as students but later even peasants and factory workers joined up. Ivy, can you tell me what the Red Guards set out to do?"

Ivy looked up from her red paper. "To get rid of all the old stuff and make way for a new China."

Benfu nodded again and looked at Linnea and Jet. Jet's face was impassive. Benfu didn't know what the boy thought about the Red Guards but supposed it might be a good time to test the boy's character by judging his reaction to the story.

"That is true, Ivy. That is true. They wanted to rid China of the Four Olds and that was their biggest mistake," Benfu said. "They planned to erase China's culture and customs and make a new way of living. But Mao's strategy turned into a vendetta of violence that wreaked havoc on our history. They destroyed antiques, books, and even famous works of art in their quest for a new, redder China!"

Jet nodded but still kept silent.

"Didn't they also kill people, Ye Ye?" Lily asked, her eyes staring blankly ahead.

Benfu took a moment to answer. The girls knew a lot about the Cultural Revolution but not so much about how it had affected him personally.

"Yes, Lily. They beat and sometimes killed innocent people they considered counter-revolutionaries. They went after anyone with any wealth, power, or education—especially teachers and professors. The lucky ones were sent out to do manual labor and learn new ways of thinking from the peasants. But even they suffered from abuse and starvation. The unlucky ones were beaten, humiliated, and sometimes even tortured."

"But what about your parents, Ye Ye? Were they tortured?" Peony asked.

The room around him was quiet at that. All the girls knew that his parents were teachers.

Calli cleared her throat from the kitchen. "Benfu dear, please don't fill the girls' heads up with scary thoughts. Today is a day of celebration, and the reign of Mao is over, remember?"

Benfu nodded. He wouldn't tell his girls about those the Red Guards murdered by having boiling water poured over them, or being forced to swallow nails. Some were killed just because of the width of their shirt cuffs or length of their hair! His parents had been lucky and escaped the physical punishments heaped on their colleagues. "Okay, Calla Lily, I'll tone it down. Girls, my parents were not treated well but they weren't beaten or tortured. They survived, which is more than many did. But who wants to hear the best part of the Cultural Revolution?"

Jasmine sat up and clapped her hands. She knew what was coming. Around the room all the girls stopped what they were doing to pay close attention. Benfu saw a confused look on Jet's face, for he had realized he was the only one not already aware of the next part of the story.

"So, after my parents brought me to Wuxi to try to hide from the Red Guards, I lived on a farm outside of town and worked in a collective."

Benfu saw Maggi scrunch her nose up in the expression that meant she was confused, and he explained further.

"During Mao's Great Leap Forward, he decided the people would no longer be able to own their own land and farm as individuals. Instead acreage was parceled out and those who weren't sent to the factories to help make steel farmed the land collectively and lived together in communes. They weren't even allowed to cook for their own families! Many of the collectives, like the one I was at, continued the tradition even after the Great Leap Forward ended. We'd all meet together each night in a giant kitchen and those on cooking duty prepared enough for everyone." He paused and lost himself for a moment in the memory of the days the kitchens could no longer produce enough food to feed the people. Those feelings of true hunger were something he was adamant his girls would never know, and the reason he continued to work hard day after day. He looked back down at them.

"Everything grown had to be turned in and divided up by the government. When the Cultural Revolution started, there were still many of these collectives operating, even though by then it was getting harder to produce enough to feed the people. Most of what was grown was shipped out; some said it was even going to Russia! The people were afraid to say anything, but everyone was becoming very suspicious of the so-called better way of living."

Benfu paused to catch his breath, allowing Lily the opportunity to add some detail to his story.

"And no one could hear birds sing any longer because Mao made the people kill them to keep them from eating the rice," Lily said, running her finger across a raised page in her new book as Maggi whispered to her that it was a turtle, then returned her attention to his story.

Benfu chuckled. "Well, that was back a few years before, but yes, that happened. The birds fell out of the sky because the people made so much noise with pots and pans they couldn't land and finally dropped to their deaths from exhaustion."

Leave it to Lily to think first of the birds and the beautiful music they could no longer make. He'd told them before of Mao's oversight that killing all the birds would result in an epidemic of insects. It was one of the stories they were most enthralled with. Even years after the war on the sparrows, the locusts and other insects were still wreaking havoc on the farms. For Benfu, the daily quota of how many flies they were required to catch was not a fond memory.

"And you got points when you worked, so you could eat," Peony said, nodding emphatically.

"And you're right, Peony—I got points for working the fields. The adults worked a full day and got about ten points. Children could make up to six points. But even though I was a teenager and worked as hard as the adults, I only got eight points. But it was enough to buy my rice, so for a long time I didn't go hungry."

"Tell us what the children did to earn points, Ye Ye?" Maggi asked.

"Well, Maggi Mei, sometimes the bigger ones carried water from the river to the fields and the little ones ladled it out on each plant. Some of them picked vegetables and others cleaned them. There were many jobs that the children took care of so the adults could do the hardest work."

"Just like you girls," Calli said. "You all pitch in so that together as a family we're able to move forward toward a better future."

Benfu felt a burst of unsettling in his gut. He really didn't want the girls thinking the revolution was a good thing in any way. He never wanted his daughters to think that allowing a dictator to control their destinies should be allowed.

"But as I worked and participated each night in reeducation classes, I began to realize that the cadres in charge were trying to brainwash us all. They told us how to work, how to learn, what we were allowed to sing and even asked us to declare our private thoughts each day!" He shook his head. "Can you imagine, we weren't even allowed to think on our own anymore? After many months of this I was unable to keep my mounting discontent a secret."

He looked across the room at Calli. She lowered her head.

"They found out other secrets, too. It was discovered that I wasn't really the son of a migrant worker far away, but rather the son of two intellectuals, what they considered a bad background."

Benfu swallowed hard. This was more than he had ever told the girls.

Peony looked confused. "Ye Ye, your parents were teachers. How is that a bad background?"

"I don't know, Peony. It just was. From then on I was considered to be from a *black* family." He remembered the classifications and how everyone strived to be marked as red families. Those were the closest to Mao because they were laborers, farmers, and uneducated people. Mao used to say the more books a person had read in his past, the more stupid he was. His entire life Benfu had been taught that education was the key to succeeding, but then everything changed and all of a sudden it was inconceivable to be smart.

"What did they do when they found out about your parents?" Linnea asked.

He shook his head and looked down at his hands—hands that had once been bound for a crime of nothing more than the claiming to be someone different than he really was. Oh, the atrocities done to him he hoped his girls never knew. "They made me regret my lies—let's just say that. But at least I was able to think freely and that is what really matters. They hated it that they couldn't control my thoughts or make me conform. After days of living in a squalid shed with barely any food, I escaped. I made my way to town and it is here that I found my heaven."

Across the room he spotted a shy smile spreading across Calli's face. He then looked over at Linnea and Jet. The boy looked humbled, as if he'd done something wrong. Benfu felt a moment of shame for using his stories to test him. This boy had done nothing but try to help Linnea and her family—all without a shred of evidence pointing to any kind of superiority.

Darker memories came forward in Benfu's mind, but he wouldn't tell the girls the details of the night the boy had set him free. He wouldn't tell them how he'd run for his life, stumbling terrified through the dark fields to find his way to town, his feet cracked and bleeding. He hadn't known what awaited him there but he did know that if Pei hadn't freed him, he would have been dead in a few days, maybe even less.

"Tell us more, Ye Ye!" Peony begged.

"Well, if it hadn't been for your Nai Nai and her family, I would have starved to death. They took me in and allowed me to stay here, right in this very house! I worked to earn the roof over my head and the food in my belly, but most importantly, I worked to earn the heart of the sweetest girl I've ever known."

Across the room Calli blushed deeper and shook her head, tsking at Benfu. He winked at her. At that the girls erupted into applauding and giggling. Benfu had once again found a way to end his sad story on a lighter note. And most of it was the truth, after all. It was just missing many details that were still better left unspoken.

Chapter Twelve

Finally the festivities were over. Jet had left for home, Calli had finally relented to Benfu's demands and was sitting with her feet up, and Benfu sat rocking Poppy to sleep as he watched the girls preparing their hair for bed. The routine was a nightly ritual that usually calmed them all before sleep—all except Jasmine who wiggled and squirmed because she'd rather wear her hair loose.

The girls all got to choose whether they wore their hair long or short, but most of them chose to wear it long because of their Nai Nai's stories. Calli had told them how when she was but a teenage girl, the party had mandated that all girls keep their hair chopped off to the level of their earlobes. Calli had specifically hated the style but in fear of retribution had complied. She'd had enough against her being distantly related to a landowner in the family; she didn't want to tempt even more attention to herself. But despite the shorn hair and the shapeless green jacket and trousers she was forced to wear, the night Benfu had met her, he had seen through it all to her true beauty. It wasn't in her clothes or hair—it was shining through her eyes and all the way down to her compassionate heart after she found him hiding in their courtyard and brought him food. Years later she decided her hair would never be cut again and now she could weave a rope with it if she pleased.

As the girls took turns braiding for one another, Benfu felt unusually unsettled. In the kitchen Linnea used her cloth to wipe down the last of the messes left behind from the meal. Sure the day had gone well, the food tasted delicious, and the gifts Jet brought had put the celebratory atmosphere back in the air. Yet Benfu couldn't shake the cloud of melancholy that talking of the old times had settled over him. Maybe it had to do with Jet and the mystery surrounding him, but it hadn't been the time to ask more questions on a day meant for celebrating.

He looked over at Lily braiding Ivy's hair and sighed. That was another subject that had made him overly contemplative this evening. There were only a few tasks that Lily felt useful doing. More and more these days the poor girl was being left behind as her twin struggled to grow into the independence that being a teenager usually brought. It was a sad situation. Ivy and Lily were identical in almost every way. They carried such a deep connection, yet Benfu could see that Ivy had given up much of her freedom to care for her sister. How could he help the two begin learning to live their lives as two separate people rather than one?

"Benfu, are you okay, dear?" Calli asked. Benfu looked up from his deep stare and met her eyes. He stood and went to her, then whispered in her ear.

She turned, her eyes searching his.

"Are you sure? You must be ready to face the memories if you do this, my love."

He nodded. "I'm sure. And I want to do something for Lily. I've thought about this for a while now and I think it's time."

"Okay, then. I stand behind your decision." She spoke softly but firmly, and with that his mind was made up.

He returned to the rocking chair.

"Girls, listen. I want to tell you another story. One that is for the ears of only our family. One your Nai Nai and I have held close to our hearts for years."

The girls' attention was immediately on him. They loved hearing his stories. But this was one they had not heard before. This was one he had kept quiet for too many years.

"Girls, I've already told you that I grew up as the child of intellectuals. My parents were educators and because my father was one of the top-tiered professors, we lived in a comfortable home in the French concession of Shanghai."

"Was your house beautiful, Ye Ye?" Peony asked, always the one to want to push the stories ahead to hear the endings more quickly.

"It was a fine home, Peony. But that isn't the story I'm going to tell tonight." Compared to the small concrete house they lived in now, tales of his childhood home of six rooms with a beautiful courtyard might be more than he should share. He didn't ever want them to feel they'd been shortchanged, and it would be hard for them to understand that they were more blessed now than he was with all his many possessions but a lack of affection and warmth when he was growing up.

Peony sat back and tucked her hands under her bottom. She bit down on her lip and Benfu could tell she was struggling to keep from asking another question. He chuckled at her expression.

"We'll talk more about the house another time. But girls, before the Cultural Revolution began, when I was only a few years into high school, my parents took me aside and told me they wanted me to go away until things calmed down in Shanghai. It was a time of chaos. At that point the Red Guards had just begun building into an organized group and Mao had given them permission to help rid the country of the Four Olds."

"No more old customs, old habits, old culture, or old thinking," Peony blurted out.

Benfu nodded. "Yes, that's right. Well, what you don't know is that I was a promising musician. I took violin lessons from a very prominent teacher in Shanghai." He paused at that and looked around to see the reaction.

"You can play the violin?" Linnea asked, her brow creased with confusion.

Beside her Benfu watched Lily's eyes light up. She was a huge lover of music and he knew she would be the most interested in his story.

"I *used* to play the violin," Benfu corrected. "But even though most all other music and instruments were banned, Mao at first allowed the violin and those who were good enough to stay in the city and perform in one of the approved music troupes. The troupes accompanied the revolutionary operas, the only bit of culture still permitted during those troubled times."

"Did you play with a troupe, Ye Ye?" Maggi asked from her bench.

"No, Maggi Mei. I didn't play with a troupe. My parents decided they didn't want anyone to know about my music, for they didn't want me taken from them only as a source of entertainment for Mao and his cadres. So they forbade me to play."

"That's so sad," Lily said.

"It *was* sad—but when my parents sent me to the country to live, they let me take the violin and told me to do whatever I could to keep it safe. I wrapped it up tightly and hid it in an old well."

Across the room he saw Calli fidgeting with her fingers. He could see that she was worried just how much of the story he would tell.

"Well, where is it? Do you still have it?" Linnea asked.

Benfu remembered vividly the night he escaped how he had first run to the old well and pulled up the rope, relieved when he saw it was still intact. Through the beatings and forced starvation his dignity had been taken from him, but the sight of the old violin had given him hope that all was not lost. Some would say he'd wasted valuable time in retrieving his belongings but Benfu would never have rested if he'd left it behind.

"As a matter of fact, I do still have it!"

The girls all watched open-mouthed as he stood and crossed over to the kitchen. Benfu bent down and opened the cabinet, then pulled out all the empty bottles, sponges, and cleaning powders and set them all on the floor all around him. Calli slowly rose from her chair and crossed the room to stand beside him.

"What are you doing, Ye Ye?" Peony asked.

Benfu didn't answer. Once the cabinet was cleared, Calli handed him an old knife and he used it to pry out the first board. The board resisted but after some tugging, it finally popped out. The rest came easier. When he'd pulled several, Benfu put the knife down and reached in and lifted something out. The first object his fingers found was his journal from tumultuous years gone past, and he set it aside. The next object he cradled like a baby as he blew the dust from the black silk that covered it.

He stood and returned to the rocking chair. It had been at least a decade since he had even laid eyes on it, and longer since he had let it release its sweet music. He unwrapped the silk material and heard the collective gasp around the room as he held the beautiful violin up for them to see. His own heart pounded with excitement, and maybe even a bit of remembered fear.

"What is it? Someone tell me, is it the violin?" Lily asked, her eyelashes fluttering in excitement, even if she couldn't see.

Benfu put his fingers to his lip and warned the other girls not to say anything. "Lily, come here, see for yourself."

She stood and shuffled over to the chair. "I smell the earth."

Benfu chuckled. "There's more than dirt here, girl. Please, come closer. I want you to sit in the chair."

He stood and guided Lily into the seat. She looked baffled, even as confused as the rest of the girls. All of them were trying to understand why he was acting so mysterious.

Benfu carefully set the violin in her lap and guided her hands to it. He watched the emotions play across her face as inch by inch she explored the instrument with her searching fingers.

Lily smiled and gently traced the contour of the neck, the body, and then the strings that were miraculously still intact.

"It's beautiful."

Ivy came to kneel beside her. "It really is, Lily. It's such a pretty wood. Ye Ye, what is this?" She put her hand on the instrument beside Lily's and together they explored it.

"Maple. My parents had it imported from Europe for me when I turned twelve." The memory of that day still played itself out in Benfu's mind. They were so proud that his teacher had told them he had reached the advanced level and would start learning the most famous classical pieces. He did learn them, too, but a lot of good that did him as years later all Western music would be banned.

"Be careful with that, Lily. It is your Ye Ye's most prized possession," Calli called out from the bed where she had moved for a better view to watch.

"No, Calla Lily. There you are wrong," Benfu said, much to Calli's confusion. "It *was* my most prized possession. Now it belongs to Lily. She will learn to make lovely music."

Benfu could see the shock register on Lily's face as she inhaled deeply.

"Mine? But . . . I can't play. Why give it to me? I can't even see to learn it." Lily looked confused and even a bit overwhelmed.

Benfu put his hand on her shoulder. Beside her he could see

Ivy well up with tears of happiness for her sister. Ivy understood what he was trying to do; this he could see in her face.

"Lily, you *will* learn to play it. You don't have to see—you only have to hear. But first you must become familiar with it. Clean it, hold it, even sleep with it. With your fingers learn every scratch, dent, and groove on it. Soon it will be your best friend and know all your secrets. Then I will get you a teacher and you will learn how to make music with it."

"But why can't you teach her, Ye Ye?" Linnea asked. "And will you play for us?"

With that request the other girls all piped in, begging and pleading for him to play.

Benfu hung his head. How could he tell the girls that he knew he could not handle the memories and emotions that playing his violin would surely bring? Memories of his privileged boyhood, the proud looks his parents gave him when he played, and later the fear that being caught with the instrument would bring. To be known as a musician in addition to an intellectual's child would have meant more persecution than he could bear. For years he dreamed of the freedom to make music whenever he wanted, but the oppression had ruined it for him. When the time came that he could freely show his gift for playing, he no longer felt he could do it. He couldn't bear the feelings the music would unearth. He'd rather pass the bow, so to speak, to let the violin make new—happier—memories.

"Please do not ask this again, girls. I no longer play. It is enough that before long we will hear your sister playing sweet music to fill our evenings. I'll find the right teacher for her, when the time is right."

Lily cradled the violin against her and smiled serenely.

"I'll call her Viola. She's part of us now because she also has a flower name."

Around the room the girls broke out in giggles and a smattering of applause. They all knew it was time that Lily had something of her own, something to help her find light through the darkness that at times threatened to envelop who she was.

In this, the family was united. The violin would become Lily's new lifeline.

Chapter Thirteen

With the final festivities over and the people of Beitang settling back into the small-town routine again—much quieter without the incessant rounds of fireworks—Benfu struggled to overcome his feeling of achiness and his persistent cough. He still went out to collect every day, as well as to patrol the usual secret places to check for abandoned children, but instead of eight-to-twelve-hour days, he'd cut back to only half days. He could only last six before he had to come home and rest. Even though he promised Calli he'd be home after lunch each day, he would always find her waiting impatiently, scurrying around him like a wet hen to get him to sit back and rest.

But today she'd just have to get her feathers in a dander because he was going to be late. As he pedaled through town, he consoled himself that the girls were all fine and even little Poppy had proven to be a healthy addition to their family—as far as he could tell, she would not need any expensive medical treatments.

Linnea's new mobile shop was still doing well and though he suspected some of the time when she was supposed to be working she was really out seeing her new beau, he approved of her newfound independence. She'd really come through and was helping with the household expenses, even if it did shame Benfu to take her contributions. Still, it was getting harder to make ends meet each month. He supposed it was his own fault, but they'd always spent their money taking care of their daughters and maintaining their home. The government gave him a small pension for being in the impoverished category, but it didn't amount to enough to make a real impact.

Today he planned to see Dr. Yu, the poor man's doctor. Many years before he was one of those very young men—not more than a student really—with a limited medical education who had been forced to travel between the country communes, treating as well as he knew how. Back then, with only a beginner's education and no experience to speak of, they fit in with the peasants and were called *barefoot doctors*. Many of them learned their techniques only from cases of trial and error. Years later when others went back to school for their medical degrees, Dr. Yu continued to build his small practice through word of mouth and his reputation for treating on credit. These days, a visit at a real hospital could cost more than Benfu would make in a month, so he hoped a visit with Yu would get him back on his feet so he could return to working full-time. He still had six girls to get raised and out of the house; he didn't have time for the cloud of misery that surrounded his bones.

He finally arrived at the block where Dr. Yu lived and had to squeeze the handbell on his handlebars several times to get the line of people waiting for the city bus to move and let him pass. Yes, everyone was back from their visits to the countryside and around China; the long lines and impatient faces proved that. Finally through, he parked his bike in the row of others and went to the old door. Though he hadn't been to Dr. Yu's office in a very long time, he could see the man hadn't gotten any richer in his absence. The door to the small concrete home still needed tightening and the trash piled up around the walkway overpowered Benfu's senses. But he wasn't here to judge his possessions; he was here with the hope of feeling better.

Luckily, Dr. Yu's daughter answered the door on the first knock and beckoned Benfu to enter their modest home that also served as an office and even operating room at times.

"*Ni hao,* Lao Benfu."

"*Ni hao* to you, Xiao An. How is your health?"

She smiled and nodded. "Very good. And Tai Tai Calli?"

"Calla Lily is just fine, thank you."

Xiao An stood with her hands on her hips, looking Benfu up and down. "What do you need today?" She was all business as usual and Benfu knew without her, the doctor's underground practice would not run half as efficiently as it did.

Sometimes she treated her father's patients to body massages to help rid them of unwanted poisons, but Benfu wasn't sure that this time her techniques would help. He hoped to be able to get Dr. Yu to perform some acupuncture.

"I have a very bad cough that won't go away, and my body aches night and day."

Xiao An giggled and covered her mouth. "Maybe because you are an old man."

Benfu nodded. "Yes, I know, but this time I think it's not old-man related."

Xiao An was only a small young woman in her early twenties, yet the energetic spark she gave off added a streak of color to the somber atmosphere of the old home. Tiny and with round apple cheeks, she smiled and told Benfu to sit down; her father would be with him soon. Benfu nodded and watched her bustle out of the room, her bright yellow skirt swishing around her ankles.

Xiao An was the only daughter of Dr. Yu and his late wife. Sadly, their teenage son had passed away many years before from an obstruction to the bowel that was not discovered until it was too late. Some would say that a doctor who couldn't cure his own son shouldn't be trusted, but Benfu knew that sometimes a person's fate was in the hands of the gods no matter what interventions were deployed. And he also knew that no one suffered more from the tragedy than Dr. Yu, and Benfu felt a loyalty to the man to keep coming, despite the talk around town that he had lost his medical prowess.

"Benfu! Comrade!" Dr. Yu came to his side quickly and patted Benfu on the shoulder. His daughter followed behind him, ready to assist.

"Ni hao, Yu *Yisheng."*

Even though he was not a recognized and certified physician, all of his patients called the doctor by the coveted Mandarin title. Dr. Yu took pride in his years of service and was never seen in anything less than a spotless white coat. Even the occasional times he was spotted out in the neighborhoods, one could still see the glitter of the shiny metal stethoscope that always hung around his neck.

First Yu asked him about Calli and inquired about the girls he was currently taking care of. After a few grunts of disapproval, the doctor asked him about his health and examined his fingernails and his tongue. He looked in his ears and listened to his chest.

"Your chest sounds very congested."

Benfu nodded. "Lately I cannot get my breath, Yisheng."

The doctor's usual cheerful face fell serious. "You need a chest X-ray. You must go to the hospital this time, Benfu."

"No, I cannot, Yisheng. It's not a good time for me to afford the hospital costs. Can you give me *zhen ci*?"

Benfu could see the doubt on the doctor's face and that scared him a bit. Dr. Yu was usually very confident. Beside him Xiao An shook her head disapprovingly but didn't offer an opinion.

"Hao le," he finally agreed. "Come to my working room and we'll give you the needles."

With that he briskly left the room. Xiao An waited for Benfu to gather his hat and then they both followed the doctor to his operating room, or so he called it when the need arose. Benfu hoped the treatment would work and have him feeling better soon. He focused his thoughts on what he'd been asking for in his prayers every day for the last ten years.

One more. Each day he asked for just one more sunset. One more look into his Calla Lily's eyes. One more butterfly kiss from each of his daughters still at home. So far his plea for just *one more* had worked—so he'd keep it up.

Twelve needles, a half dozen suction cups, and a session under the heat lamp later, Benfu straightened his clothes and prepared to leave. The procedure had been painless, other than one of the needles that went in. For the most part he didn't even feel each penetration, even though they were inserted at least two inches into his tissue, according to the nonstop narrative from Xiao An as she handed Yu the tools and watched him work. Talking through the procedure was her way of learning and her father only nodded in agreement as he wiggled the needles around for the best effect.

"Duo shao qian?" Benfu asked Xiao An as she wrote out a bill.

"Fifty reminbi if you have it. Twenty if you do not." She didn't look up from her writing and Benfu appreciated the gesture. He pulled a twenty-reminbi bill from his pocket and set it on the tabletop in front of her.

"I will bring the rest next month."

She nodded, then took the bill and put it in her apron pocket. She ripped the receipt from the pad and handed it to him.

"Just a minute. My father will bring your prescription."

Benfu sat on one of the several stools placed around the perimeter of the room. He already felt a little better and hadn't coughed once since he'd gotten up from the table. He should've come weeks ago, he thought to himself.

Dr. Yu came back in with a small packet of brown powder. "Mix one spoon of this with one cup of tea each night before you go to bed to help you sleep."

Benfu was glad to get the herbs. Maybe his daughters and Calli would finally get some rest from hearing him cough all night. He'd already tried some home remedies of his own but thus far nothing had worked.

"*Xie xie*, Yu *Yisheng*. My old lungs will appreciate this." He tucked the pouch into his pocket, not even asking what it was. His trust in the old doctor was complete and had been for decades.

"My other prescription is only advice," the doctor said. "It is time to slow down. You are old now—almost as old as me—and you need to stay away from the county dump sites and all other trash so full of bacteria and disease. Go to the park like your comrades and perform the morning *Tai qi*! Your lungs need a break and some clean air!"

Benfu chuckled at the thought of spending his time idle in the park, stretching alongside others his age. Not only was that unlikely to take place; with his responsibilities it would not be possible to have that much free time.

The doctor held his hand up. "I'm not done. You also should send those girls to the children's home in Suzhou or Nanjing and let the government take care of them. You take care of yourself and your *Tai Tai* only. This is the only way you can stop working so hard."

Benfu gave the doctor a gentle smile and shook his head.

"Yu *Yisheng,* I have only the utmost respect for you and I'm grateful for your care. But please remember those girls you talk about are my daughters. I would rather die than give them up to life in an institute. That is not an option and I would appreciate it if you never give me that advice again." He pointed at Xiao An. "And look at what a wonderful girl you've raised yourself! Would you ever dream of letting her go?"

The doctor looked at Xiao An and Benfu could see the love in his eyes for his devoted daughter. Xiao An smiled at her father and tilted her head. Benfu could see easily by her expression of compassion that she understood the comparison.

Yisheng hung his head and didn't reply. He didn't have to. Benfu could see his answer.

"That is what I thought. It is the same for me and my girls. Thank you for your care today and I'll be back around next month. Good day to you both."

With that Benfu put his hat back on his head and left the small house. Outside he breathed deeply, testing his ability to inhale. Unfortunately the effort sent him into another coughing fit. He covered his mouth and climbed on his bike, not looking forward to the long ride home. But at least there he would find his soft bed, his beloved Calla Lily, and his litter of amusing daughters.

Chapter Fourteen

Linnea ran the brush through her hair one more time and then turned to head out the door. She was lucky; her sisters had left her to get ready in peace as they went outside to enjoy the good weather and give Nai Nai a chance to get the baby to sleep. Their house was quiet—a rare phenomenon.

"I'm going out for the afternoon." She hoped there would be no questions.

Benfu sat at the table, shuffling the deck of cards. Since the few weeks before when Jet had left the gift, they'd all become quite fond of family competitions as well as short solitary games. Linnea could easily see how so many people became addicted to the sport. It was a great time filler, especially when they were probably only one of a few families left in China that didn't own a television or computer.

"Where did you say you're going, Linnea? I must have missed that." He tapped the deck of cards against the wooden table.

Linnea was almost to the door. Only steps from freedom and a half-hour walk to Jet, she looked at her Nai Nai for rescuing. She wasn't a little girl any longer and shouldn't have to report her every move. Calli ignored the plea in her eyes and continued to rock Poppy. Linnea came back to the table and pulled a chair and sat down. Usually they all spent Sunday afternoons together and she hoped her Ye Ye wouldn't object to her plans. So far she had evaded his questions about Jet's family and she was still waiting for the right time to tell her Ye Ye the truth.

"I'm going to see Jet. He wants to take me to an afternoon movie." She crossed her fingers under the table. *Not today, please don't ask me any questions today.* She hadn't seen a movie since her last birthday almost a year ago and was really looking forward to it—almost as much as she was looking forward to sitting close to him in the dark. Lately their affection had crossed a new boundary, and her face flamed when she thought of the smoothness of his hands on her body. She said a silent prayer her Ye Ye would just let her go, no more questions.

Benfu set the cards down on the table and looked up at Linnea. She could feel his eyes on her, even though she pretended not to notice.

"Linnea, you've been spending a lot of time with that boy and you have yet to tell us much about his family. Who are they? What do they do?"

So much for the afternoon. Finally she was going to have to tell him. She couldn't lie to her Ye Ye—she just couldn't do it. She took a deep breath.

"Ye Ye, you said you liked Jet after he was here for our dinner. Right?" She bit her lip, waiting on him to answer.

"*Dui le.* I think he made a fine presentation of his character." Benfu nodded. "But that doesn't tell me anything about his family."

Linnea was relieved he didn't comment on Jet's possible future in the welfare department. Maybe that meant he'd softened his stance. She looked back across the room to her Nai Nai, and saw by the pursing of her lips that she was listening, even if she wouldn't look their way. These kinds of things were always handled by her Ye Ye, and sometimes Linnea wished her Nai Nai would speak up.

"His father is an official. He works in the city government sector." She waited and watched. And hoped.

Ye Ye looked down at the deck of cards. She could see the tick in his jaw that meant he was trying to hold his tongue. She'd seen it before. She waited but he didn't say a word. Linnea suddenly felt sick to her stomach. She'd disappointed him.

"Ye Ye, I'm sorry but Jet can't help who his parents are. He's a good person, he really is."

Still he said nothing.

"He talks about his father and his mother like they are nice parents, Ye Ye. Maybe you should meet them?"

He didn't respond or even look at her.

Linnea felt her heart sink.

"Do you want me to tell him I can't see him anymore? Is that it?" She looked at him, hoping he'd tell her no. When still no reply came, she looked back at her Nai Nai, but the woman continued to rock the baby and Linnea knew she was not going to get in the middle of it. Linnea was on her own and she'd disappointed the one man who'd ever done anything for her in her whole life. But she couldn't say she didn't think this would happen. She knew it was going to cause trouble. In China, a person's family background was everything. Her Ye Ye didn't discriminate against wealth or trade, but he obviously still couldn't get over his bitterness toward the government.

She stood.

"You don't have to answer, Ye Ye. I know what I have to do."

With tears threatening to spill over, she quickly left the house and slammed the door. Her sisters looked up, startled at the noise. Ivy was sprawled on top of a blanket spread across the ground, writing as Lily sat next to her polishing her violin. Maggi was in her chair, knitting some colorful thing and Jasmine sat bouncing the ball of yarn in her hands.

"What's wrong with *you*?" Ivy asked, her pencil poised in the air. "Are you mad at us?"

Silently, Linnea walked right on by them out the gate and to the lane. Her cheeks flamed with shame. She didn't know how with only a look and without saying one word her Ye Ye had made her feel like she'd committed such a dreadful crime. And the bad part was that with all he'd been through in his life at the hands of officials, she didn't like it but she could understand why he was upset with her choice of a boyfriend.

A half hour later Linnea came upon Jet standing at the corner next to their noodle shop, his hands thrust deep in his pockets as he paced. When she broke through the crowd of pedestrians, he waved and she saw the smile spread across his face. Even when she was late, he still always seemed so happy to see her, and that made what she had to do even harder.

"Linnea! *Ni hao!*" He held his arms out to her.

Though she didn't think it was appropriate considering her intent, she gave him a quick hug, then stood back. She couldn't hide the worry on her face.

"Wait, what's wrong?" he asked. "Are you okay?"

Linnea could feel her heart beating erratically. She still felt sick to her stomach.

"Can we go in and get some tea?" She was buying time.

Jet looked at his watch, then back up at her. "We can but we're going to be late for the movie. Are you sick?"

Linnea led him through the door and to their table. Ever since that first day they'd come back to the shop frequently and if it was available, always sat in the same place. It was the beginning of *their story,* or that was what she had thought. But today would be the end.

She sat down and put her bag on the table. She took a deep breath. She would do this calmly and not act like an immature schoolgirl. He deserved that much. Quick and clean, that was the only way to go.

"Jet. I can't see you anymore."

There. She'd said it. But as she looked at the shadow cross his face she felt even worse. And he looked like she felt.

"But why? What did I do?" He held his hands out.

Linnea fought back the tears but she didn't take his hands. Instead she stared at them, remembering how comforting they felt on her skin. How could caresses that felt so right be so wrong? She looked up to see the pain in his eyes. She couldn't stand to hurt his feelings. It was killing her.

"You haven't *done* anything, Jet. It's just who we are."

"What do you mean, who we are? We're the same people we were when this all started. What's changed?" His voice rose in his frustration and he dropped his hands onto the table.

Linnea reached across and grabbed his hand. She looked around to see if anyone was listening. A man beside them lowered his newspaper and gave her a look, then raised it again.

"Shh . . . Jet, you're from a wealthy family with connections. Your parents have had your entire life planned out from the day you were conceived. I'm not a part of that plan and never will be. You know that. They'll never allow you to be serious with a girl like me, it just wouldn't be right. And my Ye Ye doesn't approve, either. He's a good man, Jet, but he still has an issue with anyone working in government positions."

Jet stared at her, blinking furiously as she babbled on.

"And you don't have to worry; I'll still pay the money back I owe you."

Jet pulled his hand away and shook his head.

"No way. You aren't going to do this to us, Lin. I'm with you because I like who you are as a person—it's not about how much money you have or what your bloodline is. This isn't 1967. I don't have to get permission for who I date. I don't care what my parents think. They'll come around one day. Or they won't—it's their choice. And I'll talk to your Ye Ye. I'll make him like me."

"It's not that simple, Jet."

Linnea could see by the scarlet tips of his ears that he was really emotional. She felt so terrible for putting him through this. She should have ended it before it even began. Now she was having second thoughts. But for his sake, she had to follow through.

"Yes, it is that simple. You make the choice. Just you, Linnea, not your family and not my parents. Just you."

He waited for her to speak again.

Linnea wanted to tell him she was sorry. She wanted to tell him to just ignore the whole thing and get up and go to the movie. She wanted to feel his hand on hers and hear him laughing in her ear. But then she thought of the deep look of disappointment on her Ye Ye's face. She'd never had that from him before. She never wanted to see it again.

She slid off the stool and picked up her bag. She pulled the strap over her shoulder. Jet silently watched her every move.

"Good-bye, Jet." She turned and walked out of the shop. She started walking and felt like her heart would break when she looked through the window and saw him still sitting there, staring down at the empty table. She hoped he'd forgive her, eventually.

Chapter Fifteen

A month later, Benfu leaned back against the cool, smooth bamboo of the chair as he sat across from Lao Gong. It had been a long time since he'd made time to just meet a friend for tea, but lately Linnea was acting so quiet that he had to admit he was worried. He knew she wasn't seeing the boy anymore but Jet was obviously still on her mind. Benfu had never seen her act so depressed and she wasn't snapping out of it, making him second-guess his inclination to rid the boy from her life. His goals were to make his daughters happy, not cause them misery, so he thought it was time he learn more about Jet. It was only natural to call Gong, as there was no one more knowledgeable about Wuxi families than the man who'd been his friend for decades.

He nodded as Lao Gong brought the kettle up to pour the first selection. He brought the cup to his lips and took three short sips of the *pu'er* tea. He grimaced. The first tastes would be bitter; then his tongue would numb and the fragrant drink would be at its best.

Benfu looked around him. The teahouse was one of the older ones and he appreciated the attention to detail in the workmanship. *Details miraculously left alone in the race to modernize everything and do away with the old traditional ways,* he thought with displeasure. He slipped his shoes off and ran his bare feet through the plush red carpeting beneath the low table. Around him he admired the dark paneling that used to be in every teahouse but was now rare to find. He was pleased to see that even the window next to their alcove looked out over a beautiful rock garden and the gentle sound of water could be heard. *So this is how the real retired men of China live,* he thought, in awe at the lavishness.

Across from him Lao Gong ignored his tea while he pinched a piece of popcorn between his fingertips and slipped it through the bamboo bars of the birdcage. His bird, just a small yellow canary, eagerly accepted the gift, then disappeared into its tiny hut in the corner of the cage.

"Ungrateful flea-ridden varmint," he affectionately muttered, then finally drank from his cup.

Benfu chuckled. "So when did you switch from crickets to birds?"

For years he had known his comrade to carry around a tiny bamboo castle-like cage with his latest cricket inside. Sometimes he took his current cricket to the park to fight and other times carried it with him to the teahouse. But this was the first time he'd seen him without one in longer than he could remember.

Lao Gong shook his head and snorted. "My last cricket fought to the death and couldn't be replaced. You should have seen him, Benfu! Such a huge head and colorful legs—he was glorious and what a reputation. With his fierce snapping jaws, that one made me a lot of money."

Benfu listened, intrigued. He himself had never had the time or money that cricket fighting demanded, and to see anything in such captivity always brought back bad memories for him. But he'd always loved to hear about Gong's adventures. Benfu was starting to see a pattern, and that was that he always seemed to live vicariously through Gong's fighting and his own daughters' travels. He didn't feel bad about it; living through others' adventures was enough. It would have to be.

Lao Gong shook his head sadly. "I wouldn't admit this to anyone but you, Benfu, but when he was killed, I was sad for a long time. When I talked about getting another one, the wife said she was sick and tired of my gambling and hearing my crickets chirp. So I got a bird. Boring, I know, but the little fellow makes me want to get up in the morning. I need that responsibility for another life to keep me going, you know. It's not like I have a house full of daughters to keep me young like you have, Benfu."

Benfu shook his head.

"I don't know about keeping me young anymore. I think I passed that description about a decade ago. Now I'm just trying to get the last ones raised and out on their own."

Lao Gong tapped the top of the birdcage, trying to prompt his bird out for another bite of popcorn. As he bent his head, Benfu noticed the gray roots sprouting from his hairline. Gong had always been a proud man, keeping his hair dyed black and wearing those formal old-man sweater vests Benfu continually rejected. But it looked like age was finally catching up with Gong. He looked back up at Benfu, a pensive look on his face.

"Old Benfu. Who would've imagined that all these years later we'd still be friends? Two men from two different worlds—overcoming a clash of classes and years of hardship. I guess we showed everyone that two young fellows from different backgrounds could be lifelong friends."

Benfu nodded in agreement. "Back when we first met, we weren't even allowed to sit in a teahouse. Old Mao thought teahouses would spur conversations about politics, and the old fool was frightened of where those discussions would lead. He knew that soon enough people would catch on to the mess he was making of our country."

Gong nodded. "Yes, he took away one of the people's biggest joys when he shut down the teahouses. I can agree with you on that."

Benfu looked up from his tea, surprised his old comrade would say something against Mao. The subject had always been one they couldn't agree on. Benfu didn't want to spar with him over politics and he looked for a way to bring the conversation back to the present day. "Now he can have his politics—I just want the tea and to be allowed to live in peace, away from the corruptness that still stands and calls itself our government."

The old memories still stung. Benfu remembered hearing about his parents and their march to the square to stand in front of everyone, wearing dunce caps and forced to declare they were insufferable scholars. Their positions as university teachers were taken from them and they had been forced to scrimp to survive. Benfu didn't hold affection for his parents any longer but he couldn't help but feel compassion for their plight so many years ago. Perhaps karma was the reason for their persecution, as later in life he felt they had much to be sorry for.

Lao Gong spat on the floor, causing a serving girl to come running with a spittoon a second too late.

Embarrassed at his friend's rudeness, Benfu cleared his throat and spoke. "Mao and his marathon swimming up the river to prove he was so strong—he wasn't so strong when the peasants started realizing the truth in his treatment of them, was he? They thought he was exalting them to pedestals of power but he was really working them to death."

Lao Gong leaned back in his seat and lit a cigarette, smiling to himself. "Boy, those were some days on the farm, weren't they? And to think, you and I started out in opposite stations and now look at us—I've become the scholar and you've been branded no better than a peasant with your livelihood as a scavenger. Life is crazy, eh?"

Benfu didn't take offense at Gong's depiction of his status in life. He had chosen his path when he'd turned his back on his parents and decided not to return to the sheltered life they had offered after Mao's revolution had ended. He wouldn't trade it if he could. His parents hadn't wanted to accept his new bride, so he'd declined his place as a professor's son and all the benefits that would come with it. What he'd found over the years was that the peace of mind his new life brought him was far more valuable than the prestige living as a scholar's son would've given him.

Sure, back then Lao Gong was a farmer's son and the first one to welcome him when he'd arrived at the collective. He was also the one Benfu had gone to for help to learn how to handle the hard life in the country. Living in Shanghai as a teacher's son hadn't left Benfu very prepared for Mao's so-called Cultural Revolution. He hadn't even known the basics of farming when he'd shown up! Without Lao Gong showing him how to survive at the commune, Benfu doubted his cover there would have lasted as long as it had. Even though Gong had not been the one to set him free that fateful day, when the revolution ended they'd both stayed around Wuxi and seen each other quite often. Despite the difference in their chosen careers, their bond had stayed strong over the years.

Ironically, when the revolution ended, Lao Gong found favor with an official and was given a job first as a guard, then later had risen through the ranks until he was a personal assistant to several consecutive officials. Lao Gong had kept in touch with Benfu, yet none of his offers of assistance were ever welcomed. Benfu had remained steadfast in his resentment of the government. He and Lao Gong had forged a truce when they'd finally come to blows over what Benfu considered disloyalty against the people by joining the ranks. After much discussion, they'd decided to remain friends but keep their career details to themselves.

Benfu set his cup down and leaned back in his chair. He didn't want to take the conversation too far in the wrong direction. Lao Gong had been wronged by his own employer, just like Benfu knew he eventually would be. After decades of service, when Lao Gong grew too old to be any good to them, they had dropped him like a hot dumpling. Benfu knew his friend was bitter, but he thought Gong should be relieved he at least was smart enough to have saved his money over the years and had enough to live on until his last days. And he did still have connections he could call on in a crisis.

"But I'm not here to talk about the old days, friend. I need some information," Benfu said.

Lao Gong gave him his full attention. Benfu knew he'd have his ear, as he had never asked for anything from him before. Even more interesting, they had never spoken about Benfu's imprisonment by the peasants and the fact that Gong could have helped him but didn't. Benfu knew that for his friend, it would have been risking too much and he didn't blame him. Even though the tables had been turned and Gong went on to pursue an important post in the government, Benfu had never tried to use his friend's position of power. Now Gong would be curious at his sudden change of heart.

"Have you heard of the family here in town named Sur, who have a son named Jet Li?"

Lao Gong creased his brow, deep in thought. An older man approached their table with a handful of cotton swabs poking from his shirt pocket, and two metal ear pickers in his hand. He tapped them together, questioning if either of them wanted their ears cleaned.

Benfu waved him away, irritated at the interruption. He also didn't have ten reminbi to waste on a task he could easily do himself.

"Yes, I think I do know of that family. I still hear things through the park-side grapevine. Lao Sur caused some tongues to wag when he named his son after a movie star. People said it was blasphemous to Mao, who would have been very offended at such a gesture. What do they think? He can hear the gossip from the grave?"

Benfu took another sip of tea. "But what else do you know? Is the man involved in black money?"

Lao Gong shook his head. "No, no. Lao Sur is clean—no corruption. Why do you ask?"

"Well, I don't want to say too much. But the son has his eye on one of my daughters. My first instinct was to dissuade her from seeing the son of an official, but this is complicated. This daughter is probably the most stubborn one I've had yet. For now the whole thing has calmed down, but I have a strong feeling by the way she is moping around that he isn't easily forgotten. If my gut is right, she might start back up with him, and I don't think she'll listen even if I do forbid it."

Lao Gong held his belly and laughed loudly. The sight of his tobacco-stained teeth made Benfu cringe. At least that was one benefit to Calli forcing him to give up smoking. He hoped his mouth looked nothing like his comrade's.

"See what you get when you decide to shake the hand of fate by taking in all those girls? Back in the old days, girls would never think to choose their own suitors. We all used matchmakers for our children. The future was based on knowledge—dates, names, and even zodiac signs known to be compatible. Marriages lasted for life! Now those of this generation go running around hog wild with anyone who catches their fancy." Gong began to play with his bird again.

Benfu frowned. His friend could rant about him being a scavenger all he wanted, but Benfu wouldn't allow him to make insinuations about his daughters. He began tapping his teaspoon against the porcelain cup as he fought to control his temper.

"And what about one of those younger ones you got living with you? I hear from the neighborhood she's got white blood in her and the colored eyes of a sorcerer!"

Benfu felt his thunderous expression forming but couldn't turn it off.

Gong held his hand up. "Now, comrade, don't get all in a dander. I was just yanking your beard. I know someone had to take in all those orphaned children. What I don't understand is why you?"

"Why *not* me? And if not me, then who?"

"Good point, Benfu, good point. Actually, I've been meaning to tell you for years now about my change of heart and my respect for how you've spent your life."

Benfu nodded and stopped his incessant tapping—listening but not yet forgiving the slight against his daughters. If he'd done anything at all, he knew he'd raised respectable girls and he wouldn't have anyone saying anything different.

Lao Gong took a deep breath and continued. "I spent my life catering to officials higher up than me and ignoring my family. They lived life without me being a part of it. Now here I sit with a damn bird for company. My only son has moved on and barely makes time for me and his mother. But you—you've done something remarkable, Benfu. You really have. Instead of spending your life being bitter about the loss you suffered so many years ago, you've worked to build a legacy of love with those daughters of yours."

Benfu's eyes filled with tears. He looked down at his cup, hoping his friend couldn't see his loss of composure. His friend's speech was touching, no doubt. He knew Lao Gong wasn't talking about the commune and his treatment there. He referred to something much worse—the biggest tragedy in Benfu's life. The incident he felt totally responsible for. Gong was the only other person still in his life who knew of his and Calli's heartbreak so many years ago, yet he had never said such kind things to him before. Now would be a good time for him to ask Gong the questions he had been dreading. He was finally going to ask him to use his connections to help him find support for the girls in case something happened to him. It was time to start facing reality—he was getting old and so very tired. He took a deep breath but instead of being ready to start, he began to cough.

"Benfu, are you okay?" Lao Gong asked, gesturing behind him to the server to bring some water.

Benfu tried to get his breath but he felt like he was drowning in phlegm. He was embarrassed but he just couldn't breathe! He grabbed his throat, coughing and coughing. The server brought the carafe and refilled his water glass. Benfu waved her away, beginning to panic at the loss of air and the sudden dizziness.

Lao Gong jumped to his feet and upset the teapot and cups in his attempt to lean over to thump Benfu on the back. His old friend's mottled face was the last thing Benfu saw as a black curtain enveloped everything around him.

Chapter Sixteen

Linnea lay staring at the water-stained ceiling over her pallet, waiting for the last of her sisters to fall asleep. It had been such a long evening. They'd been playing cards as they waited for Ye Ye to come home for dinner when his old friend had arrived instead of him. Lao Gong told them he had left their Ye Ye at the hospital after he had fainted during their afternoon tea. His announcement had caused quite a commotion and her Nai Nai had gotten so frightened that Linnea thought she might have a stroke. When Gong had finally soothed them down with words of reassurance, he took Nai Nai to the hospital to sit with Ye Ye. Before leaving, Nai Nai had warned them that she might be gone until morning. When they didn't return by nightfall, Linnea took charge to get the girls calmed and into bed.

That had proved harder than she expected. The girls were so upset they didn't want to go to bed. But she had eventually succeeded and now even little Poppy lay sleeping contently in her cradle. Linnea tried to hold back the urge to move; instead she focused on silently counting to one hundred in English—a trick that Jet had told her he did when the pressures of school and his job made him sleepless.

Just great. Now she was thinking about him again. She'd tried so hard to forget him but it wasn't happening. She missed him terribly. She missed the way he made her feel like a woman—and not a girl like her family still thought she was. She also missed his easy laugh and the way he was so protective of her in the streets and the park. She smiled in the dark, remembering their walks with his arm always snugly around her. Jet was the only other person besides her Ye Ye who had ever made her feel so safe. She wondered if she'd ever meet anyone like him again, or was she destined to be alone?

Finally, when she thought all the girls were asleep, she pulled the covers off and quietly stood. Tiptoeing to the table next to the bed, she slowly reached down and picked up the key that in all the chaos of their morning, her Nai Nai had forgotten to wear. Cradling it in her hand, she walked to the cabinet and unlocked the door. Linnea looked behind her to make sure no one had awakened and her mouth formed an O as she tried to quiet her breathing. She didn't want to wake her sisters—she was sure one of them would tell. She could feel her heart racing and once more she wondered if it would have been easier to just ask Nai Nai for permission to see her page in the book. She had always been open with the girls, but this time Linnea didn't want either of her grandparents to know that she was thinking about her mother so much. It had been years since she had asked about the details of the day they found her; she just wanted to look and see if she was forgetting anything important they had told her. Talking to Jet about it had re-opened some of the old wounds and Linnea hadn't been able to stop thinking about it since.

She reached in and gently picked up the book. She felt like a criminal but the decision was made. Holding it to her heart, she closed the cabinet door and then crept across the room, sidestepping around her sisters. She very slowly opened the door and slid out, quickly closing it behind her to keep the cold air from entering the house.

Setting the book on the bench outside the door, Linnea looked up and down the lane to be sure she was alone. Around her the crickets sang and shadows played on the low courtyard wall, and Linnea fought the urge to shiver with fear. The dark shadows looked like people to her, fluttering about and watching her. Working quickly, she settled onto the concrete seat and picked up the book. On the cover she traced the gold-embossed character of *Family,* then untied the leather cord and opened it.

Luckily it was a bright moon and Linnea could easily see the neat characters made by Nai Nai's hand. On the first page she read the familiar character of their family name. She felt a burst of quiet anticipation; she'd never seen inside the book with her very own eyes.

Book of the Official Zheng Family History. The characters swept elaborately down the page, along with a sketched trail of flowers. Nai Nai, always being fair-minded, had drawn every type of flower that her girls represented around the page. Linnea had never seen it before and she was amazed at the beautiful picture it created.

Turning to the next page, she hesitated when she saw the name Dahlia at the top. That wasn't one of her sisters—she'd never heard that name before. The page was filled with penmanship and in places, blurred by what appeared to be drops of water. Linnea's brow wrinkled as she studied the characters.

1982

Zheng Li Dahlia, born at 11:15 p.m. on February 9. A small girl of only six pounds, she fits neatly in the crook of my arm. Dark eyes and a head of wavy black hair, Dahlia looks like a dainty porcelain doll. A quiet infant, she rarely cries or makes any fuss. Thanks to the heavens! I finally have my daughter! Benfu has hopes that our Dahlia will be the salve to bring his parents to their senses and show them he made the right decision to marry me. They know a grandchild has been born and they've agreed to visit. We see it as a step toward a much-awaited reunion!

Linnea read on, mystified by the words about a reunion of her Ye Ye and his parents, but most of all by the description of a sister she had not known anything about. By the date, this child was the first one the Zhengs had taken in. Suddenly Linnea realized that if the child had been found, there wouldn't be an official birth date and weight recorded in the book.

February 10. Benfu's parents arrived to visit Dahlia. Mother Zheng refused to hold her and declared the birth a travesty. Her dashed hopes for a boy child made her ugly and she left in tears. Father Zheng refused to enter the house and followed his wife down the lane. They threatened to withhold Benfu's inheritance if he didn't follow their atrocious wishes. He doesn't want their money. Benfu held his daughter and declared her perfect, despite her gender. All is well, though my heart aches for my husband and the hurt he feels at his parents' disdain.

The realization that she was reading about Ye Ye and Nai Nai's own baby hit Linnea like a punch to her gut. She couldn't believe they had their own child and never said a word about it! She read again the part about Ye Ye declaring his daughter perfect and smiled as she recognized his actions as ones he would do today. He had been a supporter of girls for decades and ranted against anyone who tried to say girls were inferior. But what had happened to their Dahlia?

March 17. Tomorrow is Dahlia's one-month party. She has been registered and is now a citizen with a hukou. *One day she will attend school and be very successful! The red eggs are ready and will be handed out at her party to represent fertility and renewal of life. Dahlia's new name will be chosen by her grandparents and officially announced to all. Benfu has secured the banquet room at the Lotus Hotel in town. I will be sad to see her wavy black hair sheared off but it will mark her independence from the birthing process and that she is now a separate person. And I can be happy knowing that her hair will grow back much prettier! Today, after our afternoon nap, I will finish sewing her tiny red tiger outfit and attach the frog ties. Tomorrow will be a special day!*

Linnea felt another twinge of guilt that she was reading something obviously meant only for Nai Nai's eyes. But she couldn't stop herself. She still felt as if she were intruding on Nai Nai's privacy, but instead of flipping to her own page to quickly finish her task, Linnea continued to read about Dahlia.

March 19. There was no one-month party and there is no more Dahlia in our life. I awoke from my nap to find my daughter snatched from her cradle. There is no proof but I know from the familiar lingering stench of garlic just who was in my house. Mother Zheng. She took my child but swears she has done no such thing. We have traveled to every police station and orphanage within fifty miles. The local officials are of no help because Dahlia was only a girl. I can only hope that she was given to a distant cousin or uncle and that her life was not extinguished. Benfu is devastated, as am I. I have a pang in my stomach that will not go away. I never want to see Mother or Father Zheng again. I don't even know if I want to continue living, but how can I leave my grieving husband?

The words were dotted with smudges and Linnea was sure they were her Nai Nai's tears. She felt sick and fought to keep from heaving up the food in her stomach. She wondered how Nai Nai had survived all these years, not knowing what had happened to her daughter. She wanted to hug her, comfort her, and beg her forgiveness for reading her private words. But she'd do no such thing. She didn't want them to know she had done such a dishonest deed. There was another paragraph, and she had to finish. But what more could be said, she couldn't imagine.

September 3. There will be no more children for us. The officials rounded up every woman who had registered a birth in the last five years and after three days of nonstop lectures about rules for family limitations, insisted we all receive IUDs implanted for birth control. Benfu and I refused and tried to make them understand our baby was stolen, but they accused us of hiding her so that we could try for a boy. We held out for days but when Benfu got word that his parents had been rounded up and were also being detained until we complied, I relented. He didn't ask me to but I could see the fear in his eyes for what might happen to his mother. I didn't want him to carry that burden. But instead of an IUD, I was sterilized against my will. I am now a barren woman and trying to recuperate from the pain. I only hold on to the hope that my Dahlia could be out there somewhere. Maybe she will find her way back to me and her father.

Linnea wondered if all of these years, each child her Ye Ye had brought home represented his own daughter. She choked back a sob as she thought of the love and acceptance the two broken parents had selflessly given to so many girls, despite their heartbreak. She wondered what had become of the first sister. Was she alive? Out there somewhere wondering who her parents were?

November 30. Benfu now also believes his mother was responsible for the disappearance of Dahlia. They threatened terrible things if Benfu continued to barrage them with questions. His parents didn't have to disown him after all, for now he has disowned them. He said he would rather continue to pick up trash and live a life of poverty than forget what his parents have done in their attempt to lure him back to his old lifestyle. Benfu feels he is at fault for allowing his mother such control over his life and he no longer wants a part of their good fortunes. I agreed and we've committed our life to being on our own, sink or swim. Without his father's influence and reputation to back him up, it will be a hard road to take but together we will survive. Somehow I must help Benfu understand he is not responsible for his parents' deeds or the guilt will kill him.

Linnea could read no more. She felt a heavy sadness envelop her as she gently shut the book. She held it close to her heart as she reached up and wiped at the trail of tears on her face. She didn't need to read about her own details any longer. The mother who had abandoned her had done her a favor—for just as she'd always known, what she'd read proved that she couldn't have ended up with better parents than Nai Nai and Ye Ye. She looked down at the book and saw the corner of a photograph sticking out. She pulled at it and without letting it lose its place in the book, examined it closely. It was of a little girl standing in front of what appeared to be a small eating shop. The girl looked pensive, staring past the photographer with a blank look on her face. Linnea flipped it over to see if there was anything on the back but it was blank. The tiny girl looked about four years old, so was too old to be their Dahlia. It wasn't her, either, she was sure of that. But there were many other sisters it could be. In the moonlight Linnea squinted at the photo, trying to make out familiar features, but it was just too hard to tell. She poked it back down into the pages of the book.

She rose and quietly entered the house, put the book back, and locked the cabinet. Slowly she crept to the table and returned the key. She looked at the bed and shook her head in amazement. Jasmine was there, sleeping soundly while holding Ye Ye's pillow. The little girl had cried herself to sleep and refused to return to her own pallet when Linnea had explained to her that Ye Ye would be staying all night at the hospital. The bed looked huge without Ye Ye and Nai Nai in it. She imagined them there as they were every night. Ye Ye, always the protector, would be lying with his arm draped over Nai Nai. Linnea adjusted the covers over Jasmine and crawled under the light blanket beside her. Jasmine wasn't the only one who needed to feel the presence of Ye Ye and Nai Nai.

Linnea turned to the wall, closed her eyes, and pledged silently that she would find out what happened to Dahlia. Some way, someday, she'd give her Ye Ye and Nai Nai some answers. Then she began to count to one hundred again.

Chapter Seventeen

Benfu sat on the bed and looked out over his girls. He and Calli had just returned from the hospital and he was exhausted. Looking around, he marveled that his whole world sat within the small confines of the room, in the faces of those he loved. They sat quietly around him because they were afraid. He knew they were waiting for him to tell them what the doctor said but first, Benfu wanted to lie back and relax his aching body. The doctor had stopped giving him the relaxing medicine that morning and because of that, he had coughed so much that he was sore all over. The day had been long, the news grim, and he was exhausted.

"Girls, let your Ye Ye rest," Calli said, bustling over to him and helping him lift his feet up on the bed. She put a tiny basin beside him, in case he needed to cough up more blood. He hoped he could keep it back so that he didn't scare the girls any more than they already were. Linnea got him a clean handkerchief and went to see about the dinner the twins had started. As she walked away, Benfu remembered the conversation he'd had with Gong about Jet. He planned to tell Linnea that he wanted her to follow her heart and not pay any attention to an old man's prejudice. Linnea deserved to find her own way, without his interference. And if the boy was good to her and had his own stand-up character, what did it matter about his parents? But that would have to wait, as he was so tired.

He and Calli had been at the hospital for a whole day and night. Finally, after several examinations and a round of X-rays that cost them at least a week's salary, they had met with the chief doctor and he had given them the grim diagnosis. It was tuberculosis. He'd also chastised Benfu for not coming in years earlier. He said that the disease was progressed but if he'd caught it earlier, they might have been able to cure it. As it was now, the disease had damaged his lungs as well as the lining of his heart. His old ticker was having problems pumping blood, which had caused him to pass out. The doctor had said with the right drugs, and a strict regime of exercise, he could get Benfu's symptoms under control and make him more comfortable. Benfu had declined—those kinds of options were for rich men, not an old man with pennies to his name. Benfu didn't explain; he just shook his head and proudly left with Calli on his arm.

As it was now, without the costly drugs and medical attention, his time on earth was officially limited. Sure, he knew he was an old man and had lived a long life, but in China men usually lived well past his age and he had hoped to at least hold out a few more years. A strange expression the doctor had used—*without medication his time would be limited.* As to how much time that meant, the man wouldn't say; he advised only that Benfu get his affairs in order quickly. Benfu hadn't told the doctor that there wasn't anything to get in order. He would be leaving nothing to his family but the debt of burying an old man. He shook his head in disgust. If he had not had such pride, he could've reunited with his family years before and given Calli a better life. But even now he couldn't fathom ever sinking that low as to forgive them for what he knew they were guilty of.

But now what would become of his girls? Of his Calla Lily? And he had hoped to find out what had happened to Dahlia before he died. But now he had put it off too long. It was too late. He quickly reached up and wiped the moisture from the corner of his eye before it could be noticed. His only consolation was that each child had been taken to the clinic and inoculated less than a week after being found, a cost absorbed by the government, as unbelievable as that was. Even little Poppy should be safe from the dreaded tuberculosis, as Benfu had rarely handled her before her shot. But he'd been thinking about it all night and he knew what he had to do.

Calli brought Benfu a bowl of noodles and his chopsticks. "Sit up, Husband."

Benfu waved her away. The smell of the spicy shrimp broth would usually make his mouth water but he was too sick and worried to eat. He just wanted to spend a few minutes with his girls and then rest. He'd have to tell Calli about his decision soon, but he just couldn't do it yet.

"No, I'm not hungry right now, Calli. I just want to sleep for a while. Stop fussing over me!"

At that Jasmine left her perch on the stool at the table and ran across the room. First grabbing her blanket and doll from the corner, she jumped up on the bed and threw her arms around Benfu.

Benfu chuckled at the unusual show of affection. Jasmine was usually his shyest one.

"Oh! Now what is this? My little monkey missed her Ye Ye?" He unwound her arms from his neck and leaned back to look at her.

She nodded her head, her eyes big and afraid. She clutched her blankie in one tiny fist.

Benfu felt his heart tighten. Even before he had told the girls anything, the little one knew it was bad. Once again her ability to understand things that should be too mature for her amazed him. He had always said she was very intuitive for such a little girl. He dreaded to think what would happen to her without his support but he knew Calli would look out for her and the rest of them as best as she could.

He settled back on his pillow and invited her to snuggle against his arm. "Lie back here, little monkey-girl, next to your Ye Ye."

Jasmine crawled up the rest of the way until she was securely in the crook of his arm. He was sure going to miss moments such as these. But for their future, he had to let them go. After he discussed it with Calli, together they would meet with the city officials and find homes for each daughter. He swallowed the sudden lump that came up in his throat. He knew that once they were gone, his body would soon give up, as they were what kept him going. But it would be better for them not to watch an old man die little by little, then still end up without anyone to care for them. He had to see them settled. But damn if it wasn't already killing him even to contemplate it.

"I'll tell you what. You girls all get your supper and I'll tell you a short story before I go to sleep. Will that make everyone feel better?"

Around him the girls solemnly nodded. They didn't push to hear the doctor's report, and Benfu could tell they wanted to avoid the bad news. He watched as Calli served up bowls of noodles and Ivy passed them out. When almost every child had her supper, Benfu looked down at Jasmine and took a deep breath. The sudden intake of air caused another coughing fit and he held the cloth to his mouth, hiding the spatter of red. Discreetly folding it in his hand, he stuck it in his pocket and began again.

"Jasmine, girls, tonight I'm going to tell you the famous legend of Yuhua, which has been handed down from generation to generation." He touched the tip of Jasmine's nose. "The story reminds me of you and the night you became my daughter, so this one is for you, Mei Mei."

Beside him Jasmine was so quiet she couldn't even be heard breathing. The girls around the room attempted to eat their dinners without any noise, their attention focused on him.

Benfu cleared his throat and tiredly began the legendary story, pausing every few minutes to stifle a cough.

He pointed at the ceiling. "First, I haven't gotten to say it in a few days but do you know . . ."

A small smile began to play around her lips.

"That I love you to the moon and back?" Benfu finished, then looked up at his other daughters. "As I do all of you. Now"—he covered his mouth and coughed—"the story . . .

"'During the time of the Three Kingdoms period, in the Kingdom of Shu, it was rumored that a beautiful young widow with the strangest eyes of blue haunted the waters surrounding the Yangtze River. The people in the village had last seen her standing over those waters before she dived in to end her life of loneliness.'"

He looked around and smiled at the sudden expressions of fright on the girls' faces. He put his finger in the air. "No, it's not what you think. 'This young widow—Yuhua—she wasn't a frightening sort of ghost. She'd returned as a fish the color of a peach blossom, with round eyes of sapphire-blue and a swirling design of a flower on her side. Finding contentment in her new form, she frequently visited the reed-covered banks, where people would come to her with their problems. They considered her lucky, and many wishes were asked of her. Over time, her visitors noticed a pattern. Whenever someone would seek Yuhua and demand something selfish, she'd flip over and disappear into the depths of the water, refusing to return for days. Yet, when a request was made out of kindness to help another, Yuhua would swim in happy circles and many times, the desire was later granted in some way.

"'Throughout the village, Yuhua became known as the fish who taught the people it is more important to help others than themselves. It is said that many loyal followers visited her each day and brought her tidbits to snack on until she was soon fat and content.'"

At this Benfu paused and looked down at Jasmine again. She was now smiling and it made his heart lighter.

"Sounds like you with your love for the pretty fish, eh?" He bumped her with his elbow and she let out a soft giggle. He didn't have to explain; they all knew of finding Jasmine in the park pond, surrounded by colorful fish. Since that day she had remained mesmerized by the creatures. They didn't get to go often, but on the rare occasions that they went to the famous parks, it was difficult to keep the little one on the path and out of the water.

Benfu continued the story, despite his heavy eyes. He struggled on.

"'Yuhua lived through many cold seasons, disappearing when the river froze but returning each spring. One day a simple fisherman's son decided he wanted to catch her, and to wish upon her for his every whim. But Yuhua couldn't be caught. She wasn't just any old fish, you see, she still had the keen mind of a human. After teasing the young fisherman for many weeks, though, Yuhua became besotted herself and decided she might like to belong to him. . . .'" Benfu's voice trailed off, and mid-sentence he gave up the fight to keep his eyes open.

Chapter Eighteen

The next morning Benfu awakened to a sliver of sunlight beaming through the crack in the front door left ajar. He struggled to sit up, coughing as he reached for the basin on the table next to him. He spit a stream of phlegm into it and set it aside. The night had been long, full of coughs and sudden bouts of sweating. He should have felt rested after ten hours lying down, but the truth was he felt even worse than he had when he got home the day before.

"Benfu, my love? *Hao le, ma?*" Calli sat up, rubbing at her eyes.

Benfu felt guilty that his tossing and turning had kept her awake, too.

"I'm okay. Just can't stop coughing. Why is the door open?" He looked around, trying to see if Linnea or Ivy had gone outside. All the pallets were still laid out and he could see dark heads all around—understandable since it was before six in the morning and no one had stirred yet.

"Ye Ye? Is Jasmine up there with you?" Linnea sat up and asked from her pallet next to Jasmine's empty one.

Benfu sat up quickly. His feet hit the floor as he looked around.

"No. She must have gone outside to the bathroom." He stood and slid his feet into his slippers, then went to the door and called out her name. When she didn't come, he went out and around the side of the house to the small shed that was their outhouse. The door stood open and he could see she wasn't there. Puzzled, he turned back and returned to the house.

"Calli, where is Jasmine?" He looked all around the room again and went to her pallet. Using his foot, he moved the blanket aside. She wasn't there and her doll was also gone. He felt his stomach sink.

Calli looked around, a strange expression on her face. One that Benfu had seen before and didn't like.

"I don't understand. Where could she have gone?"

Linnea and the other sisters, except for Maggi, all jumped up and began tearing around the room. They looked under blankets, under the bed, and behind the table. They looked behind the curtain that was their makeshift dressing area. She wasn't in the kitchen alcove, either. Peony even looked under the kitchen sink but found the cabinet empty.

Jasmine was nowhere to be found.

Benfu went behind the curtain and dressed in his outside clothes. He came around and pointed at Linnea. He finished a coughing fit and wiped his mouth with his cloth.

"Linnea, come with me. Let's go look for her. The rest of you help your Nai Nai get the bedding picked up and breakfast started. Peony, you get Maggi situated. I'm sure Jasmine's probably just outside and we'll be back in a minute."

Linnea jumped into action and grabbed her clothes for the day. She went behind the curtain to change, moving as fast as she could.

Ivy began to cry and begged to go with him to look. She insisted at fourteen she was old enough to do whatever Linnea could do. Benfu hugged her and whispered to her that he needed her to stay and watch over her Nai Nai and Lily. She sniffled and nodded her agreement.

Benfu was frightened. Jasmine had never done this before and it wasn't safe for a young girl to be wandering around alone. Anything could happen. Anyone could snatch her and use her to beg on the streets, or sell her to an orphanage in another province, or all kinds of other horrible fates could befall such a defenseless girl. Many of his neighbors let their tiny children run free, but he'd seen what the cruel world could do to the little ones and his girls were always watched over carefully.

He felt his hands shake as he stuffed a clean cloth in his pocket. He looked over at the bed and was worried about Calli, too. She looked stricken—even confused. He was used to seeing her bustling about, getting everyone started for the day. He even expected her to try to lead the charge in the search for Jasmine. But instead she sat there still as a statue. He went to her and took her by the shoulders.

"Calli? Are you okay?" he asked. He couldn't stay and console her, and that was like a knife in his heart. But Jasmine was out there somewhere alone. He had to find her.

Calli shook her head and looked around. "*Aiya,* I smell garlic. Does anyone else smell that?"

The others sniffed and shook their heads. Benfu pulled Calli up from the bed. He hugged her, then stood back.

"You do *not* smell garlic, Calli. No one took her. Snap out of it—I need you to be strong for the girls. We'll find Jasmine."

Calli burst into tears, a sight that judging by the gasps and stricken expressions Benfu saw around the room, terrified the girls. They had never seen her break down or show such fear. Then again, they didn't know the story of the child their Nai Nai had lost long ago while she lay sleeping—the story of the child who had never been forgotten. Benfu fought a wave of dizziness and headed for the door, holding his chest.

Just before he disappeared through the doorway, Calli stood and gathered herself. "You cannot go out there walking around, Benfu. You are sick, you should be in bed."

"I'll be back when I find Jasmine. Don't worry, I'll be fine. Come on, Linnea. Let's go." He held the door and Linnea slipped through. They left the courtyard together.

Linnea followed her Ye Ye as they started with their own courtyard and then moved out into the *hutong*. They took turns calling out to Jasmine in the hopes that she was being silly and hiding somewhere near. That wasn't something she would normally do, but Linnea knew anything was possible.

Neighbors had begun to stir and a few came out to see why they were calling out. Widow Zu looked up from watering her tiny vegetable patch as they passed, her hand in midair as she searched their faces to see what was wrong.

"Zenme le?" she called out. She wasn't one to ever hold her tongue. In her book it wasn't nosiness that kept her asking questions; it was her right as the *hutong* matriarch.

Linnea looked at her Ye Ye and saw he was too preoccupied with looking around the line of trash barrels to pay attention.

"Our Mei Mei, Jasmine, is missing," she answered the old lady. "Have you seen her, Widow Zu?"

The old woman squinted. "Which one is that?" She waved her hand in the air. "Oh never mind—you all look the same to me and I haven't seen any of you girls this morning until you. But I'm sure she'll turn up."

The old woman went back to watering the small patch of grass on the edge of her dirt yard. Linnea followed along behind her Ye Ye, checking the areas he didn't. He was easy to keep up with, even with her looking in more places than he, as he struggled to get his breath while he went. Linnea kept an eye on him, too, as she looked.

At the end of the lane he stopped just before entering the street and turned to her.

"Linnea, you go that way and I'll go down to the end of this street." He pointed in the other direction.

"No, Ye Ye. I don't want to leave you. Let's look together." She was worried about him. His cheeks were flushed and she'd never seen him so upset. She was concerned because he could barely walk a few steps without attempting to muffle a cough.

She jumped when he barked back at her. His voice was much hoarser than normal, making him sound nothing like himself at all. "Just do what I say, Linnea! We don't have time to waste."

At that he took off in the opposite direction and Linnea turned down the lane, her head bent to hide her hurt feelings. She knew he was just afraid for Jasmine and wasn't mad at her, but he rarely ever yelled at them and it stung. Was he still mad at her about Jet?

Behind her she heard him start another round of coughing and she shook her head. He was too sick to be exerting himself so much. She hoped that Jasmine would beat them home and that she was only hiding somewhere around the house and was fine. When she turned up, her little sister was going to get a few yanks of the hair for the trouble she'd caused.

At the intersection, Linnea stopped to wait for traffic. She turned her head to look behind her at how far her Ye Ye had gone. She couldn't see him for the crowd that was gathering between them. Linnea wondered what they were looking at, then turned back around to cross the street. She didn't have time to be nosy; she needed to find her sister.

In front of the grocer's stand she stopped to ask if he had seen a little girl that morning. The man stood with his hand to his eyes, trying to look beyond her. By the looks of his soiled white apron and his perfectly arranged fruit bins, he'd been at work for hours already and probably would have seen Jasmine if she had come by.

"Dui bu qi." She waved her hand in front of his face, trying to get his attention. "Excuse me."

He ignored her and continued to look down the street. Linnea was irritated. They'd shopped there plenty and it wasn't like the grocer to be so rude. Her Ye Ye had told her many times how the same man used to sell his fruit and vegetables from worn baskets hanging from a pole across his neck. Ye Ye said that years of hard work and customer loyalty had finally earned the man a real storefront with shelves and crates, and he'd built his business up big enough to actually be able to take care of his family, but Linnea thought maybe he was getting too uppity. Was he too good to give her a moment of his time?

"I said *dui bu qi.*" She tried again.

Distracted, the grocer looked down at her and then his eyes widened. He pointed behind her.

"Oh, hey—aren't you one of the scavenger's daughters?"

Linnea felt her temper flare, but she needed to ask him about Jasmine and then she could just go. She didn't need to waste time defending her family.

"Because if you are, I think that's the old scavenger who just fell in the street. Can't see him anymore, too many people around him. But I'm sure that was him. He waved at me when he went by."

Linnea felt her heart in her throat. Had Ye Ye been hit by a car? She turned and began running as fast as she could. *Please let him be okay; please let him be okay.* At the curb, she darted out into the street, not even looking around her. Just a few feet from her a taxi driver slammed on his brakes and laid on the horn. A woman on a bicycle swerved and cussed at her, waving her fist at her as she fought to get her bike back in balance. Linnea kept running and covered the two blocks in seconds. Out of breath, she pushed through the crowd.

"Move! Let me through!" she cried out. "That's my Ye Ye!"

Linnea hoped she was wrong—that the grocer was wrong. But something told her they weren't. The crowd parted and she felt cold chills run up her arms as she saw her Ye Ye lying on the street, his eyes rolled back in his head. Linnea knelt down on the ground next to him. She didn't see any blood or anything to indicate he'd been hurt. He simply lay there, white as a sheet and not moving at all, despite the chaos of the street around him.

"Ye Ye! Ye Ye, are you okay? Can you hear me? What happened?" Linnea pulled her jacket off and bundled it, then slid it under his head.

He didn't answer but she could see his chest rising and falling. The people around them babbled about seeing him fall, but no one offered any help. They stared and pointed, clearly excited at the interruption to their morning. Linnea looked around, trying to find any familiar or sympathetic face. She didn't know what to do. Everyone simply stood around her, staring.

What felt like an eternity later but could only have been seconds, a young girl about Linnea's age—on her way to school by the looks of her pristine uniform—dropped to her knees beside them, holding out her cell phone.

"Do you need to use my phone to call someone? Maybe an ambulance?"

Linnea knew an ambulance crew would take one look at them and know they couldn't pay a transport fee. She didn't even have thirty yuan for a taxi—much less several hundred they'd charge for an ambulance ride. She looked at the phone in the girl's hand and suddenly remembered that Jet had made her memorize his number in case she ever needed him. He had wanted to buy her a phone, but Linnea wouldn't let him as she knew her Ye Ye would have drawn the line at such an extravagant gesture.

She looked back down at her Ye Ye, then around her for help. She thought about running the two blocks back home to get Nai Nai, but she couldn't leave him. She was on her own. She grabbed the phone from the girl and punched in the number. As she waited for it to connect, she squeezed her Ye Ye's hand and tears ran down her face and dropped on his chest.

"Please, Ye Ye, be okay. Please," she pleaded quietly as the number connected and rang once, twice, then three times. She studied her Ye Ye's face while she waited. He was pale. Too pale.

"Jet, where are you?" she mumbled just as he answered. She hoped he wasn't tied up with anything too important that he couldn't get away. The crowd around her was so loud she didn't hear him answer at first.

"Hello? Hello? Who is this?"

At the sound of his voice Linnea froze. Then she saw her Ye Ye's eyelashes flutter.

"Jet! I need you. It's an emergency. Can you come right now?" Her voice shook and she ignored the looks of pity the strangers around her cast her way. She felt a moment of panic in the lull it took him to answer; then she heard his voice.

"Just tell me where you are, Lin. You can explain when I get there."

Linnea climbed into the car and shut the door. She looked up at the hospital they had just left and shook her head, amazed at all that had transpired over the day. She hated leaving her Ye Ye there but knew that Nai Nai would stand guard and not let him get up. His second collapse in two days made it fairly clear she wouldn't let him come home until the doctor gave his approval. Still, leaving Nai Nai there alone to deal with his stubbornness made her nervous.

She peeked over at Jet and was surprised at how much older and more mature he looked sitting behind the wheel. She hadn't even known he had a driver's license. Wait, at nineteen, was he even old enough for a driver's license? He had looked so embarrassed when he'd shown up with the fancy car. But Linnea didn't care where he'd gotten it, as it had probably saved her Ye Ye's life. It had taken them both and a few recruited pedicab drivers to get the old man into the backseat and Jet had raced him to the hospital, and even signed his father's name as guarantor of any incurred charges. Linnea felt the weight of the favor and didn't know how she'd ever repay him. But first things first—and now that she'd gotten Ye Ye settled and Nai Nai there to manage him, it was time to get back and see about the rest of her family.

"We need to hurry, Jet. Nai Nai is really worried about Poppy. Ivy has taken care of her before but never totally alone. She's been there all day without me or Nai Nai."

"Okay—but Linnea, I think your sister is more than competent. I saw how she tended Poppy the other day when I was there. She was great with her. You have to calm down before you are the one collapsing."

She was also surprised that even though they had ended things badly, being around Jet didn't feel awkward. It just felt comfortable. And that made her happy, even in the midst of her panic about everything else.

Linnea swallowed the lump in her throat. "I'm glad Nai Nai came out to tell us Ye Ye is stable and resting. And the doctor isn't going to let him leave this time until he does more tests."

Suddenly she remembered the other emergency and felt a sense of urgency to get home. Nai Nai was depending on her to take care of everything. She needed to check on the baby, make sure her sisters were fed, and then go back out and try to find Jasmine. They'd already spoken to a policeman at the hospital, but he said they couldn't take a report until the child had been missing at least a day and night. Were they crazy? Jasmine wasn't much more than a baby! Did he really think they'd let the night come without trying to find her?

She had said as much to Jet as they'd stopped in the parking lot of the hospital and leaned up against the shiny black sedan. Jet had stood in front of her, his hands intertwined with both of hers, causing little jolts of electricity to shoot up through her fingers and linger low in her belly. She knew she shouldn't have let him so close but just his touch made everything seem less horrible. And he hadn't left her side since he had shown up with his father's car and transported Ye Ye to the hospital. He'd even taken her back home for her Nai Nai once Ye Ye had been stabilized and she could leave.

"Linnea, can we talk?"

"I've got so much going on in my head right now, Jet, believe me, I couldn't make sense if I wanted to. I appreciate what you've done today, but honestly, I can't think of anything but my getting Ye Ye better and finding my little sister."

Jet turned his body so he could see behind the car to back out and his arm grazed hers. She wondered if he felt the same shiver of pleasure she did when they touched; then she felt guilty for even thinking of that when her little sister was still lost.

"I don't know where else to look," Linnea said, shaking her head in frustration. One minute they were talking about the doctor's grim prognosis if Benfu refused medical care, and the next she was racking her brain to think of where Jasmine could be. In between she worried whether her other sisters were okay. She hoped Ivy was also looking out for Maggi's needs, as well as the baby's. But first and foremost, she worried for Jasmine.

"What?" Jet glanced over at her as he pulled out of the parking lot.

"Oh, I'm sorry. Just thinking out loud. I don't know where else to look for Jasmine. But I've got to find her. That'll be the first thing Ye Ye asks when he wakes up. If she's still lost, it might send him into another relapse."

Jet thumped the steering wheel, his brow furrowed in deep concentration. Ahead of him a man on a motorcycle carried a woman and a small boy, and Jet paused to let them through to the other lane.

"Think, Linnea. What does she like to do? What does she talk about?"

"She doesn't talk, Jet. She never has."

"Oh, I forgot. Sorry."

Linnea wished the little girl *would* talk. Instead all she seemed interested in was her doll and playing with Ye Ye. She remembered just the night before how she had watched him in adoration while he told them—

"Jet!"

Jet jumped and jerked the wheel. Linnea grabbed the door handle and held on. She had never even ridden in a car and she could already see she hadn't been missing much. She'd much rather be on a bigger, safe city bus than in the small, fragile vehicle.

"What, Linnea? You scared the crap out of me."

"I'm so sorry. Forget going home. The girls will be fine. I have somewhere I want to check first. You know Plum Garden? Go there."

Jet scrunched up his face. "Plum Garden? Why? Isn't that a bit far for her to wander?"

"For most kids her age, maybe yes, but not Jasmine. That's where Ye Ye and Nai Nai found her and it's her favorite place to go on family outings. She could possibly remember how to get there. There're too many of us for a taxi, so we've always walked together. I have a feeling she might go there to talk to her beloved fish."

"Fish?" Jet looked puzzled. "Okay, if you say so. Let me find a place to turn around. But I do hope you know that garden has over seventy thousand square meters of land. It will take us hours to search the entire seventeen acres."

Linnea shook her head. "No, it won't. I know exactly where I want to look."

Jet turned into a supermarket parking lot and then circled around to exit the opposite way.

Linnea clutched the door handle nervously with one hand and with the other she crossed her fingers under her leg. She hoped her gut instinct was right. If Jasmine wasn't there, she was at a loss for what to do next to find the girl.

In front of the park Jet rolled his window down and handed the parking attendant ten yuan. The man waved them into the small space and tore a stub from his roll, giving it to Jet even as he looked the car up and down, admiring the sleek black lines.

Linnea struggled to sit taller in the seat, trying to peer through the windshield at the elaborate entrance gates. It was useless. Too many people were in the way and she couldn't see any small children wandering alone.

She felt the tires hit the curb and was out of the car and on the sidewalk before Jet even shut off the ignition. She shifted from foot to foot, waiting for him. Dusk was coming and the park would soon close. She didn't want to get locked out before she could take a look.

"Come on, Jet. Hurry!"

Jet joined her on the sidewalk and they hurried through the gate and toward the area where Jasmine had been found the year before. All of the girls knew their finding places; it was just one more way for her grandparents to help them know their history. Jasmine probably had the prettiest finding place of all—but this time Linnea ignored the beauty of the hanging trees, winding vines, and rock gardens as she searched through it all for a sign of the tiny girl. She kept walking, a pace that she could tell Jet was having trouble meeting, even though his legs were much longer than hers and he should have been running to keep up. She was getting impatient with him.

"Linnea," he heaved, just a step behind. "Slow down. Wait. So this is where your little sister was found?"

Linnea paused for half a second, letting him catch up. "Yes, this is it. Well, this is the park—Jasmine was found just outside of the Huoran Cave." She picked up to a jog again. "We need to run, Jet. But that's where we're going. It's a beautiful place to start a new life, right? Much better than my finding place." Her words came out in jagged breaths with each stride.

She didn't have to explain. By now Jet understood the term *finding place* meant where she was found after being abandoned.

"Wow, do you think her birth parents just left her here?" Jet asked, his tone incredulous.

Linnea sighed. She'd always found that people from the other side of town who had no experiences with abandonment or poverty also had no sense of reality for what desperate people could and would do. It wasn't his fault; it was just the bubble that the rich lived in.

"We don't know. There is a possibility she got lost, but no one came forward when the officials ran the ad in the local newspaper. So if they lost her, they sure didn't try too hard to find her again."

Around them they dodged open umbrellas held by women trying to shield their skin from what little light the setting sun gave off. They darted around strolling couples, children, and elderly men and women. Most were on their way out of the park and Linnea was frustrated at the slowness of everyone around her. Didn't they understand this was an emergency situation? Her grandfather lay possibly dying, her little sister was lost, and the people around her were going on with their evenings like everything was fine with the world. Linnea thought she would explode with frustration.

As she left the path to take a shortcut to the cave, Jet must have felt the vibrations of stress coming from her, because he reached over and squeezed her hand.

"Linnea. Calm down. If she's not here, we'll keep looking. I'll help you find her."

Linnea was embarrassed when she felt the wet tears begin sliding down her cheek. Lately she'd really had a hard time shutting away her emotions. Jet was going to think she was nothing but a baby, but she couldn't help it. The situation was desperate.

She was desperate. It was getting dark fast and Jasmine was out there somewhere alone.

"Jet, everything is falling apart. Jasmine is lost. And what am I going to do about Ye Ye? What about all of us? He's dying and what are we going to do? What will Nai Nai do without him? They're never apart—it's unthinkable, Jet."

Linnea felt Jet trying to pull her to a stop, probably to hug her and give her comfort.

"Linnea, shhh . . . shhh . . . no one said he's dying."

She pulled back. They didn't have to say it; she wasn't stupid. And she didn't have time for comfort. Everyone was depending on her. She pulled away and ducked under the low branches of a majestic plum tree.

Beside her she heard Jet take a sharp breath.

"Lin, is that—?"

There was a flash of pink through the branches, surrounded by the blue of the swirling water. Linnea swatted the hanging willows from in front of her face and trudged ahead. Could it be?

She broke through the branches and breathed a sigh of relief. Just as she'd hoped, outside the cave, squatting in the koi pond amidst the lily pads and flowers was Jasmine, the tiny pink doll dangling from one hand as she intently searched the water beneath her.

Linnea's hand flew to her mouth and she attempted to muffle the sob that tore from her. Jasmine didn't hear them; she was in her own little world. All around her the colorful fish swam, oblivious to the child who proved no threat to them. Linnea shook her head—in the fading light of the day and the silence of the scene, it looked almost dreamlike and she could imagine it was exactly the same as Ye Ye had described it when he first found the small girl.

"We're going to frighten her, aren't we? She sure is intent on touching those fish," Jet whispered, his arm around Linnea's shoulders. "She's lucky the park attendant hasn't seen her wading around in his pond—he'd have given her a scare for sure."

"I'll get her." Linnea sighed in relief. Finally, there was one positive thing in a day that had felt like one long, bad dream. She bent down and pulled off her shoes and socks, throwing them on the grass. She waded into the water, ignoring the cold sensation creeping up the bottoms of her jeans. Behind her Jet squatted on the bank, quietly waiting and watching.

"Jasmine?" Linnea called out softly, trying not to startle her. She didn't want her to slip in the water and be soaked.

The little girl looked up, her eyes widened in surprise at seeing her big sister there. She wrinkled her brow in confusion, looking around Linnea.

"It's just me, Mei Mei. And Jet. Remember him? We've come to take you home. Ye Ye and Nai Nai are worried about you, baby. You've been gone all day." Linnea spoke to her softly and moved in closer, one slow step at a time as she felt along the slimy bottom of the pond to gain traction.

Jasmine pointed down to the fish, her face scrunched up as if she were about to cry. Linnea remembered the story from the night before and knew exactly what Jasmine had come to do. In her mind, just like in the legend, Jasmine thought her beloved fish could make her Ye Ye well. She was going to give the fish her greatest wish and wait for them to grant it. Linnea looked behind her and saw one of Nai Nai's jars on the bank. Obviously, catching some of the fish was in the plan, too. Linnea cringed; she hoped the girl hadn't planned to find a way to get to their bones.

Her heart broke when Jasmine followed her attention and also looked at the jar. The little girl held her arms up to Linnea and began crying in huge racking sobs. Linnea grabbed her out of the water and held her close, stroking her hair. They cried together, Jasmine for fear of her Ye Ye's health and Linnea for fear of that, as well as what would happen to them all when he was gone. But Jasmine's cries were the most pitiful thing she'd ever heard. She wished the girl could talk and release some of her fears with words. Linnea couldn't imagine how scary it was to keep everything locked inside, unable to communicate them. Carrying her, she waded out of the water toward the bank. Jet held his hand out and caught her elbow, guiding her up the steep side. A few people gathered around them to point and stare. One couple generously handed them a worn blanket to wrap around Jasmine and muttered for them to just keep it. Jet accepted the gesture and draped it over both Linnea and Jasmine.

"There, there, Mei Mei. Ye Ye's in the hospital and the doctors are working hard to make him better. See what you did? You made it possible for him to go back and get the care he needs. See—your fish *are* magic." She looked over Jasmine's head at Jet. She hoped he knew that she wasn't really giving the girl credit, as it was he who had stepped in and been a hero all that day. She didn't know what she would have done without him.

Jet smiled knowingly at her. "Come on, girls. Let's get you home."

Chapter Nineteen

Linnea worked her way through the house with her willow broom, sweeping the pile of dust out the door and into the courtyard. They had a lot to do before Friday and she needed all her sisters to work hard. Judging by the number of get-well wishes from the neighbors and Ye Ye's colleagues who had stopped by since he had been staying in the hospital, there would be a lot of people in and out to welcome him home and she wanted to make him proud. Three weeks had passed—three long weeks during which Ye Ye had remained at the hospital to take treatments, with Nai Nai by his side. During that time Linnea had taken full responsibility for everything. She left home early each day to catch the business from the morning's commuters, then returned to the house by midmorning. The rest of the day was spent cleaning, cooking, and taking care of Poppy and her sisters. Thank goodness they had always been taught to pull their share, as the burden alone would have been much too heavy. She, Lily, and Ivy had teamed up to make everything run smoothly. Peony was the only one who didn't help, but they were used to her orneriness and just let her sit and write out her postcards, safely out of their way.

"Ivy, have you finished outside?" She had put Ivy in charge of cleaning up all the collections of trash from their front yard. She was supposed to sort it by type and then Linnea was going to load Ye Ye's bike cart and take the collection to exchange it for yuan.

"Yes, Linnea. We've got everything bagged or boxed. Maggi and Peony have peeled all the bottle labels, too. It's ready to go. Stop worrying so much. And quit being so bossy."

Linnea went to the alcove, put the broom up, and retrieved the bucket. She handed it to Ivy. "Here, go fill this up. I'll mop. I'm trying to finish by the time Jet gets here."

Ivy disappeared outside to go to the pump.

Linnea pushed the damp tendrils of hair off her face and stood tall, stretching the kinks out of her tight shoulders as she waited for her sister to get the water ready. At the sink, Lily stood, carefully washing their morning dishes, a new chore she had taken over in Nai Nai's absence. Even without sight, the girl had thus far never dropped a single dish and they found that she did a much better job at it than the others. Linnea knew Lily still wanted to finish quickly so she could get back to practicing on her violin. So far the girl had self-taught herself quite a bit, much to their Ye Ye's astonishment. And these days he had taken to giving her lessons, albeit only oral directions thus far. He still stubbornly refused to play the instrument.

Linnea looked over at Maggi and smiled at the way she had the baby nestled against her chest, feeding her a bottle. In Calli's absence, Maggi had proved invaluable in helping with the baby. Jasmine knelt beside them, playing with the baby's fingers as she quietly stared into her eyes. Linnea was glad to see a small smile playing across her lips, a rare occurrence since Ye Ye had been gone.

"Jasmine, you've been so good with Poppy lately. Thank you so much for helping me care for the baby. You are such a big girl now."

Jasmine looked up at Linnea and gave her a shy smile.

Maggi snorted. "Helping you? Look who's feeding her, Linnea!"

Linnea knew that was true, but though Ye Ye's absence had been hard on all of them, little Jasmine had been absolutely lost without him. Every night she lay in his spot on the bed and clutched his pillow, inhaling the lingering scent of his shaving lotion as she fought back tears. Linnea could only imagine that the few weeks had felt like forever to the five-year-old girl.

Maggi looked up. "Is Jet coming over tonight?"

With Nai Nai's permission, Jet had been a frequent visitor to the house during Ye Ye's hospital stay and Linnea couldn't have been happier. Part of her was afraid to start something again that might not be able to work, but with all the chaos of her life at the moment, letting him near again just felt right. More than right—it made her almost sickeningly cheerful.

In the evenings when he finished at work he came straight over, lending a hand with dinner and sometimes even bringing treats. Linnea tried to discourage him from spoiling the girls, but most nights he pulled something from his pockets that was sure to bring peals of giggles from her sisters. He even let the girls take turns playing games on his cell phone, something they all fought over. At night they all sat outside and looked at the stars as he took Ye Ye's place and told them stories. And on the lucky nights, they'd even been able to steal a few private moments alone—moments that still left her blushing if she thought on it too much.

Linnea felt like her sisters were as much as or even more in love with him than she was—a sentiment she hadn't allowed herself to completely embrace yet out of her fear of rejection. She still couldn't imagine why he continued to come around them, a family so different from his own. She also didn't trust herself to get too deep into the relationship yet, as Ye Ye didn't know they were seeing each other again. But with Nai Nai's stamp of approval, she was hopeful it would all work out.

"He's coming, but only to pick me up." Linnea sighed. She was so very nervous. Tonight was the night she'd finally meet his parents. Jet had insisted, and no amount of pleading could get her out of it.

Maggi, Peony, and Lily all moaned their disappointment. They loved Jet and looked forward to his card games, teasing, and just the diversion from their usual routine that he gave them.

Ivy returned just in time to hear Linnea. She put her hands on her hips.

"And I'm stuck watching everyone again, I suppose?" she demanded.

Linnea shook her head, laughing. "No, Ivy, how about I stay and you take my place and go meet his terrifying parents?"

Ivy laughed and set the bucket down. "In that case, have fun, Linnea."

Linnea stuck her mop in the water, then wrung it out and began sweeping it in wide arcs across the floor.

"Hmph. Fun? I don't think so. They're going to take one look at me and think I'm nothing but a simple peasant from the wrong side of town." *And they'd be right,* she thought to herself.

As she finished cleaning the floor she tried to avoid thinking about the upcoming inquisition—or dinner, as Jet called it. Now Linnea felt nauseated as she thought about the rest of the evening and how she'd probably have to see pity in the eyes of Jet's parents as she described their life. As she set pans of hot water on the stove to prepare for a bath, she lost herself in a make-believe story of a pampered little rich girl—a fairy tale she'd love to use as her own if she only had the guts to do it.

Linnea took a deep breath as she tried to calm the butterflies wreaking havoc in her stomach. They were on their way to Jet's family home and she felt faint from anxiety. It was only a short drive into Wuxi, where they lived, and Linnea wished it was much farther to give her time to settle herself.

Jet stopped to wait for a traffic light. He turned to her and smiled, showing the dimple in his right cheek. "Don't worry, Linnea. They aren't monsters—they aren't going to eat you for dinner or anything."

Sure they aren't, she thought. But they might try to hire her to do their laundry.

"I know, Jet. I'm just nervous. I just know they aren't going to like me." She picked at an invisible thread on her sweater. She had taken extra time in the shower, despite the freezing air, and Lily had braided her hair so that it would lie over one shoulder. She'd borrowed one tiny squirt of Nai Nai's perfume and hoped the scent of wildflowers wasn't too strong. As for clothing, she didn't have much to choose from but Jet said he liked the way the midnight blue sweater set off her dark hair. Lily had given Linnea her special gift for the night, tucking a small fabric yellow lily into her hair. She said Linnea felt stiff and formal and she hoped the flower would soften her up. It would have to do—she wasn't trying to prove anything after all. Or was she?

"Of course they'll like you. Don't be ridiculous. Anyway, *I* like you and that's all that counts."

Giving a clue that his statement needed no response, he turned up the radio and drummed his fingers on the steering wheel to the beat as he guided the car over the bridge and into the turning lane. Linnea looked over at him and shook her head. She wanted to pinch him for being so blasted relaxed. She still couldn't figure out why Jet liked her, so how was she supposed to believe his parents would follow suit? She tried to imagine what they'd think when they saw her, or found out she wasn't a student, or discovered her past. Linnea suddenly felt ill again and wiped the sheen of perspiration from over her eyebrows.

"Dao le." Jet declared their arrival as he turned into the parking deck of a large apartment building.

Linnea looked around, confused. There weren't any houses around—only high-rises and parking lots. This was a part of town she wasn't used to, that was for sure.

"This? I thought you lived in a house?"

He laughed. "No, we call it our house but it's really considered an apartment. My parents bought it when I was born. They said they wanted a modern, new place to raise their son. You know—golden child and all that?"

Linnea rolled her eyes at him. His coddling was a joke between them by now, and really she knew he hated that he was the only child and expected to continue the family name. Speaking of it with humor was his way of coping with the constant pressure. Sometimes when he was really giving himself a pity party, she reminded him that there were many orphans or other kids from poor families who would trade places with him in a heartbeat.

Jet let a rare moment of pride slip. "We—along with hundreds of other families—were one of the first ones to buy from this property development when Wuxi offered a discount to Beitang residents. Just wait till you see what my mom has done with it. It's amazing."

That sure didn't make Linnea feel any better. She was walking into a setting she had no idea how to adapt to. She flipped her visor down and looked in the mirror one more time as Jet exited the car and came around to open her door. She grimaced at her reflection. Without the luxury of makeup or extravagant hair accessories, she just looked plain. But it was too late to do anything about it now. She flipped the visor back up and took a deep breath. *Time to enter the lion's den,* she thought as she tried to still the trembling in her hands. She climbed out and looked at the fancy building in front of her. She looked down once more at her cheap sweater and worn jeans. She suddenly wished for her simple home on the wrong side of town.

Chapter Twenty

Linnea straightened to her full height as they approached the door to the building. She reached up and smoothed her hair one more time, hoping the stubborn tendrils would stay in place for once. Outside, a young man about her age and dressed much nicer than she, in pressed pants and a white tailored shirt, stood at attention. When they came close enough, he opened the door and held it for them. Jet nodded at the boy as he guided her through, but the boy didn't respond other than giving a curt nod without making eye contact.

"That's Max," he said as they walked by.

Linnea thought Max was a strange name but more curious was the fact that he looked to be the exact age and build as Jet. Didn't Jet think it weird to pass a doorman who looked like him every day?

Jet stopped in front of the elevators and pushed the button. He turned to Linnea and grinned. "Don't be nervous."

She didn't respond. Instead she concentrated on breathing while she hoped the elevator would suddenly stop on another floor, to give her more time to prepare. She looked in the mirrored doors and examined the foyer behind her. Every surface shined and the furniture in it alone probably cost more than her Ye Ye made in a year. Possibly two.

The elevator door opened and she followed Jet in. He pushed the number seven button and reached for her hand. Linnea cringed as she heard the sound of her own heartbeat pounding in her ears. She glanced over at Jet but he didn't look like he heard it.

The doors opened and they stepped out. In the hallway was only one ornate door with a huge brass knocker on it. Linnea looked around.

"Where're the doors to the other apartments?" she asked, confused.

Jet laughed. "There aren't any other apartments on this floor. Just ours."

"You own the entire floor?" Linnea shook her head from side to side slowly.

Jet ignored her question and led her to the elaborate wooden door. He opened it and immediately a small white dog charged—or more accurately, pranced—toward them. The dog stopped and stood on two legs as he pawed Jet, begging for attention.

"This is Pang Pang." Jet reached down and picked up the dog. He held him up for Linnea to see.

The dog's tongue darted out and before Linnea could react, he had licked her across her face. She gasped and stepped back, wiping at the moistness he left behind.

Jet dropped his head back and laughed loudly. Linnea didn't appreciate that she was the source of his amusement, especially since she didn't see what was so funny.

"You should see your expression! It's priceless—haven't you ever been licked by a dog, Linnea?"

Linnea blushed crimson.

"Well . . . no, I can't say that I have. Um, he is . . . um . . . cute."

Linnea did indeed think the dog was cute but she'd never before been around a dog that was a house pet. The only ones she had encountered were strays on the street. With it being hard enough just to feed their own family, the thoughts of having a dog as a pet had never even been discussed in her home. It just wasn't even a thought. And actually, her Ye Ye had read them an article from the *People's Daily* recently that talked about the latest fashion accessory in China being small dogs and they had all laughed. It was a hard thing for them to imagine.

Jet put the dog down and crouched beside the animal. He began scratching him behind the ears as the dog's hind foot shook with rapture. Linnea had to admit, the furry bundle was really adorable.

"Pang Pang's harmless. He's almost as old as I am, Linnea."

The introduction was interrupted when a petite woman came around the corner and joined them in the hall. Jet stood quickly and draped his arm around Linnea. She felt a moment of relief that quickly reverted back to barely hidden panic.

"Jet, you two are five minutes late and that is unlike you. Why didn't you call?" She turned her attention to Linnea. "*Ni hao,* Linnea, I've heard quite a bit about you. I'm glad Jet has finally brought you around so I can see if you live up to all he has told us."

Linnea stopped herself from cringing at her brisk tone. She stood frozen in place as the woman reached for her hand, then looked her over, head to toe. Linnea felt uncomfortable under the intense inspection and could feel her hand begin to dampen.

The dog hopped around their legs, begging to be included in the attention until Jet's mother snapped a command at him to sit. She didn't look old enough to be Jet's mother. Her bobbed black hair hung straight and glossy, the strands cut diagonally to end right below her jawline in a fashionable city style. Her eyes were perfectly lined in kohl and her lips were stained a deep red. She was beautiful.

Linnea could see that beneath the apron she wore some sort of silk pantsuit in a pale ivory color. Peeking out from the top of the apron was an exquisite porcelain lily pinned to her blouse. Linnea took a deep breath and after the woman let go of her hand, she discreetly reached up and pulled the fabric flower from her hair, then tucked it into her back pocket. She felt like a peasant standing in front of the woman.

"Linnea? This is my mother. And yes, Mother, this is the girl I've told you so much about and she definitely can live up to all I've said."

Linnea laughed nervously. "So very nice to meet you, Sur Tai Tai."

Jet's mother turned to him and beckoned toward the room behind her. From what Linnea could see, she didn't look impressed with her son's choice of a dinner date.

"Jet, bring your little friend in here so I can get a better look at her." She swatted at him with the small dish towel in her hand. "Hurry up, I've got to get back to the kitchen."

Linnea felt overwhelmed as Jet led her behind his mother to the living room. She looked around, amazed at the décor of the apartment. A combination of Western and Asian, the room looked like the pages of an interior design magazine. Her attention was immediately drawn to an elaborately carved wooden screen. She thought she recognized it as mahogany and could pick out the curves of a dragon and phoenix in each of the four panels. It was the most beautiful piece of furniture Linnea had ever seen. In front of it they had artfully placed a Western-sized sofa and chair, and she looked at the lush yellow soft-looking leather and visualized her Nai Nai's rocking chair, the only piece in her home that she could be proud of. On every wall there were paintings of old Chinese scenery, flowers, and other subjects. The paintings were so stunning they took

Linnea's breath away. One particular piece with a sun setting behind a pagoda was especially mesmerizing.

"Please, sit down and make yourself at home. I see you are interested in art? That is only some of my collection." Li Jing gestured toward the couch. "Have a seat. I have to check on dinner. I'll be back."

Jet led Linnea to the couch as his mother hurried out of the room. "She's not really cooking dinner," he whispered. "She's just making sure the *ayi* does it like she wants it. Right now she's in there hovering over poor Xiao Fei, probably making her a nervous wreck."

Linnea looked at him, embarrassed that she found herself unable to think of anything to say even though she had a million questions swirling in her mind. She couldn't help but feel as if Jet's mother disapproved of her. She'd known that would most likely be the case, but the tense atmosphere when she approached was something Linnea hadn't prepared for. She hoped the woman stayed in the kitchen.

She looked over Jet's shoulder to a door that was obviously a bedroom. She marveled at the piles of pillows and luxurious-looking silk covers on the bed. For just a moment she felt a touch of envy as she thought of the simple bamboo pallet she used each night. Then she pushed back a flash of guilt when she remembered the quilt sewn with love especially for her by her Nai Nai.

"My father will be here shortly. That will be a different experience. He is the total opposite of my mother."

Linnea's fascination with the bed quickly evaporated.

"What do you mean?"

Jet shook his head. "You'll see. Don't worry about it. Hey—you want to see some of our family photos?"

Linnea started to nod but her attention was interrupted with the opening of the front door. She turned to see a tall, handsome man enter the room. He set his keys in a dish on the side table and immediately zoned in on her and Jet. His face darkened in a scowl.

"Baba. Hello—please come and meet Linnea," Jet said. Linnea looked at him, surprised at the uneasy sound of his voice. She had never heard him speak with a lack of confidence before. He quickly shut the drawer to the coffee table he was opening for the photo books. Instead he stood and beckoned for her to join him as they faced his father.

Linnea felt a shiver of foreboding as the man stomped his way through the foyer and headed toward them. She thought she was going to be in for a long, uncomfortable night.

Linnea leaned back in her chair and sighed in relief when she spotted the *ayi* approaching the table with a heaping dish of rice. Ironic that in her home the rice was usually the meal but in this home, the steaming *mifan* signaled the *end* of the meal. It couldn't have come any sooner. Along with her desire to get the evening over with, she didn't think she could eat one more morsel. Amusingly, the dog had decided he liked her and was asleep right on top of her feet under the table, adding to the warmth she already felt from a full belly.

"Sur Tai Tai, once again, I'd like to say how amazing this meal was," Linnea complimented Jet's mother. Across from her Lao Sur nodded in agreement, his mouth still full of the sliced watermelon from the last entrée served.

Jet's mother put her nose higher into the air and folded her hands on the table in front of her. "I suppose you don't eat food like this too often? It's quite a culinary treat that most hired help can't pull off. But we like to employ the best in this household."

Linnea didn't know how to answer what was so obviously a cut against her. Thankfully, Jet swooped in and added to the conversation.

"So what was your favorite dish, Linnea?" he asked.

Though she was happy for a diversion, Linnea could have strangled him for asking that—as she didn't know which one would be the most proper to compliment. Everything in China was based on tradition, but unfortunately she was severely lacking in remembering most of the lessons her Nai Nai and Ye Ye had tried to teach her about the many symbolisms of each dish.

"Um, I really liked the *Gong Bao Jiding,*" Linnea answered, feeling her cheeks get hot.

Lao Sur looked up from his bowl with his serious expression. "That's my favorite, too. Nothing beats spicy chicken with peanuts, except maybe Mandarin squirrel fish."

Linnea smiled. She couldn't believe she'd been so intimidated by him. The man who'd caused her ripples of apprehension had turned out to be a big teddy bear of a father. He was just a quiet man, more thoughtful than most Linnea had known. She still noticed that Jet was more reserved around him, but now she realized it was because he wanted to show his respect. It was obvious that he valued his father's opinion much more so than his mother's.

"It's a shame that we're going to lose one of the best cooks we've ever had," Jet's mother said, tsking her disappointment into her napkin.

The maid blushed as Jet explained to Linnea that in a few months Xiao Fei was leaving to join her children in her home province. They'd been living with their grandparents for years while she sent money for their care, but finally she'd saved enough to be reunited with them.

After going around and dropping a serving of rice in each bowl, the maid began to gather dishes and take them to the kitchen.

Linnea stood. "Let me help clean this up." She reached for a half-empty platter of celery and shrimp from the middle of the table.

Jet's mother stood and put her cold hand on Linnea's wrist.

"Absolutely not. Xiao Fei would be completely offended. Let's move out to the balcony and talk. You all go on and I'll bring the tea." Without waiting for an answer she was gone in a flurry of energy, barking orders to the *ayi* about setting up the tea set on her way into the kitchen.

Jet's father slowly rose from the table and headed for the door leading outside. Jet and Linnea followed—the little dog right on their heels. Even before they joined his father, she could smell the rich aroma of the cigar he lit.

On the balcony, Linnea was once again stunned by the beauty of their home. They stood on a cedar-lined terrace overlooking the river and a small park below. The edges of the terrace were lined with clay pots of various flowers, small bushes, and a few miniature Bonsai trees. In the distance, the twinkling strings of lights draped on bridges and buildings gave off quite a show against the moonlit night. To Linnea's right, a line of terra-cotta soldiers stood guard against the wall to the apartment. To the other side, a small tropical garden and waterfall added the final touch of sophistication to the outside area. Linnea sighed. To live in a place of such beauty was something she couldn't imagine. She leaned over the railing of the balcony and watched a couple on the sidewalk at the park, holding the hands of a little boy between them. The boy toddled along in his split pants, a glimpse of his pale backside flashing with every step.

"Here, Linnea. Sit down." Jet pointed to a love seat and plopped down, patting the cushion next to him. He left her only a tiny square of seat.

Linnea was embarrassed to sit so close to him in front of his parents but did so anyway.

Lao Sur cleared his throat just as his wife bustled in and set the tea tray on the table in front of them. She sat down and began pouring tea. The aroma of sweet jasmine wafted under Linnea's nose as she waited for the man to speak, and she looked down at her watch. She wondered if her little sister was already asleep or still waiting up for her. She needed to go and hoped they'd understand that she was responsible for getting her sisters to bed at a decent hour.

"Linnea, so tell us a bit about your family." He leaned in and picked up his cup, taking a deep drink from it.

Linnea took a deep breath. Here was the conversation she had dreaded. Now there was nowhere to run and no way to avoid it. What would Jet do if she really told his parents a more-polished version of her life than he knew to be true? Would he rat her out? Or would his ingrained eagerness to please his parents allow for her to embellish the truth? But more importantly, would it be an insult to her Ye Ye and Nai Nai to claim she was anyone but her true self?

She looked down as Jet reached over and patted her leg. She brushed his hand away, embarrassed to see his mom looking their way. "Well, I was raised by a man who found me years ago wandering around a market. He and his wife became my Ye Ye and Nai Nai."

Linnea stopped talking and looked down into the amber swirls of tea. She didn't know what else to say.

Jet's mother made what she must have thought was a sympathetic clucking in her throat. Jet glanced quickly at Linnea, then began speaking. She was glad he jumped in again, as she wasn't sure she could hide the dismay in her voice if she heard pity coming from his mother.

"Baba, you have to meet them to understand how amazing they are. Her grandfather has taken in more than two dozen girls over the years. Girls that no one else wanted. They've raised them and loved them as their own. Honestly, it beats all I've ever seen. And Linnea here—she has her own business. She's a designer of the coolest T-shirts you've ever seen. She just started and is already bringing in enough income to support her family right now while her Ye Ye is sick!"

Linnea cringed as Jet babbled on. She hoped he wasn't going to tell them that he gave her a loan. And he made it sound like she was making so much money!

"And she's so competitive. . . . Let me tell you about the day I met her . . . ," he began.

Oh no! Don't tell them I used to change bicycle tires! Linnea thought frantically.

Lao Sur held his hand up for Jet to stop speaking. He began to nod his head.

"*Dui,* I've heard of Lao Zheng. I've never met the man, a miracle in itself, seeing how I am the director of social development. Nevertheless, word gets around. I know of his deeds and have a lot of respect for him and his wife."

Jet's mother sighed and clinked her spoon against her cup. "I'm sure they were only doing what they deemed appropriate as citizens of Wuxi. You know, it takes a village and all that. . . ."

Linnea ignored the obvious sarcasm from Jet's mother and instead stared at Lao Sur, her eyes wide with surprise. She'd known Jet's father worked in some official branch of government but she had no idea it was in a department that had a direct connection to girls like herself. *And he knew of her grandfather? How?*

She was speechless, and also relieved that she hadn't stretched the truth after all.

Lao Sur chuckled. "Don't look so surprised, girl. Did you think I wouldn't investigate who our son was spending so much time with? I was pleased when I discovered you were one of Lao Zheng's girls. I've tried to tell my wife that he's a legend around here. He's been taking homeless children in for over two decades! We've always planned to staff and open the orphanage, but over the years since it's been finished, I've come to believe that institutional care is not the best option for orphans. They should be cared for by relatives, adoptive families, or foster care. That is where they'll thrive—not cold institutions. So I've stonewalled opening the orphanage."

"An orphanage is just what this town—"

Jet interrupted his mother, cutting her off in midsentence. "*Dui le,* Baba. That is so right. I can't believe some of these cities that have the huge orphanages and children there are still hungry and neglected. The townspeople in those areas need to step up, like Lao Zheng has, and take care of the children of their community. Especially with the one-child policy restrictions in place, foster care would be a great option for some who want to add to their families but cannot."

Linnea could only nod her head. She was speechless. Never had she thought that Jet's father would not only know of her family, but respect them and from what it sounded like, be in total awe of her grandfather. And the way his father felt about abandoned children was puzzling. This man was unlike any official she'd ever known or heard of. Shocked was too mild to describe how she felt and she looked down to hide the confusion in her eyes.

When she looked up, Jet's mother smiled brightly, but in the dim light of the balcony Linnea couldn't tell if she was looking at her or Jet. She could only see that the woman looked uncomfortable, as if she wished the conversation would take a different turn.

Jet turned to Linnea. "My father is the one who originally implemented the program to give stipends for children living in foster care and adoptive families."

Linnea shot Jet a scolding look. She couldn't believe that he hadn't mentioned this before.

"My next plan is to pilot a program that'll give abandoned children ongoing benefits like adequate medical care and education. And later they'll be eligible for employment and housing benefits. But we have a ways to go to get that approved all the way up through the many tiers. I've been working on my proposal and budget ideas for at least two years."

Linnea thought she should come out with something—anything—as a response to such a statement. She didn't want to sound like an uneducated idiot but also didn't want to push the subject along. Her status was usually something she tried to hide, not explore for dinner conversation.

"Well, um . . . I'm sure when my Ye Ye gets out of the hospital and I tell him all about this, he'll be pleased."

Sur Tai Tai leaned over and refilled Linnea's teacup. She clicked her tongue, feigning sympathy. By now Linnea knew that she'd only successfully gained approval from one of Jet's parents, not both.

Lao Sur shook his head. "It's a shame that a man who has given so much to his community has had such bad luck. There must be some way we can show him our gratitude for his commitment to the children."

Jet's mother crossed her legs first one way, then the other. "Can't we move on to a more pleasant subject, everyone?"

Linnea thought Jet's mother looked a bit panicked at her husband's words; then she thought about all their money and shook her head. The small stipend her Ye Ye received from the government barely met their needs for clothing and food, but she knew he'd never consider accepting money from anyone else. "No, we are fine, but thank you. Ye Ye is supposed to come home soon."

Jet's father shot her a stern look. "Don't let one's sense of pride steal another's gift of generosity," Lao Sur said.

She looked at Jet for guidance. What was she supposed to say to that? Beside her Jet cleared his throat and Linnea thought finally he sensed her unease.

"Baba, I was thinking. I have an idea of how we can show Lao Zheng our gratitude. As a matter of fact, I have already formed somewhat of a plan. I wanted you to meet Linnea first and see how amazing she is, because we need your help."

Linnea looked from Jet to his parents, puzzled at his statement. She saw his mother shoot him a quick look of disapproval before setting her cup down with a clatter.

"Jet, can you help me for a moment in the kitchen?" she asked.

Jet sighed, wadded his napkin, and tossed it on the table. "Linnea, I'll be right back." He stood and followed his mother into the house.

Lao Sur cleared his throat. "So, Linnea, while they're away, I'd like to thank you."

"Thank me?"

"Yes. Since you and Jet have been friends, I've seen a total transformation in my son. No longer does he beg for the latest gadgets, or try to bribe me to increase his allowance. Lately he has matured—become more of the man I was hoping he would be. I can't imagine that you haven't had anything to do with it."

Linnea smiled at him and once again marveled at how different he was than she'd thought he'd be. He was so much more—accepting.

"I'm sure it's nothing to do with me, Lao Sur. Your son is just growing up."

Lao Sur waved his hand in the air impatiently. "Well, whatever you say, but all of a sudden he's showing concern for someone other than himself and I'm going to enjoy hearing about this grand idea of his—if his mother ever lets him tell it."

Something told Linnea that Jet had been scheming for quite a while to come up with whatever had pasted the self-satisfied smile across his face before his mother's interruption had wiped it clean. Whatever it was he had in mind, if he was able to get it past his mother, Linnea was going to have to be on board. Either that or it would steal his thunder—that she could see clearly. Linnea looked down at her watch and grimaced at the time just as Jet returned.

"Jet, I really need to get home."

Jet pulled up in front of the lane that led to her house and switched the motor off.

Linnea was getting used to riding in the car now and it didn't scare her so much. Even the queasy feeling had gone away. Now that he had let her know his secret—that he had a license and could drive his father's car—he didn't want her to take the local transportation if he was available to ride her around. He was so protective of her, but to be honest, it made her feel good. She'd never felt so spoiled before.

"Jet, thank you for saying all those nice things about me to your father."

His cheeks reddened. "I meant everything I said. You *are* seriously awesome, Linnea."

Linnea shook her head. "*Sui bian*—whatever. But you have to admit, your mother doesn't like me. And that's putting it mildly. At times I felt like she wanted to jump across the table and claw my eyes out for daring to be a part of your life."

Jet chuckled, then paused. Linnea had to give him credit; he didn't try to lie.

"I know she can be overly protective of me, but she doesn't *not* like you, Lin. She just needs time to get to know you like I do. But my father is very impressed with your accomplishments."

She looked out the dark window. She guessed it was too much to hope that both his parents would see past her modest background and just like her for who she was. She almost wished it was his mother who liked her instead of his father, as in China, the mother usually had the last word—or more accurately whispered it in her husband's ear and let him speak it.

She turned to look at him. "I really need to go."

"Not yet, you don't." He reached over the console and gathered her in his arms.

Linnea wanted to resist but she felt her protests melt away in her mouth when he pressed his lips to hers. He kissed her, so smoothly and effortlessly that her head spun. Just as smoothly, she felt his warm hand creep under her sweater and travel up until it was planted firmly where it shouldn't be. She couldn't help but arch her back, her body ignoring all thoughts of retreating that fluttered through her mind and then back out again.

"Linnea, please," he whispered.

She thought she knew what he was asking but couldn't reply as he slowly moved away from her lips to run his tongue deliciously up her neck, somehow finding the one spot that made her pulse beat wildly.

Yes—yes—yes, her body begged for more of his touch, even as she finally found a small piece of sanity and pushed him gently away. "Not here, Jet."

She pulled her sweater down, checking the window to see if any of her neighbors were out even as she reached up to smooth her hair.

"No one's out there," Jet said, reading her thoughts like he always did.

She laughed nervously. "Good thing—or we'd be the talk of the *hutong* by tomorrow morning. That's all Ye Ye needs to hear when he gets home."

"Oh yeah, he's coming home Friday, isn't he? How is he doing?"

"A lot better now that they've started treating him. Nai Nai said he's been doing less coughing and is resting more."

Jet nodded. "You know, Lin, that your Ye Ye carries the weight of the world on his shoulders, right?"

"Yeah, he always has. He works much too hard for his age. I keep telling him that but he doesn't listen. You don't have to remind me, Jet. I know he's under a lot of pressure to take care of all of us."

"I'm just saying that there are ways for him to get help, if he'd just fight harder to get it. But anyway, have you told him about us, yet?"

Linnea released a long sigh. "No, not yet. I thought I'd wait until he's out of the hospital."

Jet tapped the steering wheel for a minute, then she looked back at Linnea.

"I've got an idea. Let me pick him up."

"You?"

"Yes, it'll be more convenient anyway; he won't have to take a taxi. And it'll give me a chance to talk to him."

Linnea could just see Ye Ye's face if Jet showed up to bring him home. She shook her head. "I don't think that's a good idea, Jet."

"Listen. Your Ye Ye is from the older generation when things were done differently. I should've realized it before, but we need to discuss things man-to-man. It's the only way I'm going to convince him my intentions are good."

"Are they?" Linnea teased.

"They are if my intention to get you into my bed and ravish you until you beg for mercy can be considered good."

Linnea laughed at the mischievous tone he took on. "Just keep that part to yourself."

"Seriously, Linnea. I want to start spending some time with you at my apartment, away from your sisters, or strangers in the park—just you and me and some privacy."

Linnea gave him a slow smile. "But what about your parents?"

"I've got that covered. Friday nights. They're out every week, same night and same friends. They won't be home until at least midnight. Next week—that's our night. Promise me."

Linnea picked at an invisible piece of lint on her sweater.

"Maybe."

Jet slammed his hand on the steering wheel and gave a joyful yell. "*Aiya!* That's enough. I'll take it. But beware, by Friday when I start working my magic on you, I'll tell you now that you won't even be able to utter the word no."

She laughed again. "Okay, so you're going to the hospital Friday morning?"

"Absolutely," Jet answered, the cheesy grin still pasted on his face.

"Stop looking at me like that!" Linnea hoped her cheeks didn't look as scarlet as they felt. She fiddled with the door.

"Do you want me to walk you to your house?" he asked. "Help you carry all the goodies for your sisters?"

Linnea shook her head. She knew if he came in, her sisters would never let him leave. They needed to get up early and get started on the rest of the cleanup list and gathering the information Jet's mother had asked for.

"No, that's okay, Jet. Please thank your mother again for wrapping up all these leftovers for the girls. They'll go crazy when they see what I've got." She perched the bag on her lap. "But will I see you tomorrow?"

Jet lowered his voice and raised his eyebrows a few times, really flirting with her now. "Do you *want* to see me tomorrow?"

Linnea sighed. He didn't have a clue how much she wanted to see him tomorrow—and the next day and the next day after that. She still wanted to ask him why *he* wanted to see *her*. Especially after witnessing the way his family lived, it was hard to believe that he would be interested in her, just a girl from the poor side of town. For the first time in her life, she wished she lived in a grand house with a decent courtyard.

"Sure, if you want to come by, we can go over everything we talked about with your mom. I can give you the information she asked for." She fiddled with the door handle. She still couldn't get over how amazing Jet's parents were.

"Will we have any *alone* time?" he asked, his voice low and sexy.

"No. But you'll have pesky little girls climbing all over you. That should take care of your constant need for attention." She squinted at him for effect.

"I don't mind. I'll do whatever it takes, Linnea, to spend time with you. Here, let me get that." He leaned over her to open the door. As his head passed close to her face he paused.

Linnea breathed deeply, inhaling the clean, crisp smell of him. She felt that familiar fluttering again. It intensified tenfold when his hand brushed over her lap as he unlocked the door for her.

"How about one more kiss, Lin?"

He leaned in and once again, planted his burning hot mouth over hers. As usual, all logical thought drained from her brain immediately. When he pulled back, she felt an instant of weakness, then kissed him softly on the cheek before he could move. She didn't know why she did it—she just did. Then she immediately felt stupid.

Jet put his hand to his face and his eyes widened with mock surprise.

"*Aiya,* girl. That's gonna leave a mark."

Linnea was confused. She reached up and touched her mouth. "A mark? But I'm not wearing anything on my lips."

"That's not what I'm talking about," he answered, smiling. "I meant it's gonna leave a mark on my heart. Who knew under all that sass was a little bit of sweetness?"

Linnea felt her face turn hot, and she opened the door and quickly climbed out.

"Good night, Jet," she said as she pushed the door and walked away, too embarrassed to look him in the eye. She couldn't believe she'd just given him a silly little butterfly kiss. She suddenly wished she was more experienced than she actually was.

Just before the door shut behind her, she thought she heard him chuckle.

Chapter Twenty One

Benfu sat impatiently on the side of the bed as Calli bent to tie his shoes for him. She'd already packed up all of his clothes and things and now they waited for the discharge nurse to come with his papers. His patience was just about gone.

It had been a long night full of dreams—or memories—as he supposed they were one and the same. The nurse had come in halfway through the night and given him something to help him sleep. Instead of the blissful rest he craved, he'd spent the next few hours reliving the nightmare of being imprisoned in the collective so many years ago. It was so real he felt he could still smell the putrid waste from the outhouse that was his jail cell. He had woken himself up a few times by tossing and turning to shake the invisible mites and flies from his skin. The shame and resentment had welled up in him again, as fresh as it was decades ago when his only transgression was being born to intellectual parents. Even in his dream he fretted that they'd find his possessions and he'd lose the one thing that held his sanity together, the hope that his precious violin still waited.

The dream had finally ended but he'd woken feeling that desperate need to run that had fueled him the night he'd escaped. He realized that it all probably had to do with his urge to get out of the hospital. Then his thoughts of losing his daughters filled his head and made him miserable—so asleep he was tortured by memories and awake he was bothered by what he must do. He supposed a life of no peace was now what remained of his short future.

"There you are. Now, do we have everything?" Calli asked, straightening up and putting her hands on her hips.

"I guess so, everything except my pride."

Benfu raised his eyebrows as Calli giggled. She had already teased him that morning that at least half a dozen young, pretty girls had seen his backside in the few weeks he'd been there. He'd had so many shots he felt like a human pincushion.

He was so relieved he was finally going home. After almost a month of hospital care, he wanted to see his girls, even if it was only temporary. The hospital guidelines were so strict that they hadn't been allowed to come up to his floor to see him, and he had been too sick to venture to the bottom floor. Linnea was the only one allowed in, as she could pass for much older. The girls had stayed at home but at least Linnea had been able to bring several cards and letters from his grown daughters, a welcome distraction of anecdotes and snippets of their lives from far away. The message had spread that he was sick and his daughters were showing their concern the only way they could, with words of encouragement.

Benfu hoped they weren't too worried. Most of them led difficult enough lives without worrying about a fragile old man such as he.

Calli finished with his shoes and stood in front of him, making him think she could read his mind with her next words. "You ready to go home, old man?"

She didn't know just how ready he was. He was so tired of looking at the same soiled walls and ceiling in the small, sterile room. He was tired of hearing the incessant clicking of heels up and down the halls at all hours day and night. He was sick of having too much time to think, and most of all, he was tired of being poked, prodded, and treated like an invalid. He wasn't naïve. He knew he had a long road ahead of him to recuperate—if he even stood a chance at getting better. But first he needed to get home and figure out how he was going to get some income flowing to buy the needed medication to keep him going. And from what Calli had told him, Linnea had been making ends meet to feed everyone, but there were bills to pay and things that she didn't even know to worry about. Her help was appreciated but would soon stop, as once things were settled, she'd be living under a new roof. That thought sliced through him like a razor and he pushed it away.

He nodded to Calli in response to her question. He didn't feel like talking. He had too much on his mind.

"Now you get that look off your face, *Laoren*. You're worried and already thinking of how you are going to fix everything. And you wonder where Linnea gets her stubbornness from. You cannot be doing anything; you have to concentrate on getting better," she scolded.

"*Hao le,* I know, I know," he reassured her. He was concerned about her, too. She wouldn't admit it but she was exhausted from her vigil and weeks of caring for him. He looked at her familiar wrinkled face, her dark hair streaked with gray and pulled into the elegant bun, and his eyes misted over. When he looked at her he didn't see the lines of worry she'd earned over the years or the brittle hair. He still saw the creamy-skinned, dark-haired girl who had selflessly hid him in the back of their home until she could talk her parents into allowing him to stay. He'd never forget how she cared for the deep wounds around his wrists, wrapped his ribs, and brought him his first bites of real food he'd had in weeks—food that was taken from her own daily allowance and given to him without even a spark of regret. She'd saved his life; there was no other way to put it.

A few days ago he'd begged her to go home and get some rest. But in her usual stubborn fashion she'd retorted that they'd never spent a night apart in all of their years together, and they weren't going to start such nonsense now.

Benfu knew he was a lucky old man. How he'd ever earned enough good karma to deserve her devotion he would never know. The old saying that women were weak and made of water must have been dreamed up by someone who'd never met someone like his own Calla Lily.

"What are you thinking of now, Benfu? That serious expression you are giving is worrying me."

Benfu reached over and took both of Calli's hands in his. He rubbed his thumbs over her soft palms. A woman such as she deserved to be bejeweled in precious jade and dressed in the finest silks. But here she sat, simple yet beautiful in her worn cotton and tiny white pearl earrings.

The same question he'd pondered for years now burned inside of him. He just had to ask. He needed to finally know.

She gave him a small smile; then when he didn't return it, it disappeared.

"Calli, I need to ask you something."

"What, Benfu? You're scaring me."

"You would tell me, wouldn't you, if I haven't been enough?" He searched her eyes.

"Enough what?" She shook her head in confusion.

"Just"—he paused—*"enough."*

Calli gave a small laugh, then let go of his hands and leaned in, kissing him softly on the cheek.

"You silly old man, of course you've been enough. As a matter of fact, you've been more than enough. You've been *everything* I've ever wanted or needed," she whispered in his ear.

Benfu felt tears spring to his eyes; then he heard plastic shoes slapping in the hall.

He cleared the lump in his throat and brushed away the moistness just as the nurse came through the door and stood next to the bed. She fiddled with the papers on the clipboard, then handed Benfu the pen.

"Sign everywhere I marked an *X*," she said. Her voice matched the briskness of her crisp white nurse's uniform. Benfu thought she didn't appear much older than Linnea, but he was impressed with her diligence. As a matter of fact, his stay in the hospital had shown him just how much the nurses ran the place. He had rarely even seen the doctors.

"What's the total amount owed?" Benfu asked with a confident voice that hid his anxiety at the expected answer. He began signing at the appropriate places as the nurse pointed them out.

The nurse shook her head, her tiny white cap bobbing back and forth. "We'll send you a copy of the bill. I've been told it is still being processed."

Benfu looked at her and raised his eyebrows. It was unusual for a hospital not to demand payment before services and downright strange to still prolong it at the time of discharge. They had bypassed the admitting deposit with the official chop of Jet's family name, but Benfu had expected to get hit with the final billing on the last day. Even the heavy ball of stress in his stomach had been anticipating the numbers all morning.

"Can I see someone in charge? I don't even know what I'm signing for!" He didn't want to leave without knowing what was going on with his debt.

"Not today. There's a big meeting going on—all the doctors are there." The nurse efficiently took the clipboard from him, then waved on her way out the door. "You're free to go."

"Come on, Benfu. We can worry about this later." Calli nudged him toward the door. She picked up the plastic bags carrying his clothes and supplies, and followed him out the door.

In the hall they stood to the side to allow a team of staff to fly by them with somebody on a stretcher. Benfu pushed himself flat against the wall to give them room, and as they passed, he briefly locked eyes with the old man who struggled to breathe under an oxygen mask. It shook him up, as he imagined that was just what he looked like on the day he was admitted. He was scared; he didn't want to die and leave his girls, especially his Calli. And he never wanted them to see him look like that.

"Which way?" Benfu asked. He didn't even remember arriving at the hospital. His world had been limited to only the small room and the window overlooking the crowded parking lot. He'd spent a lot of time staring out over the smog-covered street while wondering if his stay in the hospital had resulted in lost children not being found. But he hadn't ventured out of the room. How was he supposed to know how to get out of the hospital? He reached and grabbed the largest bag from Calli as she moved to get in front of him. He wasn't totally incapable and didn't want her straining to carry everything, even if he did have to follow behind her like a darned baby chick.

"This way, and stop being so cranky. Linnea is supposed to be waiting downstairs for us. She said she'd arranged a car service."

Benfu muttered under his breath. He didn't need a ride home in some fancy car. He'd rather take a taxi or the bus, like they always did. But on the other hand, it would get him there faster and he could see his girls.

He kept his grumbling to himself and slowly followed Calli to the set of elevators. She pushed the button and watched his face as they waited. He was winded even more than he let on as he tried to control his breathing. He knew she was wondering if he was really feeling better or just faking. For sure he was weak, but he was going to fight hard to get stronger. He needed to get her and the girls into better shape before the tuberculosis overtook him or completely shut down his heart. He had to—he just had to find a way to leave behind something other than a trail of debt to the hospital.

Calli smiled affectionately. "There you go with all that dark thinking again. Can you just relax for a while? At least let me get you home, old man."

The elevator doors opened and to their surprise there stood Jet, a polite smile pasted on his face. He stepped out and patted Benfu on the shoulder.

"Good afternoon, Lao Zheng. Ready to go?"

Benfu looked around him but didn't see Linnea.

"What are you doing up here? I thought Linnea was meeting us in the parking lot? Where is she?" he asked. He hadn't yet had a chance to tell Linnea to make her own decisions about the boy and yet here he was, showing up to drive him home, of all things!

Calli nervously beckoned for them both to get in the elevator. "Come on, you two. We need to get going." They followed her in and the doors closed.

The silence was awkward until Jet finally broke it.

"Linnea couldn't come. She's waiting at home with the girls. I hope you don't mind that it's just me. They've been real busy preparing for your homecoming."

"Oh, that's fine, Jet. But you didn't have to come up here. We could've taken a taxi," Calli fretted. Benfu silently fumed.

Jet smiled. "That's okay, Lao Calli. It's no trouble at all. Seriously."

The boy lowered his eyes and fiddled with the zipper on his light jacket, avoiding eye contact.

Benfu frowned. Jet was up to something sneaky and he didn't like it. And Linnea couldn't tear herself away to come meet him? That was strange. He hoped they hadn't gone to too much trouble just for his return. He imagined that they had probably done more paper cutting and the house was probably a flutter of girly red and yellow designs. He didn't care; as long as he could get to his bed, they could fill the whole place with paper dragons and rainbows. He sighed, fidgeted from one foot to the other, and wished the elevator would hurry to the lobby floor before he lost his fight against the deep cough that threatened to erupt from his lungs.

On the bottom floor the elevator doors opened and they all stepped out with Jet in the lead. He led them toward a small sitting area and turned around.

"Lao Calli, can I have a moment with Lao Zheng?" he asked.

Calli nodded. "I'll just go find a bottle of water to wet my lips. I'll be back in a few minutes."

Benfu reached his hand out to stop her but she skirted on by. "Wait, no, we need—"

Calli put her finger to her lip. "Please Benfu, just listen to what the boy has to say. Can you do that much for Linnea? For me, please?"

Benfu sat down heavily in the plastic chair behind him. He'd listen because what choice did he have? He felt sure with or without his blessing, this relationship was going to have to run its course. He'd give the boy a minute and see what he had to say.

Jet sat in a chair across from him and propped his elbows on his knees. Benfu could see he was nervous by the way he was breathing, but he wouldn't make it easy on him. He waited. He wouldn't be the first to speak.

He watched Jet's Adam's apple jump up and down as he swallowed a few times, then took a deep breath. "Lao Zheng, I'm aware that you do not approve of me. As you know, without your approval, Linnea doesn't want to continue a relationship."

Benfu stared at the floor. Jet waited on him to say something and when he didn't, the boy began to talk again.

"I can't promise you that I am worthy of being anywhere near your daughter. And I can't promise you that we'll never have cross words between us. But what I can promise you is that I am my own person and many of the philosophies that people around me have tried to drill into my head about differences in class mean nothing to me."

That got Benfu's attention. He had to give it to him; the boy didn't beat around the bush. He got right to what he knew was the thorn under the saddle between them.

"How do I know you aren't using my daughter as a plaything to add some interest to your pampered life? And when you tire of her, you won't just drop her and move on to the next pretty—but more acceptable—girl?" Benfu stared Jet right in the eye.

As he watched, he saw a boy trying to be a man. More than that, he saw a man's anger threatening to explode from the boy. Jet's face turned red and Benfu held his ground as the boy struggled to bring his emotions under control, a fight that was obvious from the expressions that flitted across his face.

Finally Jet nodded his head and maintained the direct stare. "I can understand your concerns, Lao Zheng. I really can. But I can only tell you that Linnea means more to me than any girl I've ever met. I don't care if she decides to make a living by planting shoots in a rice paddy. If I have to, I'll stand right beside her with muck up to my ankles. I'll do anything to be near her." He dropped his gaze and sighed.

Benfu was impressed at the boy's self-control and his passionate speech, even if he didn't want to admit it, and he sure wasn't ready to show it. He waited to see if he had anything else to add.

Jet looked up again at Benfu. "I just can't live without her. But I can only give you my word as a man that I won't hurt her. Can you just give me a chance to prove to you that I mean what I say?"

Benfu continued to glare unwaveringly at Jet. And to his astonishment, he saw honesty and sincerity staring back at him. Benfu realized suddenly that he had been judging the boy only based on his family background. It was ironic that what had been done to him so many years ago had now come full circle. So what if Jet had family involved in the government? That didn't make him a criminal or a bad person. From what he knew the boy hadn't done anything to wrong anyone—of any class. Benfu felt a streak of shame at his unfounded prejudice. But still, he had to make sure the boy knew he meant business.

"You do know that if you hurt my daughter, you cannot possibly run far enough or fast enough to avoid my wrath, right?"

Jet chuckled. "I sure do know that, Lao Benfu. I've already heard about your encounter with the bike man. You can bet I won't put myself in jeopardy like that."

Benfu stretched out his hand. Jet hesitated, then took it and they shook, knowing a silent oath had just taken place. Jet would promise to respect and treat Linnea like she should be treated, and Benfu would withhold judgment until the boy had a chance to prove himself.

Calli returned with a bottle of water for Benfu and handed it over. He stood and took off the cap, then took a long swig. Looking at Jet, he nodded.

"Now get me home so I can see my girls," he said gruffly, and with that he led the way out of the hospital, struggling to put his spine straight and shoulders back as Calli and Jet followed him. He might be exhausted, sore, and homesick but he'd leave the hospital like a man—the way it should be.

Chapter Twenty Two

Benfu breathed a sigh of relief as Jet turned the corner and came to a screeching stop at the entrance to a parking lot near the end of his *hutong*. After Jet handed a ten-yuan bill out the window to the attendant, the surly man finally directed him to the other side of the lot.

Jet guided the car into the small space and turned off the ignition. He turned to look at Benfu and Calli in the backseat. Traffic had been chaotic and Benfu just wanted to get home. In his current shape it was going to be rough, but they'd have to walk the rest of the way, as a car couldn't fit through the small lane.

"Wait right here for a minute. Don't get out."

Benfu immediately sat up straighter. He didn't like to be told what to do, especially by someone only a third of his age.

"Don't get out? Now look here, son. I've been waiting to see my girls for almost a month now and I'm ready to go home. Open this blasted door."

Calli reached over and patted his leg, trying to shush him before he got angry. He hated it when she did that and was about to tell her so.

Jet interrupted. "Please, Lao Zheng. Just one minute. I promised Jasmine."

Benfu sighed. The kid knew where to hit him. If it was for Jasmine, he'd wait and see what he was up to.

Jet opened the door and jumped out. Benfu strained to see what he was doing and saw him beckon at someone around the corner. A dark-skinned small man rode up on his pedicab, stopping just outside the car. Benfu opened the door and stepped out.

"Why didn't you say so? I'm not so stubborn to refuse a ride that'll save me that long walk. My old legs are tired, boy. Come on, Calli. Climb in so we can get on home. Jet—we can take it from here. Thanks for your help."

Jet chuckled and helped Calli into the pedicab. He settled their bags around their feet and whispered to the driver. They took off, with Jet jogging behind. Benfu looked back and shook his head. He just couldn't get rid of the boy. Now he was going to follow them all the way home?

The driver guided the pedicab out of the parking lot and turned the corner to go down to the street where the *hutong* began. Benfu was relieved to see all the familiar sights, except he didn't see the usual old men out playing their sidewalk games, and most of the usual shopkeepers were absent from their posts. He sighed. He would have liked to greet them, seeing how he hadn't seen them in weeks. But they were nowhere to be found.

"Where is everybody?" he wondered out loud. "Is today some sort of holiday?"

Calli looked puzzled and she shook her head. "No, I don't think so."

As they neared their street, Benfu struggled to see around the driver's head. He could see a crowd standing around the entrance of the *hutong,* and he wanted to know why. And he wanted to know now. He hoped there hadn't been some sort of accident, and his heart lurched as he wondered if something had happened to one of his girls.

"What's going on up there?" he yelled out to the driver.

The man ignored him and continued to pedal. Benfu glanced back at Jet jogging behind them but the boy shrugged his shoulders as if he didn't know.

As they neared the *hutong* entrance, Benfu realized where all the usual people from the street were. They were standing around in his alley. Something must have happened and he felt nauseated with dread. Ahead Widow Zu stood in the line, waving at him and smiling a toothless grin. Seeing how it was the first time he'd seen her smile in a decade, it sent his apprehension up even another notch.

Suddenly Calli grabbed his arm.

"Benfu! Is that—"

"Mari!" Benfu exclaimed. Dressed in colorful gypsy-looking garb, she stood out in the crowd and he saw her at the same time as Calli did. He couldn't believe it. His dear daughter Mari had left her station at the Great Wall to come home! His heart soared with joy at the sight of her familiar face.

"But who are all those other people and what's going on?" Benfu squinted. Standing on both sides of the *hutong* were two lines of people. He saw a few of his favorite shopkeepers, some of the old retired men, and there was even Lao Gong standing their waving at him. His friend had never come to his home before!

Beside him he heard a sniffle and jerked his head to look at Calli. She was crying! What in the world was going on?

"Calli? What is it?"

"Benfu. They're here for *you,* my love. Look, there's Lotus. And I see Camellia. I don't know how they've done it but it's not only our neighbors; it's all of our daughters, too. They've come to welcome you home, dear."

Closer to the gate Benfu looked around. Gathered around Linnea, Ivy, Lily, and Peony he saw his other older daughters.

Among those waving at him were Hyacinth and Blossom, and even Daisy had come all the way from Chengdu! He couldn't believe it. How did they all manage to get here? How had they afforded it? He shook his head, unable to speak.

He turned to Calli and could clearly see that she was just as speechless as he to see all of their daughters together, a feat they both thought would never happen in their lifetime.

"*Aiya,* Benfu, look what they've done!" Calli gasped as she pointed to a new stone archway that was erected over the entrance to their tiny courtyard. In beautiful carved calligraphy that Benfu recognized immediately as Linnea's work, it read ZHENG'S FLOWER GARDEN.

Two tall panels of lattice bordered the gate, entwined with many different types and colors of flowers and ivy. Along the courtyard wall sat small colored pots holding every array of blooms possible, the containers painted with childlike designs. The concrete wall had been given a fresh coat of gray paint, making it look almost new. Benfu was speechless. His entire courtyard had been transformed; it was no longer just a barren square of dirt and trash. It was now a sight to behold. Somehow even a large tree had been planted and from the branches hung several wicker birdcages that held various colorful birds hopping around. Benfu thought it was a beautiful sight but knew he would have to release the birds to their freedom as soon as possible. As he and Calli sat there in total shock, taking in the sight of the new garden and their many daughters, friends, and neighbors, the entire crowd broke into applause.

Benfu shook his head frantically and waved his arms at them, trying to stop them. Then his heart lurched when he saw his little Maggi. In the midst of all the sisters, she sat beaming with pride in a wheelchair. It wasn't new, Benfu could see that, but the chair fit her perfectly and he'd never seen such a beautiful sight. Someone had tied ribbons through the spokes of the wheels, and the same colors were also threaded through her hair to match. When she saw him look at her, a smile began to spread across her little face.

He looked at Calli to see if she had been keeping the secret from him. *Where had the chair come from?* She sat with her hand held over her mouth, her eyes open wide in surprise. He watched her gaze linger on Maggi and knew she was touched; they had always wanted to get Maggi a chair, but there just hadn't ever been the money to do it.

"But where—why . . . how?" He couldn't form full sentences. He stopped trying.

Jet finally caught up and stood beside the pedicab. Linnea walked up with Poppy snuggled in her arms, and stood beside Jet.

Linnea smiled at him and a tear ran down her face. Around her all his daughters chattered loudly, some laughing and others still clapping. Small boys and girls ran around; Benfu startled when he realized they were probably the grandchildren he hadn't yet met, and he searched their features to try to match them up to their mothers. He marveled at the plump faces and sparkling eyes, gifts the world would have missed out on if their mothers hadn't survived their harsh beginnings.

"Welcome home, Ye Ye," Linnea said, her voice shaky. "I hope you like what we've done to the courtyard. All of your daughters and grandchildren contributed, and our neighbors helped us pull it all together. Even your old buddies from the plant and flower market came through and donated all this!" She waved her hand through the air.

Benfu climbed down from the pedicab and hugged Linnea. Calli climbed down and took Poppy, snuggling her close and inhaling the scent of her. The driver laughed loudly, nodding his head as if he were a part of the entire event. Benfu let go of

Linnea and looked around again, trying to clear his mind. He was confused—*and so happy to see all of his daughters in one place*—but still confused.

"Linnea? What have you done, girl? What's all this fuss about?"

"Everyone is here, Ye Ye. All the girls, their children, even your friends. We're going to have a feast! Everyone brought food. We're so glad you are home, Ye Ye. We've missed you so."

Linnea turned and waved at the door to their home. A well-dressed young man approached.

Jet stepped forward. "Lao Zheng, this is my father's assistant, Yang Fu."

Yang Fu cleared his throat. "First, let me say that I am here on official business."

At his announcement Benfu felt his first indication of dread. What was an official—even one as wet behind the ears as this one appeared to be—doing at his home uninvited? Was he going to take away one of the girls?

Yang continued. "I know you aren't very happy with the local and not-so-local branches of government, and I've come to show you that we indeed do care. I'm here on behalf of the director of social development to thank you for your contribution to our city."

Benfu looked at Calli, an unspoken question in his eyes. *Why had an official sent his lapdog to their home? And Jet's father worked in the same department that basically dictated how Benfu built and supported his family?* That was a revelation. Calli shook her head in confusion as she swayed back and forth with the baby.

The crowd quieted down and everyone listened as the young man pulled a piece of paper from his jacket pocket and nervously began to read it. Benfu could easily tell he was not accustomed to speaking on behalf of anyone, let alone in an official capacity.

"Since evidence of your contributions was recently brought to our attention, we want to acknowledge that you are the epitome of the example we hope our future generations will grow into. You will go down in history not as a scavenger, but as a model citizen. You have shown all of us how to accept one another based on the person—not the gender, or the absence or presence of disabilities."

All around everyone began to choke up, some pulling tissue from their bags and pockets. His daughters hushed their children as they waited for him to speak. Benfu heard several of them remark to their children that he was their grandfather—an important man—and they needed to show respect.

Benfu sighed as he looked around at their faces. It was an emotional announcement for all of them, as many had been abandoned because of disabilities and some just because they were girls. He knew his daughters would always harbor feelings of being unwanted, despite the care he and Calli had shown them.

Benfu didn't really know what to say. He hadn't done anything out of duty. He loved each and every one of his daughters and they had brought immeasurable joy to his simple life. He was also selfish; the girls at various ages had given him a peek into what his Dahlia may have looked like or been like at each year of her life that he had missed. He couldn't tell them that, but he had to say something.

"Thank you, Yang Fu. I appreciate the sentiment." He looked around at all his daughters and grandchildren. Could it be possible that the world saw him as much more than a lowly trash collector? He felt his heart swell with emotion, tinged with a bit of embarrassment for such a show put on just for him. "I'm not much on being recognized, but I'm thankful to see all of you! Finally you have all come home for a visit!"

The girls started to clap again until Yang held his hand up.

"My supervisors wouldn't have known the extent of your contributions without your daughter, Linnea, and her friend, Jet. They are a formidable team," Yang Fu said.

Benfu glanced at Jet and wondered just how cooperative his father was in the sudden acknowledgment of his efforts. His absence and the trainee he'd sent in his place made Benfu suspicious. But he'd think on that later. He looked at Linnea and shook his head. "I always said you were the most resourceful daughter of them all."

Linnea giggled at the approval and all around Benfu's other daughters nodded their agreement.

Yang Fu stepped closer. "I'm not done yet, Lao Zheng. We also want to announce that the children still in your care will *all* be receiving monthly stipends, as well as a full education. They will no longer be penalized because they are orphans. This is the new program my department has been working on, and it's still not approved for total rollout, but we've decided to kick it off using your children as our test case."

Calli nodded. "Thank you, Yang Fu. We appreciate any assistance you can offer."

Yang Fu nodded in acknowledgment of her gratitude and bowed low.

Then Calli leaned in and whispered to Benfu. He strained to hear her over the sudden murmuring from the girls and the neighbors. "Benfu, can you believe all this is happening? It's a miracle—nothing less."

Benfu heard the tears of joy in her voice and handed her his handkerchief. He felt the stress of his burdens slowly begin to lift from his shoulders. It sounded like his girls were going to be okay—even if he wasn't around a lot longer. He felt his face flush at the many times he'd cursed officials under his breath. He realized now that just like in every sect of humanity, there were good men mixed among the corrupt in the different tiers of government. He'd unfairly generalized too many people.

Suddenly the young man stepped back and Lao Gong moved closer. He patted Benfu on the shoulder and leaned in to speak quietly, giving a message only for Benfu to hear.

"You really gave me a scare at the teahouse, Benfu. But you also made me realize how much stress you have been under. Linnea told me what's been going on and I'm going to help you apply for some additional benefits. I still have a few contacts in place and you may not have tapped out what the system has to offer you. You just need someone to walk you through the steps. We'll find you the best doctor and I'll help you work out a way to pay for it."

At this news Benfu had to sit down. He realized his pride and his aversion to dealing with the government had made life much harder, and he wished he'd come to Gong earlier to ask his help. He faltered and Calli led him to the bench outside their door. He shook his head. It was too much to hope for—that he would possibly be able to get the drugs and care needed to live a few more years. He'd not even allowed himself to consider it before. But now, perhaps he would see the last of his girls grow up after all. He wouldn't have to give them up. Sure, life would continue to be difficult but in all his misery, he'd forgotten that there was always a thread of hope to hold on to.

Gong leaned in and whispered in his ear. "And all your neighbors and I took up a collection for your hospital stay and we cleared your bill this morning. There were so many that wanted to contribute, no one had to put up more than they could afford, including me." Gong playfully punched him in his arm. "Who knew you were so popular, old friend?"

Benfu was embarrassed to feel a sob of gratitude rising up.

Mari, their daughter from Beijing, stepped forward and pointed to the corner of the courtyard.

"Look, Ye Ye. We all pitched in to make you and Nai Nai a koi pond, too. It's small but I hope you like it. Our little ones all placed the rocks, so you may have to do a bit of rearranging."

Benfu looked to the corner that usually held his piles of collections to be sorted. It had been transformed into a garden area lined with rocks and anchored by a small fishpond. Benfu smiled and felt the joy all the way down to his toes. Of course, sitting on the edge of the pond was his little Jasmine. As usual, she was oblivious to the crowd as she swirled her tiny fingers in the water, playing with the fish. His heart flooded with love for her and he realized why. It was the young innocence in her face that reminded him of every girl he had raised—all his daughters who had propelled him through his difficult life, the hopes for their futures always pushing him to do more and be more.

He stood. "Jasmine?"

At the sound of her name being called, the girl looked up.

Benfu pointed to her, then his nose and then the sky. Jasmine jumped up and flew across the courtyard. She threw herself into his arms and burst into tears.

Benfu sat back down with her on his lap, rocking her back and forth as he held her tightly. Linnea had told him about Jasmine's adventure to find her fish, and knowing how much sadness and fear she held inside because of him tore at his heart.

"Now, now. What is this? I am home, little one. *Bu ku le.* You don't have to cry anymore." He reached down and wiped the tears from her cheeks. He was amazed. In her usual way she had ignored the chaos around her and instead sat entertaining herself in her own silent world. Until she'd seen him, that was.

His heart swelled with love.

Jasmine pointed over at the fishpond, making sure he'd seen it.

"Yes, your fish brought me home, Jasmine. And guess what? Who do you think is getting a new bedtime story tonight?"

At his touch on her cheek, Jasmine looked up at him and sniffled. With the amazing gift of childlike trust, and the promise of a new story, his lengthy absence was forgiven.

Benfu felt something at his side and found Lily there, holding the violin.

"Ye Ye. It is time. The music is waiting." She laid the violin in his lap, handed him the bow, and moved back. Jasmine scooted off his lap and sat between him and Calli, waiting impatiently.

Benfu shook his head and tried to push the violin back into Lily's hands. "Oh no. My time has passed."

Lily shook her head, stubbornly refusing to take the violin back. Benfu looked around at the girls and then at Calli. He didn't think he could do it. It had been years since he'd allowed himself to feel the cool comfort of the wood against his chin. He'd been forced to keep the violin and his gift secret for so long that he'd told himself he would never play again, and he had meant it. But now, with the unexpected blessings this day had brought, his heart rebelled against that oath.

Calli gave him a reassuring nod and Benfu put the violin against his shoulder. He found that it still fit there comfortably, as if it had never left. He picked up the bow and laid it against the strings. With one tiny movement he felt first a pang of regret; then another movement brought him a stirring of relief. Memories flooded him and though some were painful, the glimpse into his past allowed him to see how precious his life now was. He played the first chords of a once-forbidden classic and felt a rush of energy. Beside him he heard the laughter bubbling up from Calli, making her sound seventeen again. The sound took him back to those long-ago stolen moments with her, moments full of hope and plans for their future—plans to marry and have a big family. But fate had only given them one child and she had been taken from them. Then those government monsters had taken away their opportunity to ever have another.

With that thought he paused, then began to play a slow, soulful song. It was one that he had loved for many years and the dramatic chords came to him quickly. He closed his eyes to hold back the tears and his little Dahlia's round face suddenly showed itself to him again. In his mind he could see her pressed against Calli's breast and saw again the look of content they had both carried. It had been years since he'd allowed himself to remember those treasured moments.

With hot tears escaping from his closed eyes, he began to release the sorrows he'd carried for so long. His bow seemed to take on a life of its own; then he couldn't believe it but from his own hands he heard the sweetest and purest music he had ever before made.

He looked around and saw respect mirrored in the eyes of his friends and neighbors, and he felt a flash of pride that finally he was able to show them he was more than they had perhaps thought. Then he searched the faces of the girls all gathered round and was filled with a sense of inexplicable joy. These *were* his children! Fate had not stripped him of fatherhood—just because they didn't come from his loins didn't mean a thing. He felt the smile spreading across his face, and he closed his eyes and inhaled the music and the feeling of love that settled over him like a warm cloak.

All around the courtyard the only sound to be heard over the song was the sound of muffled crying as they all shared in the special and unexpected miracle. Even Gong stood with his head cocked to one side, listening as the sun reflected off his wide forehead.

When Benfu finished playing the piece and rested the bow, he looked over Jasmine's head and locked eyes with his Calla Lily. Deep within her dark brown eyes he saw the girl who'd accepted and trusted in him so many years before—the same girl who had given him reason to live when she'd promised him forever.

He couldn't believe the life they'd built together. He reached over and rubbed at the tear moving slowly through a deep line on her lovely face. He shook his head in amazement—he wasn't such an old fool that he didn't realize the gods had surely smiled down on him. Why they'd want to bestow such a life to just a wretched old man he didn't understand. But in that instant he also knew there was no other place in the world he'd rather be than in his garden with his beautiful flowers, known as the Scavenger's Daughters.

Tangled Vines

Enjoy a Sneak Peek of Book II
of The Scavenger's Daughters series.
Coming soon from Lake Union Publishing.

Chapter One

Suzhou, China, 2011

Li Jin ducked to the left as the familiar but dreaded fist flew toward her face and hit the concrete wall behind her. It was getting easier to predict his actions and sometimes her quick moves helped her avoid the pain. But not always.

"You'll do what you're told and if you don't, Jojo will pay the price."

Li Jin was glad Jojo was at school and not there to witness her shame. The man she'd once considered her rescuer cradled his bleeding knuckles against his chest and glared at her as if his pain were her fault. She huddled in the corner of the room, transfixed by the dots of spittle on his upper lip. Erik knew how to get her to do what he wanted. Her son meant the world to her, and she'd do anything to protect him, even if it meant jeopardizing her freedom. She'd already lost a lot to keep the façade of normalcy in place for him but mostly it was her dignity that was irreplaceable.

"Okay. I'll do it," she answered, careful to keep her eyes downcast. If she looked straight at him when he was angry, he'd take it as a challenge.

Erik snorted in disgust and pushed the piece of paper into her face, crushing it against her nose. She took it and slapped his hand away. He turned to leave, throwing out one last warning.

"Be there by noon. Don't make me come find you, Li Jin. You're an old woman, now. You can't hide from me."

The bitter sound of her name rolling off his foreign tongue made her glad once again that she hadn't shared her secret with him. *Dahlia*—just a name but it was the only clue about her birth that she'd been able to ferret out from the director at the orphanage. The nontraditional name had been given to her by parents who didn't want her, but it at least made her wonder if they may have loved her even a little. She'd almost told Erik about it when he'd asked about the tattoo on her foot, but now she never would. He didn't deserve to know and she didn't want to hear something so special come from such an angry person.

Surprisingly, Erik spoke good Chinese and his South African accent made it sound almost poetic. When he had swept her off her feet a year ago, he'd told her she was lovely and didn't look all of her thirty years. Now that he'd been in China long enough to understand much of the culture, he knew being an unmarried mother at her age was a social stigma. In the eyes of her people, she was a disappointment to society.

He'd used that weakness and longing for respectability against her. He was younger than her, though not a lot, but his muscular body had immediately attracted her attention. She hadn't encountered too many foreigners and his golden boy looks, blond hair, and blue eyes had startled her at first. He'd approached her as she sat watching Jojo play in the park. At first she was wary but he won her over with his smooth way of talking. After some flirting, he'd told her he was an investor. They'd hit it off and she couldn't believe such a worldly man would choose her. He had smothered her with attention and for the first time in her life, she had felt what it meant to be romanced. They'd moved fast—too fast, she now knew. Within weeks she had helped him secure an apartment for a great local price and he'd begged her to move in with him. At the time she and Jojo had been staying in a hostel and barely making it. With the new living arrangements, she'd felt like finally fate had sent her a reprieve.

Unfortunately, Erik's behavior had changed quickly once she was securely ensnared in his web. Those blue eyes that had captivated her now turned icy when he was having one of his fits. And these days he constantly made remarks that he could easily get a younger, more beautiful girl to do his bidding.

Now that she knew who—or what—he really was, Li Jin wished he *would* find someone else. But then who would pay for Jojo to go to school? Without an education he'd just be another kid on the street, forced to hustle to make a living like the migrant workers' children. The support from Erik had allowed her to put Jojo in school for the first time and he had flourished ever since. To Jojo, school was a constant adventure and source of entertainment. And she loved her son more than life itself. He was her only spot of light in what before him had been a world of darkness. This was her only chance to provide for his future. She'd suffer the abuse as long as it didn't touch her son. There was no limit to what a mother would do for her child and she was determined Jojo would never have a childhood like hers. He would have a family and feel protected and wanted.

When she heard the front door slam, she stood. She released a ragged sigh of relief. He'd be gone for the rest of the morning. She rubbed her hands down her clothes to wipe away the invisible feeling of filth from Erik's latest demand. She didn't approve of what she had to do, even if she'd done it several times already. The truth was that it never got easier. She resolved herself to just get it over with and not think about it. She'd focus on the face of her son and pretend she was just a normal mother out to finish her daily errands. She'd done it before and she could do it again. But only for Jojo. And just maybe before the next round she'd find a way to stop the madness.

Chapter Two

Old Town Wuxi, China

Linnea exhaled a big breath to move the sweaty strands of hair off her forehead while she rummaged in the deep recesses of her bag to find her keys. Too many commuters and the lack of space had made her morning bus ride miserable and hot. Now she could breathe a sigh of relief because she was here, at *her* store. She still couldn't get used to the words! Feeling another burst of impatience, she dug beneath the old packs of chewing gum, a few folded love notes from Jet, and a half-empty bottle of water until she finally touched metal.

She pulled the key ring out and took a step back to look up at the sign over the door: VINTAGE MUSE. Jet had hung it the day before and Linnea had stepped outside at least a dozen times to look at it. She'd painted it herself and loved the elaborate characters and the buds of pink Linnea flowers etched around the border. It was a little piece of her up there, and she couldn't be more proud.

It was hard to believe, but she was finally getting her chance to rise above the low expectations that society had set for her as an orphan. More importantly, if she succeeded, she would make her Nai Nai and Ye Ye proud—and show them the years of love and care they'd given her after finding her abandoned on the street was all worth it. She felt a lump rise in her throat as she realized she'd no longer have to bow down to obnoxious boss men, or work in the streets in the freezing winter or the scorching summers. She'd done it! Or at least she'd almost done it—time would tell if she'd be a success or have to go back to slinging tires or hawking wares from the sidewalk.

She quickly looked around at the other shops and by the still-dark store windows realized she was the first one on the block to arrive. It had been hard to get up so early but today was the most important day of her life thus far. If she didn't get going, her *grand opening* wasn't going to be so *grand*.

She looked through her large but empty picture window and sighed. The bare space gave her yet another huge project to throw together before her opening. She wished she'd asked some of her sisters for help but in her usual stubborn way, she hadn't wanted to burden anyone else. Now she had a long list of tasks befitting at least a dozen workers to be accomplished on her very own, all in only a few hours. Frustrating, but it would be a while before she could actually afford to hire employees, so she'd just have to make do with her own two hands.

Ready to tackle the day, she unlocked the door and walked through.

She stood in the middle of the room and put her hands on her hips. There was so much to do! She approached the box that she'd toppled over, opened the flaps, and began to pull out shirts and stack them on the shelves next to it, trying to sort by size. The shirts were her signature item—and the main resource that had helped her pay back the original loan to Jet.

She held up one of her favorite shirts. Printed across the front was a graphic she had sketched of what used to be called a *Tiger Kitchen Range*. In the old days, the Wuxi people would line up at local shops to buy hot water to shower with. On the shirt, the huge pipe—what they called the fuel mouths—that brought in the water looked like the head of a tiger, the two big pots it poured into resembled the body, and the chimney mimicked a swishing tail. From afar it was simply a tiger, but close up the detail on the shirt was amazing. Now there were only eight such kitchens left remaining in all of Wuxi. Linnea didn't want those pieces of history to disappear—and with the sudden success of her shirts, obviously neither did the Wuxi residents who had bought from her.

Other shirts sported graphics of old street signs, subway tickets, and other Old China memorabilia. Her shirts had been categorized as urban vintage—and Linnea was still astounded at the popularity of them. Somehow without any real advertising she had sold out repeatedly until she'd finally found a supplier to help her keep up.

But now that she had a real store with walls and a door, in addition to her shirts she was going to collect and sell other vintage pieces. She had already collected many things that were scattered around the room, waiting to be displayed in just the right way to entice a buyer. Linnea wiped the sweat from her brow and picked up the pace. She had left too much undone the day before. She'd never finish in time.

An hour later Linnea looked up when the bell hanging over her door jangled. Backup had arrived and leading the charge of her sisters was her feisty Nai Nai, pushing a wheelchair through the narrow entrance with such energy that the gray bun on top of her head jiggled back and forth. Over her plump middle she wore her blue gingham going-out apron, but Linnea noticed by the bulges that she'd still packed her pockets full of odds and ends.

"We've got to talk to the city about the buses being inadequate to get wheelchairs in and out. You should have seen what we just went through." She fussed as she pushed the chair into the store, then broke into a wide smile that crinkled her face into a thousand tiny lines.

Her sister, Maggi, waved from her wheelchair as Nai Nai pushed it over the doorjamb. On Maggi's lap, Poppy, their youngest addition, sat wide-eyed and curious, just happy to be out for a ride.

"Linnea! Nai Nai brought us to help you. What can I do?" Maggi asked, her pigtails bouncing up and down as she looked around the store, taking it all in. At nine years old, she acted like she was big enough to tackle any task.

Linnea laughed. "You mean you're going to stop knitting long enough to do something else with those talented little hands?"

She was relieved that despite her stubbornness in not asking for help, they'd come anyway. She should've known they would. And her army of sisters was just what she needed to help her out of the time crunch she had created. She was speechless with gratitude.

"Linnea," her Nai Nai began, her face set in determination, "we'll whip this place into shape in no time. You just give the orders. Where's Jet?"

"Oh, he was going to be here but this is the day he already promised to help his father with some special project. He'll be here tomorrow. He was so upset to miss this." At least, that's what he'd said when he broke the news to her last night. Sometimes Linnea got so frustrated with his busy schedule but then he'd flash those twinkling eyes at her and make her forget why she was even irritated. And he always went out of his way to make it up to her—she felt her cheeks warm as she thought of some of the ways he went about it.

Linnea dropped the T-shirt she was folding and jumped up. She ran to the old woman and, skirting around the chair, hugged her tightly. "Nai Nai. Thanks for coming. I thought I was going to have to do this alone!"

Nai Nai shooed her away and pulled a wrapped steamed bun from her apron pocket. "*Bah.* Of course I was coming. Do you think I'd miss your grand opening? This is a big moment for the Zheng family. You're going to be a business owner—and at only nineteen. *Aiyo!* We're so proud of you, Linnea. And here, eat your breakfast and don't be sneaking out on an empty stomach again. Ivy, hand me that playpen for Poppy."

Behind her Ivy deposited the playpen against the wall as she and the other girls bickered about who would get to do what. Lily, Ivy's twin, kept her hand on Ivy's arm as the girl guided her around the unfamiliar territory. Lily swung her new walking cane to find her way, but she wasn't quite used to it yet and still depended on her sister to help her around unfamiliar areas.

Linnea still recalled when the girls had been brought to them at only five years old. Officers had brought them by after their mother had been taken away by the police. The girls were meant to be transferred to the orphanage in the next city over, but knowing their Ye Ye like they did, the officers asked if he'd take them in. The girls had huddled behind the officer, bedraggled and reeking of smoke. Nai Nai had shuffled them through the door and tried to comfort them. Even then Ivy had protected Lily and refused to allow anyone else to touch her. She'd helped her sister eat, bathe, dress—everything, until she'd finally felt like they were in a safe place.

Now they were fifteen, and Ivy was the loudest. Her voice carried over everyone else as she walked to the front window display box.

"I want to work in the window!"

Lily followed along. She never complained about being blind, probably because she'd always had Ivy to depend on. The two were so connected that many times she didn't even need to hold on; she could just feel where her sister was leading.

"But what about their lessons?" Linnea asked, knowing that since the year before when the city had begun sending a tutor for the girls who couldn't go to regular school, it was considered top priority in the Zheng household.

Calli shook her head. "The only lesson they'll learn today is how to follow their hearts and keep at their dreams until they come true. And Peony is thrilled to skip school. You can probably get her to do anything you want."

Linnea scanned the room and saw Peony busy on the other side of the store, already scoping out the new items and probably trying to figure out how she could swipe some new things for herself. Linnea thought Peony at ten years old the most beautiful of all her sisters with her mixed blood that gave her golden eyes and fair coloring. Even the natural auburn highlights in her hair added to her exotic look and Linnea knew that when Peony grew older, she would be even prettier. But the most amazing thing was that her little sister didn't have a clue of her own beauty; instead she acted like a tomboy—and was into everything. She usually went to the local elementary school, but she didn't like it and wanted to stay home and be tutored, too.

Linnea stopped looking at her so intently before Peony noticed.

"Where's Ye Ye?" she asked Nai Nai.

"He's coming. Jasmine pulled him over to watch those old buzzards on the lane playing mahjong. Now that he's feeling better I can't get him to stop all his *socializing*." She waved her hand dismissively in the air. "You'd think he was a celebrity or something the way everyone wants to have time with him."

Linnea smiled at her Nai Nai's words that she knew hid a deep affection for Ye Ye. She had never seen two people more in love; even after all their years together they were still totally devoted to each other. And she should have guessed her little sister, Jasmine, would have gotten Ye Ye sidetracked. Even though she'd never spoken a single word, the almost-six-year-old had Ye Ye wrapped around her little finger. And her grandfather *was* a celebrity of sorts—but then so was her Nai Nai. They'd both been recognized a year ago for their contribution to the community for taking in abandoned girls and raising them as their own over the course of a few decades. Linnea was one of those orphaned girls—but she couldn't love the two old folks more if they were blood related. In her mind, she wasn't an orphan because she had Nai Nai and Ye Ye, as well as her sisters, and they were a family.

She left those thoughts behind and put her hands on her hips. "Okay, we have two hours before the doors open. Peony, you and Ivy are in charge of that display window. I want you to find a way to display my T-shirts but also add some of the antique items sitting over there next to the wall. Make it look like an old Chinese living room with a flash of urban."

The two girls came back to get the box of T-shirts, racing against each other to be first to look through the styles. Linnea figured she'd let them work for a little while before she intervened to explain to them the definition of urban.

"Maggi," Linnea began again, "it'll be a huge help if you just entertain Poppy while Nai Nai helps me clean up." Her sister was doing great after her recent surgery by the Shanghai doctor to remove the sac of membranes from her spine, and Linnea was surprised that the operation had given Maggi such a different outlook on her future. Spina bifida could be cruel and her sister might not ever be able to walk, but at least now she had control over her bladder and no longer had to wear the embarrassing diapers. And since the surgery had done so much to minimize her pain, Maggi was gaining more strength in her lower body and had even learned to lift herself up and could get in and out of her chair by herself. And Linnea couldn't believe how talented she was with the knitting needles! She was even learning how to embroider and crochet. In her eyes, Maggi was nothing short of amazing.

"Nai Nai, the broom's back in the storeroom. You can sweep, or I'll sweep while you polish the glass countertop. As soon as the girls get the display going, I'll help them get it perfect."

Nai Nai answered her by immediately going to the storeroom for the broom.

Linnea looked at Lily, her other sister. What could she have her do to feel helpful?

"Lily, I have a box of porcelain teapots and cups over there in the corner. There's a shelf right in front of the box. Please unwrap everything and set them up. I'll put them in the right places after you get them all out."

Lily would probably be even more careful than her sighted sisters, Linnea thought to herself as she watched Ivy lead Lily to the corner where the box of porcelain sat. The empty wall behind the girl caught her attention and she sighed. She'd forgotten she needed to hang one example of all her vintage shirts across the wall for a display. Luckily her Ye Ye would be there shortly. He could help her attach the lines and then clip the shirts up. He could also open the register and get her starter money situated. *He'll feel important to be handling my money,* she mused.

With her hand on her chin, she stared up at the wall, imagining the best way to hang the shirts to get the most attention from shoppers.

Behind her she felt a jolt of something prickly on her backside and turned around.

"What are you standing around gawking at, girl? You've got work to do!" Nai Nai prodded her again with the broom and smiled, showing the gap between her two front teeth.

Linnea jumped into action. She felt a shiver of excitement that traveled up her spine and tingled through her fingertips. Thanks to her family it was all going to be okay—everything was coming together and in a few hours she would embark on the next stage in her life. Vintage Muse was going to be a smashing success—she'd settle for nothing less.

Glossary

Great Leap Forward

An economic and social campaign of the Communist Party of China, reflected in planning decisions from 1958 to 1961, which aimed to use China's vast population to rapidly transform the country from an agrarian economy into a modern communist society through the process of rapid industrialization and collectivization.

Cultural Revolution

A social-political movement that took place in the People's Republic of China from 1966 through 1976. Set into motion by Mao Zedong, then chairman of the Communist Party of China, its stated goal was to enforce communism in the country by removing capitalist, traditional, and cultural elements from Chinese society, and to impose Maoist orthodoxy within the party. The revolution marked the return of Mao Zedong to a position of power after the failed Great Leap Forward.

Aiya (pronounced I-yah)	Expresses surprise or other sudden emotion
Anjing (Ann jing)	A command to be quiet
Ayi (I-yee)	Auntie or a woman performing house help
Bushi (Boo sher)	No
Dao le (Dow luh)	We've arrived.
Dui bu qi (Dway boo chee)	Sorry

Dui le (Dway luh)	Right/Correct
Duo shao qian (Dwoh sh-oww chee an)	How much?
Gong xi fa ca (Gong she fa tsa)	Happy New Year
Guo lai (Gwoh lie)	Come here.
Hao-bu-hao (How boo how)	Is okay or not?
Hao de? (How duh)	Okay?
Hui jia le (Hway jah luh)	Has come home
Hukou (Who koh)	Residential permit all Chinese must carry
Hutong (Who tong)	Lane or residential area
Jie Jie (Jay Jay)	Big sister
Laoban (L-oww ban)	Manager or boss
Laoren (L-oww run)	Respectful way to address the elderly
Li Jin (Lee-Jean)	Girl's name meaning beautiful, gold
Mahjong (Ma jong)	A Chinese game
Mei Mei (May may)	Little sister
Mifan (mee fon)	Rice
Nai Nai (pronounced Nie Nie)	Grandmother or other elderly female
Ni hao (Knee how)	Hello
Ni hao ma (Knee how ma)	How are you?
Nuer (New are)	Daughter
Sui bian (Sway bee ann)	Slang expression for "whatever"
Xie Xie (She she)	Thank you
Ye Ye (Yay Yay)	Grandfather or other elderly male
Yisheng (E-shung)	Doctor

Zaijian (Zie gee an)	Good-bye
Zao (Zow)	A short morning greeting
Zenme le (Zun muh luh)	What's wrong?
Zhen ci (Jen tsuh)	Acupuncture
Zhu ni haoyun (Joo nee how yoon)	Good luck

Author's Note

I was inspired to write *The Scavenger's Daughters* after reading online articles about scavengers in China who have opened their modest homes to children from the street, raising them as their own. Lou Xiaoying, an amazing woman who has raised over thirty children she has found on the street, had this to say in the July 31, 2012, edition of *What's on Shenzhen* magazine: "I realized if we had strength enough to collect garbage, how could we not recycle something as important as human lives?" This book is for her and others like her.

With Benfu's story, it is my hope to highlight those in China who, because of their enormous capacity to love the unwanted, are an inspiration to the rest of the world. There will be more books in this series because I have much more to tell in *The Scavenger's Daughters* family saga. If you enjoyed this book, a short review posted on Amazon or GoodReads would be very much appreciated. Also, please go to the Kay Bratt website to sign up for my newsletter to notify you of new releases.

I hope this story will raise awareness about the difficulties that children and adults from the working-class families in China face on a daily basis. If you would like to support an organization that benefits orphans, you can check out the nonprofit I volunteer for called An Orphan's Wish.

Acknowledgments

These projects are never completed alone, and I couldn't do without my critique partners. This time my go-to girls were my friends and fellow authors Gina Barlean and Denise Grover Swank. Many times we can't see the story for all the words, and you both helped me dig deep and find what I really wanted to say.

To my developmental editor, Charlotte Herscher, it's amazing how you crawl into the story and guide me to tell the most important parts while cutting the fluff. Jane Steele, your attention to detail is an asset to every book that lands in your path. Thank you both, for your contributions to *The Scavenger's Daughters*.

Many thanks to my acquisitions editor, Terry Goodman, who saw the potential and had the idea to turn the initial short story into a much more detailed and interesting series. I can't thank you enough for your guidance and continued belief in the value of my work. To Jessica Poore, Nikki, and the rest of my team at Amazon; you guys already know this, but I'll tell you again—you rock.

Ben and Amanda, you'll never know how much your encouragement helps me continue this journey as an author. When I don't believe in myself, you two always stand strong behind me, sometimes even shoving me reluctantly forward. Lou Hsu, thank you again for always being there for me. Your insight into the Chinese culture is vital and much appreciated. I'm so glad my first book was the introduction to our friendship. To my readers; I owe you the *greatest* gratitude. So many of you have been loyal to read everything I write. Your support means the world to me and I hope you will continue to read my work and tell others about it.

About the Author

ECLIPSE PHOTOGRAPHY STUDIO (GAINESVILLE, GA)

KAY BRATT was born in the Midwest and lived in many different states of the USA before settling down in the South. Always ready for adventure, she and her family later accepted an overseas assignment that landed them in China for almost five years. It was there that her life was changed forever when she discovered a passion for the Chinese people, their land, and culture. In 2009 Kay released a poignant memoir detailing her work with the children of a local orphanage. Now she uses her love of writing to continue to give the rest of the world a glimpse into the mysterious culture of China, and to raise awareness of issues that affect its women and children. Please visit her website at www.kaybratt.com for more information on current and upcoming books, contests, and ways to help make a difference.